COLD SANCTUARY

DAVID J. GATWARD

WEIRDSTONE PUBLISHING

Cold Sanctuary
By
David J. Gatward

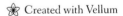 Created with Vellum

Grimm: nickname for a dour and forbidding individual, from Old High German grim [meaning] 'stern', 'severe'. From a Germanic personal name, Grima, [meaning] 'mask'. (*www.ancestory.co.uk*)

To Christian ...
without whom I wouldn't have been stupid enough
to try and run an off-road marathon.
And succeed.

CHAPTER ONE

Oʟᴅ Bɪʟʟ Dɪɴsᴅᴀʟᴇ's ʟɪꜰᴇ ᴡᴀs ᴊᴜsᴛ ᴀ ꜰᴇᴡ ᴍɪɴᴜᴛᴇs away from ending in such an appalling, violent, and apparently random way, that it would undoubtedly haunt the Dales for years to come. Right now though, he was having the best of days. And, like most of us in those fragile final moments of life, he was utterly oblivious to the sound of Death's scythe cutting through the ether as it rushed towards him, keen and sharp.

The day was bright and warm. May's late sun had burned off most of the early morning moisture from the fields. Bill had been up early, as was his lot, being a hill farmer in North Yorkshire. But he wasn't complaining. Never had, never would. Just wasn't in his nature. 'Above all things, be grateful,' his dad had taught him, and with good reason, because as a family, they had so much to be grateful for—being alive, for one. So, Bill had followed this advice his whole life, and done his best to pass it on to others.

Breathing deep the rich Wensleydale air he had known his whole life, Bill loved the place more than words could ever say. From the moment they'd arrived all those years ago, he'd never wanted to be anywhere else. The Dales had welcomed them with open arms. It was more than just the sanctuary they had so needed in such desperate times, it had become home.

As Bill often pointed out to anyone who asked, as well as plenty of those who didn't, 'When you realise you're lucky enough to live in a place that other folk come to visit on their holidays, going elsewhere just doesn't make much sense, now, does it?'

Like a good number of folk his age, the furthest Bill had ever travelled beyond the Dales themselves was Blackpool, and that was to see the world-famous Illuminations. Bill knew from experience that if he tried to explain that spectacle to those who hadn't been lucky enough to live most of their life in the Dales, then it really didn't sound very exciting at all. And perhaps it wasn't. But for Bill, it was a yearly trip, which his dad had started and he'd continued, even after his own son had left home.

Heading off across the Dales, usually at the end of harvest, to drive along the promenade and witness over six miles of displays showing all manner of things done with millions of coloured lightbulbs, was a wonder. Those lights, the smells of the place, the sounds, it all held so many memories for him that sometimes it was as though he was a child again, leaning forward between the front seats of his parents' car, to stare wide-eyed at this magical wonderland.

This annual trip wasn't a holiday as such, because Bill didn't take holidays, but it was a little break from the norm and he'd loved it ever since he was a boy. And he'd always bring something a bit naughty back for his wife Hannah because nothing said 'I love you' more than a kiss-me-quick hat and a rudely-shaped stick of candy rock.

Today, though, was going to be nothing more than spending a few hours bumbling around some of the paddocks in the lower valley, sat in his 1951 Ferguson TE20, more commonly known as the Grey Fergie, with the baler hitched onto the back. He'd had it for years, kept the thing running sweetly, and only used it for easy trips out like this one. Sometimes he'd just take it out for a spin, if only to remind him of his old dad doing the same, having been the original owner of both the tractor and the farm.

The farm ... And what a place it was, Bill thought, as he looked forward to the day ahead. His parents had worked so hard and without complaint to save up and buy it, toiling through the hottest summers and those days of winter now long gone, where the snow had swallowed flocks of sheep and quietly buried barn and home. It was a family thing and his very blood was in the soil feeding the roots.

The grass had been cut and Bill had been over it a few times with the spinner to whip the stuff up into the air to help it dry under the heat of a golden sun riding a light breeze. On those days he would imagine that the plumes of cut grass were great clouds of green drifting across his land, bringing with them the promise of yet another year in heaven.

Bill's lunch was already made, nothing more than a cheese and pickle sandwich, a pork pie, an apple, and a flask of tea. And a kiss on the cheek from his wife would be just enough to send him on his way.

God, life was good, he thought, and he whispered this sentiment as a little prayer, grinning at the day before him, because he was lucky beyond measure, in life and love. And now, with age getting the better of him, he was going to share that luck with those who needed it, just as he and his parents had, arriving one dark, rain-cast night with desperate terror chasing them to new shores.

With the old tractor's engine rumbling sweetly through the yard, Bill saw the love of his life step out through the kitchen door and into the yard, wearing a smile that even now, so many years on, could bring a heat to his soul like nothing else. She waved and Bill waved back, walking over to have a final word and perhaps, he hoped, to steal a kiss to keep him going just long enough to return that evening to her warmth and her love.

'Now, you'll be back in time, won't you?' Hannah asked.

'When am I ever anything else?' Bill replied.

'The choir are singing in the chapel,' Hannah continued. 'We can't be turning up late, now. Wouldn't look right. Not to Mary, anyway, and I don't want to be giving her any good reason to come over and bark at us.'

Bill laughed.

'Mary's harmless.'

'That may be,' Hannah said, shaking her head, 'and her bite may have lost its teeth, but there's still that tongue of hers, and it's as sharp as it ever was, you mark my words.'

'Don't worry, pet,' Bill said, not really listening, because Mary was an old windbag and gossip, though there were fewer now left to listen, unless of course, she fancied a natter at the cemetery in Hawes. And Bill laughed to himself at this, imagining the woman berating the dead.

Hannah approached the tractor in worn jeans and a threadbare jacket and Bill knew that he hadn't exactly kept her in riches all her life. But there were riches in the farm, in the land, and she always remembered that. Riches to share.

Always.

'You're a good man, Bill,' Hannah said. 'You know I've always thought that, don't you? And I always will. Always.'

Bill smiled, leaned over, then removed his flat cap and kissed his wife of fifty years. Not on the cheek, either, but full on the lips, and with a tenderness that belied his rough hands and hard, weather-worn face. Then, with a boyish wink, which even now in his twilight years could get him into trouble, he played smoothly with the Grey Fergie's gear lever. Easing it into second, he then gently pushed the throttle arm, a thin stick of metal sat just underneath the steering wheel, and he was off into the golden promise of what he would only ever see as the happiest and the best of times.

Waving him off, Hannah gave no thought to the notion that, unless it was in a far off place beyond death, where time is held in the palm of God's hand, and all of life's love and goodness is around you, she would never again see her husband alive, or feel the warmth of his soft, loving embrace one last time.

CHAPTER TWO

Harry Grimm was up early to face the day. Freshly showered, he was standing in the bathroom staring at someone he didn't exactly recognise: himself.

As reflections went, it wasn't the best, Harry thought, rubbing his stubbly chin, noting an altogether new ache in his left elbow. The pain subsided, but he had no doubt that it was making itself at home among friends.

Harry's hair was a mess, but he always kept it short enough for that to not really matter. He had never once in his life asked for a specific style of cut, instead, sticking to a once-a-month grade-one buzz cut on the back and sides, and a neatening up of whatever was still left on top. He wasn't thinning, exactly, but neither was he sporting enough on his head to warrant fussing with it like his brother, Ben, who seemed to be more preoccupied with how he looked now, what with his blossoming relationship with Liz, one of Harry's own team. Harry was pretty sure there was no direct correlation between haircare and relationship status. At least, he hoped there wasn't.

As for the scars, well, they weren't going anywhere, were they? When an IED decides to ruin your day, the marks it leaves behind are permanent. And the memory of that day was forever with him, though the fit young man he had been in the Paras was becoming increasingly hidden by the gradual war of attrition being waged on him by time, work, and not enough exercise. Plastic surgeons had done their best, but no one could work miracles.

So, what exactly was it? he thought. Harry moved in for a closer look, reaching up with a hand to stretch the skin beneath his cheekbones, leaning his head left and right, as though attempting to dislodge a thought he couldn't quite reach.

Like lightning bursting from a hellish cloud, the lines reaching out from his eyes were unchanged, and Harry noticed how his skin didn't exactly spring back into place like it once had a long time ago. There were blemishes, too, he saw, not just scar tissue either, but mottled marks of age, no doubt made worse by stress. But there was a difference there, wasn't there? And yet, for better or worse, he looked the same.

Harry leaned back and stood up straight, staring himself straight in the eyes. This allowed him to see more than he really wanted to, despite the mirror being at head height above the sink. He was still well-muscled, at least that's what he told himself. Unfortunately, his on-off relationship with exercise, which was now limited to running around the undulating Dales lanes that wrapped around Hawes like loose ribbons, when he could fit it into his busy life, was having little impact on the body mass hiding it all. But it was the start of a new week tomorrow, so he would begin afresh. Perhaps he'd have a word with Jen to draw him up another plan to try and stick to. Fewer bacon butties might help, to say nothing of the cheese and cake.

From behind, a warm hand slipped across Harry's stomach and was then joined by another. When they reached each other they clasped and gave him a tight squeeze and he felt a gentle kiss on his right shoulder blade.

Harry watched in the mirror as Grace, having sneaked in through the open door, leaned to the side to reveal herself from behind him, the side of her face against his shoulder. But then, it was her door, in her house, Harry thought, so she could do all the sneaking that she wanted.

'Something the matter?' Grace asked, her arms still around him.

'No, it's nothing, I'm sure,' Harry said, looking now at the woman who over so few weeks had become increasingly important to him. He wasn't one for emotion, and feelings confused the hell out of him, but she was somehow doing something with both. It was all as unnerving as it was enjoyable.

'You look serious.'

'I always look serious,' Harry said. 'Comes with the face.'

'Well, I rather like that face,' Grace said, stepping out from behind Harry.

Harry grinned. Couldn't help himself, not with Grace staring back at him, bright eyes glinting.

'That's a smile by the way,' Harry said. 'In case you were wondering. Sometimes, well, all the time if I'm honest, it can be pretty hard to tell.'

'Suits you,' Grace said.

Grace stepped back and Harry turned around to face her.

'You busy today?' he asked.

'Let me think, now,' Grace replied, her eyes looking up a little. 'It's a Sunday, so after I've walked the dogs I'll be going to church with my dad.'

'Oh, right,' Harry said, having not expected that as an answer. 'Er, I can join you, if you want?'

Grace laughed.

'I'm joking,' she said. 'Dad's a regular, but I'm not. He's a local preacher, actually, so he's often out, up and down the dale, preaching to a handful of people in the few chapels that are still going.'

Harry pictured Arthur, Grace's gamekeeper father, in a pulpit, throwing out hell and damnation to a congregation of sleepy pensioners.

'He's a preacher? Really?'

Grace gave a nod.

'Hard to believe, I know, but he's worth a listen.'

'Not really my thing,' Harry said.

Grace left the bathroom and headed out onto the landing and through to the bedroom. Harry followed.

'He spends most of his time telling stories and bad jokes,' Grace said with a laugh just tickling the edges of her voice. 'And he doesn't half know how to get folk to enjoy a good sing-song. You should hear him when he's on with Amazing Grace. He bellows that out, loud enough to rattle windows! Though that's probably just because I was named after it, and I'm the apple of his eye, obviously.'

In the bedroom, Harry spotted something furry and black curled up on the bed. He shook his head.

'Rule Number One,' he said. 'You're not allowed in the bedroom. And that rule applies even if this isn't my bedroom.'

The furry black thing didn't move.

'Ignoring me won't change Rule Number One,' Harry said, heaving on some clean clothes, his brain telling him to search for coffee, and quickly.

The furry black thing let out the biggest of sighs. It still didn't move.

Harry stared at the bed and found himself whistling.

'Great,' he said, pulling on some socks, and looking up at Grace. 'Now that tune's going to be stuck in my head for the rest of the day!'

Grace laughed.

At last, the furry black thing moved, stretching out to nudge Harry with two soft paws.

'Morning, Smudge...' Harry said.

The young dog thumped her tail softly on the bed.

Grace stroked the dog's now upturned belly.

'Gets away with murder, that one,' she said.

'Well, I'm not the one who let her upstairs, am I?' replied Harry.

Downstairs, with a breakfast of boiled eggs, toast, and the coffee he'd craved almost finished, Harry said, 'So, you're not busy then? Today, I mean.'

Grace shook her head as Smudge, at last, decided to join them from the bedroom, dropping herself down on the floor at Harry's feet.

'My diary's empty,' she said. 'Dog walk first, though Jess won't be joining us; she's tired enough as it is with the pups.'

Harry smiled. Grace's dog, Jess, was the only one of her working dogs allowed in the house. This was because she'd recently popped out a litter of seven tiny squeaking, scrabbling, funny balls of fur. The other dogs were all outside in a purpose-built kennel and dog run at the end of the garden.

'Ever been over to Hardraw?' Harry asked.

'The waterfall, you mean?' Grace asked. 'Hardraw Force? Not since I was a kid. A school trip from Primary School, then mucking about up there as a teenager now and again. It's a pretty place. Why?'

'No, it doesn't matter,' Harry said, shaking his head. 'Not if you've already been...'

'You mean you've been here almost a year now, and you've never been yourself?'

'We'll do something else,' Harry said. 'It's fine, honestly.'

'No, we won't,' Grace replied. 'And on the way, we'll swing by your flat.'

'My flat? Why?' Harry asked.

Grace grinned.

'You'll see...'

CHAPTER THREE

Hannah was sitting at the kitchen table deep in thought. The morning she'd had planned was now somewhat in turmoil on account of a phone call she'd received a few minutes ago. The trill of her phone had shattered the blissful quiet of the morning, giving her a start, and she'd answered it more to shut it up than to have an actual conversation.

'Yes?'

'Hannah? It's Richard. Bill's not around, is he?'

'No,' Hannah replied.

'Out in the fields then. I saw him on Friday and he said that he probably would be, depending on the weather, obviously. That's good.'

'Why is it? What's up?'

'I don't suppose you're free, are you?'

'Actually, yes, I am,' Hannah said, a little confused. 'Why?'

'I think there's something we need to talk about. Something Bill hasn't mentioned to you.

'What?'

'Probably best if you come over.'

'This isn't making much sense.'

'And this won't either. Bill's jacket, the one he was wearing Friday evening.'

'His posh one, you mean?'

'That's the one. Can you just go and have a look in the pockets for me, please. I think you'll find something there that you need to look at.'

Hannah's confusion was growing exponentially.

'What's this about, Richard?'

'Please, just go and check his pockets and call me back.'

Hannah hung up, went to find the jacket, and in one of the inside pockets had found an envelope. And inside that? Notes. Disturbing ones. Threats.

She'd rang Richard back immediately, arranged to go around, but now she was just sitting in her kitchen, trying to work out just what the hell was going on.

They had never kept secrets from each other, her and Bill. Not ever! And she supposed that in over fifty years of marriage, to have this be the first time? Well, that was a good sign of sorts. She understood why he'd kept what she'd found a secret, his concern for worrying her overriding everything else, no doubt, but still... Bill! You old fool!

She thought back to how happy he had been to head off to the fields, one of his favourite jobs on the farm. The smile on his face, a picture to remember forever, the boy in the man shining through so clearly. Perhaps that meant something? she thought. The secret of the notes, maybe they weren't as serious as she thought. And if Bill hadn't told her about them, then maybe that's all there was to it, that there was nothing actually to worry about at all.

Still, Richard wanted to talk about it and she'd said she

would go over now, so she went to reach for the envelope when a sharp knock rapped at the door. Before Hannah even had a chance to get out of her chair to answer, the ageing wood was creaking open, the hinges vocal about their need for a drop or two of oil. It brought with it a scent of summer to come, borne on the morning breeze that Bill had followed earlier. Quickly, Hannah threw a tea towel over the envelope she'd found in Bill's jacket and turned her face to the new arrival now standing in silhouette against the morning sun, a puddle of gold at his feet.

'Now then, Mum,' said the man as he stepped into the kitchen. He didn't wait for a welcome. Didn't need to. 'Nice day for it, isn't it?'

Danny was a big man, bigger than both of his parents, and the shadow he cast across the kitchen floor seemed to roll itself out like a thick, black rug.

'It is,' Hannah replied, standing up to give her only son a kiss. As she did so, she wondered if he could see her racing heart beating in her chest. 'You gave me a start!'

'Did I? Why? Expecting someone else, were you?'

'I was half asleep,' Hannah said, the lie coming with surprising ease to her lips. She yawned just enough to add a touch of realism. 'And who would I be expecting out here at this time, and on a Sunday?'

'Yeah, fair point,' Danny said. 'Dad about?'

Hannah shook her head.

'He's out in the fields,' she said. 'Where else would he be on a day like this?'

'Of course, on with the hay, then. The weather's looking good for it, as well, I think. Still his favourite job.'

'He is, and yes, it is.'

Danny raised an eyebrow in mock surprise.

'But what about church?'

'What about it?'

'He'll be missing it if he's out. Can't be having that.'

'God doesn't keep a tally, Daniel. And I think your father's been plenty enough over his years to have Saint Peter let him in when the day comes, don't you?'

Danny said nothing and instead was over to the kettle. After quickly filling it, he switched it on. He patted his stomach, which bulged a little through his jumper.

'Any bread in?'

'Do you not feed yourself at your own house?' Hannah asked.

'Of course I do,' Danny said. 'But I'm peckish. You know how it is.'

'You're always peckish.'

'I'm a growing lad,' Danny replied.

'You're forty-five years old!' Hannah retorted, aware of the keen edge her voice was showing, a blade pulled just shy of leaving the scabbard. 'The only way you're growing is out.'

Hannah pressed a hard finger into Danny's stomach. It gave just enough.

Danny stared at Hannah for a moment, then walked over to the bread bin. He popped a couple of slices into the toaster then searched for and found butter and jam.

'Sometimes, it's almost as though you don't want me here,' he said, as he made himself a mug of tea.

Hannah wouldn't have minded a brew herself, but she wasn't about to ask for one.

'I've never said that,' she said. 'Neither of us have. And neither of us ever will. You're our son, remember?'

'There's a but there though, isn't there?' Danny said.

'A but? What are you talking about?'

Danny shook his head, leaned against the table, waiting for his toast to pop.

'There's always a but. So, what's it going to be this time? That I'm away too much still? That I'm not working hard enough at settling down?'

'Daniel...'

Hannah hadn't the energy for an argument, not this early in the day. She had other things on her mind as it was. No space for any of her son's usual nonsense.

'There's a life beyond this farm, Mum. I may have come back, like I always said I would, but that doesn't mean I have to stop living, does it?'

'If that's what you think being back here and working on the farm means, stopping living, then...'

Hannah's voice trailed off. She didn't want to be angry, but sometimes? It was so difficult to be anything else.

'You know that's not what I mean,' Danny said. 'At all.'

'A farm needs dedication,' Hannah explained, her eyes firmly set on her son's own. 'We don't mind you going away, but still, you need to be here more than you are. You know that.'

Daniel spread his arms wide.

'And here I am, Mother,' he said, and Hannah flinched not just at the change of tone, but the name he used, so formal, so cold. 'Ready to take on the day!'

For a moment, Hannah said nothing, the quietness of the kitchen disturbed only by the gentle sounds of the house

'I'm assuming you've popped around for more than a snack?' Hannah said eventually, her eyes straying for a moment to what was hidden under the tea towel.

'I didn't have to come back, you know,' Danny said, not

answering her question. 'I wanted to, though. And I'm pleased that I did.'

The toaster pinged. Daniel placed his mug down on the side, grabbed for the toast and, with a quick trip to the fridge, covered both pieces thickly with butter and his mum's home-made raspberry jam.

'We're thrilled that you did,' Hannah said.

'I know,' Danny said, and Hannah saw the smile which had always melted her heart.

'It really is the truth, you know that, don't you?'

'I do,' Danny said. 'I just wish you'd see sense a bit more, that's all. And really, that's all I'm trying to do, to help you see what you should do. Farming, it's tough, Mum, for every-one. You and Dad, you've done it for so long, you need to rest now, don't you think? Just ease back a little?'

'Ease back?' Hannah laughed. 'Can you really ever imagine your dad easing back, honestly? I certainly can't.'

Danny finished off his toast, drank some tea.

'Look, I'm only saying this because I care,' Danny said. 'About all of us. About what we should be doing instead of whatever the hell this is supposed to be. It's why I came over now, this morning, to chat with Dad and you. Mainly Dad, though. To try to make him see sense, to think really care-fully about what he's planning to do.'

Hannah made to rise from her chair, but Danny held out a hand, stopping her.

'Please,' he said, and Hannah sat back down. 'I came back because you asked me to, like I said, remember? Because you both need me. And I need you, too, so don't forget that. But don't go thinking I'm just going to stand by and watch you both ruin what we have!'

This time, Hannah was on her feet, and no signal or sign from her son was going to stop her.

'And just what do you mean by that, what *we* have? Who's this *we*?'

Daniel rubbed his temples as though dealing with a sudden sharp headache.

'You just can't see it, can you, either of you? What you're sitting on, what we could do with it, how happy we could be. No stress, a good life. Doesn't that mean something?'

'There you go again, mentioning this *we*,' said Hannah.

'*We* are family,' Danny said. 'There's only the three of us, after all. And I'm not going to stand by and watch you and Dad farm yourselves into an early grave! You can't expect me to, either.'

It was the same arguments, all the time, Hannah thought, as she stared at Daniel. When he'd come home, a couple of years ago now, both she and Bill had hoped he'd seen sense at last. He'd certainly had long enough to do so, that was for sure. First, it had been university, a degree in Drama, of all things. Then it had been away to the city with him, to London, would you believe it! Following the nursery-rhyme promise of streets paved with gold, of auditions and small parts and the hope of Hollywood. Visits had grown less frequent, and they'd soon lost count of the number of jobs their son had tried, and the places he'd lived, both here and abroad, chasing that dream.

His return had brought with it so much promise and so many memories, too, of happier, more content times. When their boy was in love with the Dales and the fells were in his blood. But beneath the surface, something else had been hiding. And Hannah knew that if Daniel learned what was in that envelope just an arm's reach away, he'd lose it completely, and ultimately have something to support exactly what he was saying. Right now, though, and regard-less of Daniel's behaviour, her son was home, and losing him again to the world that lay outside of the Dales, well, that would be just too much to bear. Especially after all the trouble they'd had with getting him in the first place all those years ago. Where on earth had the time gone?

Hannah sat down and weariness fell upon her as though it were a thick blanket, like the kind her own mother had once tucked her into bed under.

'Look,' she said, her voice calm now, and quiet, 'I do understand, Daniel. I really do. This farm, you see its worth, but not as we do, well, not in the same way, maybe. And we somehow need to meet in the middle, can't you see? We've been here our whole lives. Change, well, it's something we see with the passing seasons, a slow thing it is, not quick, like you would have it.'

Danny placed his empty plate over by the sink, drained his mug, then rested it on the plate.

'It's a millstone,' Danny said. 'And I didn't come home to have it tied around my neck as well, you know. I came back to help cut us free of it, before it's too late. I don't want to lose you to it, to this little patch of grass and hill.'

'That's not how your dad sees it. Nor I.'

Danny laughed, but the sound was humourless, a cold bark on an iced tongue.

'He needs to let go of the past,' he said. 'You both do.'

'You know he can't do that,' Hannah replied. 'He won't. It's not in his blood. The past, *his* past, it's important to him, part of who and what he is, what he believes in.'

'This farm didn't save him!' Danny said, his voice rising again. 'Neither did the Dales and neither did any of the people up here. That was Grandma and Grandad, the risks they took in coming here, way back when, their hard work. And it's time he moved on. Time we all did!'

'And we will, when we're ready,' Hannah said. 'You just need to be patient, love, that's all.'

Danny opened his mouth to say something, but no words came. Instead, he just stared at his mother, then shook his head and walked back to the door.

'Time's running out, Mum,' he said. 'And I know it's self-ish, I really do, but I don't want to wake up one day, both of you gone, and my only memories to be of time spent throwing bales around or fixing a broken tractor.'

Hannah walked over to her son and hugged him. He hugged her back and for a moment they stood there, together, in unspoken love.

'He's out in the field then, is he?' Danny asked, finally breaking free.

'He is,' Hannah said.

'Then maybe I'll just wait till later...'

There was a pause then, an odd silence which rolled between them, pushing them both back.

Danny opened the door and made to leave. But as he stepped out into the day, he turned back and said, 'You know what keeps me awake at night, Mum? The thought that one day, Dad'll be out there, and you, too, perhaps. And you won't come back. I'm not ready for that. I'm just not.'

Then he was gone, the door swinging closed behind him.

Hannah hugged herself then, as a chill cast its way across her from the yard outside, turning her skin to goose flesh. Tears were in her eyes, cold jewels chasing down her cheeks.

She rose to her feet, paced over to the door, and heaved it closed. When she sat down again, she pondered for a while on the words Danny had left her with. In a strange way, it was comforting to know that he worried about when they would be gone, and perhaps he had a point. Bill really was a bit of a silly old bugger and maybe they should listen to Daniel a little. And considering what she'd found, what Richard had told her to look for, the sooner the better.

On the table, Hannah pulled away the tea towel and rested a hand on the envelope. Its contents worried her, Daniel worried her, and time itself, or the lack of it, worried her. Perhaps, then, we should all start listening to each other a little more, she thought. So, she grabbed the papers and followed after her son out into the day.

CHAPTER FOUR

BILL'S RIDE TO THE FIELDS WAS ONLY HALF AN HOUR, the journey anything but rushed, and his old tractor rolled along at a speed not much faster than a gentle jog. Though that was plenty fast enough for a mode of transport that was pretty much the same age as himself.

Unusually for an early morning, and as he was coming into a sharp corner, a car sped past and Bill swore under his breath at the driver, wondering how on earth anyone could ever want to be in such a rush, particularly on a day like this.

Yes, it was true that most of the locals drove like complete idiots in the Dales, the lanes as good as any challenging section in a rally, but it was rare for folk to be up and about at this time unless, like him, they were farmers. But then again, what did it matter? He certainly wasn't going to let someone else's death wish ruin his day.

Reaching his destination, Bill clambered out of the tractor, swooshed the gate open, its wooden bars creaking a little, then drove through, popping back round to shut the gate behind him again. Back at the wheel, he gazed at the wondrous sea of mown hay before him, the grass turned now to a greenish-gold. The air was thick with the sweet, dry scent of it. This field, and those beyond it, were all crowned with dry stone walls, ancient and rugged and silent. Trees jutted up at intervals, their boughs filled with the gentle calling of birds. And beyond this, the fells filled the horizon, their slumber undisturbed by the life turning beneath them.

This was going to be a very good day, Bill thought, a very good day indeed. But then it had been a good week, hadn't it? Now that his plans had finally been put into play. He would talk to Hannah about them later. She would no doubt be a little cross that he hadn't consulted her, but she would understand, he was sure. And it was all a surprise, too, wasn't it? She would be excited and his secrecy would be forgiven. So, with a grin on his face as wide and happy as it could ever be, Bill engaged the baler, eased forward again on the throttle arm, and trundled off into the morning. And behind him, small, oblong bales of light green hay began to lay themselves out in a thin line, the morse code of an early summer.

The day was close to switching from morning to afternoon, the sun having risen to its highest peak, when a metallic clunk spluttered itself out from the baler. Bill quickly pulled the tractor to a halt, turned off the engine, and swung himself down from his seat. He'd been meaning to stop soon anyway, his stomach rumbling something terrible for lunch. He also rather fancied a nap. He was only a few paces away from that little spinney of gnarly old trees in the middle of the field, the ones the sheep always appreciated on the sunniest of days. He could've cut them down years ago, but never did. There were few enough trees in the Dales as it was, and it was a perfect place for a kip.

Opening the baler, Bill stared into a mess of metallic

jaws and strange levers, partly formed bales of hay, and strands of orange binding twine. To the inexperienced eye, it meant nothing, but to Bill, it was usually easy to see what the problem was. Though, looking at it now, he was a little bit baffled. He'd check the baler over the night before, as always, to make sure there was enough twine for the day, and to give the 'old mechanicals', as his dad had always referred to anything even slightly engineered, the once over. And everything had seemed fine. Now though, it was obvious something had gone wrong, he just wasn't sure what exactly.

Bill pushed back his cap, wiped his brow, and sighed. Whatever the problem was, he knew that the best way to deal with it was to do so on a full stomach. Knowing that there was a pork pie waiting for him would not put him in the best of minds to solve whatever little problem the baler had decided to throw at him. So, lunch it was.

Grabbing his small pack, Bill wandered off towards the shade of the spinney. There were other trees he could use, like the old oak tree at the other end of the field. It sat directly in the line of a drystone wall. He had always admired how the builders of that wall had, instead of cutting down the tree, simply left it alone and constructed the neatest, smallest bend in the wall itself to accommodate it. But the spinney was the closest so that's where he headed to rest.

The packed lunch Hannah had prepared for him didn't last long and the urge Bill had felt earlier to take a nap became overwhelming. So, he gave in, leaning back against the tree, his cap pulled forward over his eyes, the warmth of the day sending him quickly to sleep.

A voice woke Bill, which was probably a good job, he thought, because although time wasn't exactly money, the weather could always change, and wet hay bales were no use to anyone.

Bill leaned forward to see how this new arrival was shielding his eyes against the sun.

'Now then, Dad.'

'Daniel?'

'Thought I'd come and give you a hand, if that's okay?'

'Really? Well, that's a nice surprise, if you don't mind me saying so,' Bill said, pushing himself up and onto his feet. 'I'm not sure what you'll be getting on with while you're here, though. Is there nowt up at the farm to be on with?'

'Probably,' Danny said. 'You must be tired, though, doing this on your own. A job shared, right?'

'A hot sun on my head and a pie in my stomach, that's all the tiredness is,' Bill said with a laugh. 'Did you see your mum, then?'

Danny gave a nod as Bill started to make his way back over to the tractor and baler.

'I had nothing planned for the day,' he said, 'so just thought I'd head over and see if anything needed doing.'

'On a farm, there's always something that needs doing,' Bill said, then gave a nod over at the baler. 'Like this, for example.'

'Something up?'

'It's probably nowt,' Bill said. 'Baler's just old, that's all. Probably needed a rest, like me.'

Danny laughed, but Bill noticed how the sound seemed to be lacking something. Not warmth as such, just that it sounded forced, like his son was distracted by something. He had a good idea what, too, but he wasn't in the mood to be talking about any of that, because it would just spoil his day.

He and Hannah both knew Daniel's heart was in the right place, but they weren't for being told how to live their lives.

'Want me to take a look?'

'Know all about balers now, do you?' Bill said and was immediately annoyed that his voice betrayed just enough of his irritation at Danny's as-yet unvoiced intentions for visiting him in the field.

Danny stared at his dad, shrugged.

'Two pairs of eyes and all that,' he said. 'That's all.'

Bill walked over to the baler for another look. Danny joined him, leaning into the machinery, reaching in to poke at something.

'I won't learn unless you show me,' Danny said.

'Well take your bloody hand out of there for a start,' Bill said, reaching for Danny's arm and pulling it out of the baler. 'The hell do you think you're doing?'

Danny looked shocked.

'What did you do that for?'

'Did you check if the tractor was off? Well, did you? What if it wasn't? What if the power was on, something went twang, the baler started up, and you ended up with your arm getting caught? Then what?'

Danny's mouth dropped open, but no words fell out.

'You'd be in there, that's what!' Bill said. 'Dragged in there, kicking and screaming, that's for sure. You'd lose an arm, and that's if things turned out well. Damn it, lad, I thought you knew better!'

Danny, smarting from the telling off, rubbed his arm where he'd caught it on the baler as Bill had pulled at it.

'If you want to learn then you have to listen and you have to use some common sense.'

'I've always said that I want to help,' Danny said. 'You know that. It's why I came home, isn't it?'

Bill said nothing. He had baling to be getting on with, and he was fairly sure that once he was moving, the baler would start working. It had happened before, it would happen again.

'I know I've said it before, but you can't keep on with this the way you are,' Danny said, as Bill headed over to climb back up onto the tractor.

'And what do you mean by that?' Bill asked, turning around to face his son. He loved the lad, always had. So much so, in fact, that sometimes he could feel the pain of it in his chest when he thought about how much he'd missed him when he'd left home all those years ago. Where the hell had the time gone? Away, that was then, and there was no way to get it back, neither.

'Only that you need to ease off, Dad, that's all.'

'Ease off?'

'Downsize.'

Bill laughed. Bless the lad for trying and not giving up.

'Downsize?' he said. 'That's a fancy word, now, isn't it? A fancy word that means sell up and move into a bungalow and take up golf.'

'That's not what I meant.'

'Can you imagine?'

Bill pretended to swing a club.

'Dad...'

'Four!'

'You're not listening, you never do. Damn it, can't you just, for one minute, hear me out?'

'I'm listening and I'm hearing,' Bill said. 'We both are. We just need to do things our own way, you know that.'

Bill saw the frustration on Daniel's face, his eyes betraying so much, as they always had.

'I care, that's why I'm here,' Danny said. 'But you know what, if you want to send yourself into the grave, don't let me stop you. Mum and I will be fine, I'm sure, just fine!'

'Daniel...'

'Though, I guess Mum will just follow you soon after, won't she?' Danny said, talking over his dad. 'Trying to keep this place going on her own, refusing to let me help, because that's the way you both are; stubborn to the end!'

Bill gave his son a few moments to calm down. Then he thought to himself how perhaps now was as good a time as any, and turned away from the tractor to stand in front of his son.

'We have been listening,' he said. 'We both have. And, well, things are going to change pretty soon, lad, so whatever worries you have, you can just let go of them, you hear? It's all going to be fine and dandy.'

'Fine and dandy?' Danny said, his face trying to handle a sudden change in emotion, from anger and frustration to confusion. 'What do you mean by that? How are things going to change? What have you done?'

'Done?' Bill said. 'Well, nowt yet, really, but it's all in motion now, that's for sure.'

'What's in motion? What are you talking about? You need to spell it out for me, Dad. No riddles.'

Bill laid a hand on his son's shoulder.

'Don't get so het up,' he said. 'The farm, it's ours, isn't it? It will always be our home. And yours, too, even more so now that you're back. That's important.'

'Get to the point.'

'I'm just, well, changing things a bit, that's all. So that I can look after your mum and me, give you what you need, and also do my bit to help folk, like. Give back a little of what was given to me, if you know what I mean.'

'No, I don't know what you mean,' Danny said, though Bill saw a change in his son then; he didn't look as surprised as he was professing.

'Like I said, you don't need to worry. There's plenty left for you, I've made sure of that.'

'And what do you mean by there's plenty left?'

'For you,' Bill said. 'Once it's all arranged—and it nearly is now—you'll have a good farm to be going on with, to do with as you see fit. What was it you were on about, glamping pods, wasn't it? You could do that, no bother.'

'What has been arranged? And why am I only finding out about all this now?'

'Because we've been sorting it out, that's why,' Bill replied. 'And we didn't want you worrying yourself about it. In fact, we wanted it to be a surprise, a handing over of the keys, once we were happy with what we were handing over, like.'

'I need you to get to the point,' Danny said. 'Spell it out for me, Dad, nice and clear.'

Bill leaned against the rear wheel of his tractor, stretched a little, heard his joints pop and creak.

'I've managed to get planning permission on a couple of barns,' Bill explained. 'They'll make a nice few houses for some young folks, because that's what's needed round here, and you know that better than most, I'm sure. And I'm putting up some of the land for sale as well. We don't need all of it, never have, really. And then we'll have enough of a farm for you to be going on with, the house for us all, some money left over for me and your mum to step back and relax and maybe even go on a holiday, eh? And the rest I'll be using to do my bit to help, like me and my parents were helped. There, you see? Not as bad as you were worrying, am I right? What do you think?'

Danny went to speak, but nothing came out.

'Come on, lad, out with it,' Bill said.

Danny scratched his head.

'Just give me a moment to get my head around what you've just said, Dad, okay?'

'Of course,' Bill said with a firm nod.

Danny walked away from Bill, scratching his head, kicking at the odd clump of grass. Then he turned back and came to stand with his dad.

'What do you mean by doing your bit to help? And what do Grandma and Grandad have to do with any of this? I mean, I hate to break it to you, Dad, but they're not around anymore.'

'We were given a home,' Bill said. 'Not the farm, obviously. I don't mean that, because dad had to work for that, build it up. Took a good few years, too, but he did it.'

'Dad, get to the point.'

'What I mean is, when we came over, back in forty-one, escaping from God knows what, this place, the people, welcomed us. And I want to do the same, provide a home. Like we did with you, remember?'

'What you did with me? That has nothing to do with whatever this is that you're talking about right now, that's for sure. And don't go pretending that it does.'

'You know the old chapel in Hawes?' asked Bill.

'The one that's not been in use for years? Of course I do. What about it?'

There it was again, Bill thought, a flicker behind his son's eyes, a tell that suggested he knew more than he was letting on.

'Well, the thing is, your mum and me, and a couple of others, we've raised some money, with the backing from the local church as well, and we've bought it.'

Bill saw shock etch itself into Danny's face then crack and crumble to reveal hot anger beneath.

'You've done it then, have you? You've bought the chapel? Is that what you're saying?'

'You knew, then?' Bill asked.

'I'm not an idiot, Dad!' Danny said.

'And you never said?'

'Because I hoped you'd see sense, I hoped you'd be persuaded to see how the whole thing was mad!'

'Persuaded?' Bill said. 'What do you mean by that?'

Danny hesitated, then said, 'The whole idea, it's madness, you know it is!'

'We'll have to go through the usual planning stuff, but we've already done some preliminary investigations and it shouldn't be a problem.'

'What shouldn't be a problem?'

'Us turning it into sort of a halfway house I suppose is the best way to think about it,' Bill said. 'Somewhere that folk who've got nowt can come to, get a roof over their heads, food in their bellies, that kind of thing. Not just locals either, but those from all over.'

'A hostel for the homeless, is that what you mean?' Danny asked.

'More than that,' Bill said.

Danny went to interrupt but Bill just kept on talking, holding out a hand to still his son's complaints.

'There's kids and families from all over who need help,'

he said, passion in his voice now. 'You know it as well as I do. Being washed up on our shores, just like I was, remember?'

'Dad...'

'You've seen them on telly, we all have. It's wrong! No, it's worse than that; it's bloody disgusting is what it is, and I'll not stand by, son, I just won't!'

'I understand, Dad, I really do, it's just that...'

Just that what?' Bill asked. 'Some people might not agree with it? Well, sod them, that's what I say! We're going to do our bit and make a difference. We can't help everyone, of course we can't, but we can sure as hell help someone, can't we?'

'But like this, Dad? Really? You're not thinking this through. This isn't the place for it.'

'It's the perfect place for it,' Bill said. 'The fells, the Dales, this place is heaven! It can heal. And just think on this: if someone hadn't helped me and my mum and dad all those years ago, then where would I be now? Where?'

Danny shrugged.

'Nowhere,' Bill said. 'Because neither of us would even be here to have this conversation.'

Danny stepped back from his dad, stumbled a little.

'You're absolutely serious, aren't you?'

'Of course I am,' Bill said. 'I'm looking after you, after Hannah, and I'm giving back a little like I always said I would. Like everyone should, in my opinion, not that it's worth much I know. And yes, I know some folks won't understand. They've told me as much, some of them, but I've no time for that. This is the right thing to do. And it's about time folk around here, around everywhere, started to care a little bit bloody more about everyone else instead of themselves and nowt else.'

'A little?' Danny's voice was full of disbelief. 'At what point is what you're talking about a little? You're giving away Mum's money, my inheritance, just like that!' He clicked his fingers right in Bill's face, so close that the old man blinked. 'Well, you can't, Dad. you just can't do this. I won't allow it.'

'I can and I have,' Bill said. 'You say that as though there's nowt left. Well, there's plenty, and enough to do the chapel, too.'

Danny turned from his dad and walked off, rubbing his head, swearing at the sky. When he turned around Bill could see hurt in his son's eyes.

'I'm leaving you the farm,' Bill said. 'Can't you see that? It's yours! You can do with it what you want. You've nowt to be so upset about, at all! The rest, well, that's our business and that's all there is to it.'

Danny strode over to Bill.

'You should've told me, Dad,' he said. 'You both should've told me! Can't you see that? This kind of thing, it's too big, too bloody important! You were wrong! You *are* wrong!'

'That's as may be in your eyes,' Bill said climbing onto the tractor, aware now that the day was getting on and that the hay wouldn't bale itself, 'but the outcome would've been the same. And you'll understand eventually.'

Sitting up in his tractor, Bill looked down at his son.

'I'd best be getting on with the rest of the hay,' he said. 'Won't be baling itself now, will it? Not that I'd want it to, taking away one of my favourite jobs.'

'And that's how you're leaving it, is it?' Danny said.

'We'll talk later,' Bill said, starting the engine.

Moving off, Bill gave a last glance back to his son. The love he had for him was immeasurable and unchanged, but the lad still had a few things to learn in life, didn't he? Perhaps, though, with all that they'd just spoken about, he'd understand a little more eventually. And surely, of them all, he should understand the most.

With that final hope in mind, Bill went on his way, the baler now back to working again, and the rest of the day calling him on.

CHAPTER FIVE

HANNAH PARKED UP OUTSIDE WHAT WAS A VERY impressive and desirable house indeed, walked up to the grand and somewhat imposing front door, and pushed the bell.

She heard not a sound, no indication at all as to whether the bell had chimed inside the house.

The door opened.

'Oh, hello,' Hannah said. 'Your father's in, yes?'

The lad standing in front of her was in his mid-teens and doing his best to look older. He looked down at Hannah from above a puffed up chest.

'Why?'

'He invited me over,' Hannah said. 'He's expecting me. So, can you just tell him that Mrs Hannah Dinsdale is here?'

'S'pose,' the lad said, turned, and shut the door in Hannah's face.

Hannah waited then, as she was about to ring the bell once again, the door opened.

'Hannah?'

'Richard,' Hannah said. 'I came as soon as I could. Daniel turned up unannounced, you see, so if I'm late, that's the reason. He goes on a bit, you know? He means well, I know he does. Sorry, I'm rambling.'

'Don't apologise,' Richard said. 'Come on in. Please.'

Hannah stepped up into the house, the front porch of which she noticed was getting on for the size of her own lounge.

'I'll just take these off.'

She leaned over and, with a little effort, managed to pull off her Wellington boots.

'Would you like some tea?' Richard asked, as Hannah followed him deeper into the house. Beneath her feet, the carpet was like stepping onto a marshmallow.

'I've never said no to a brew,' Hannah smiled.

'Why don't you make yourself comfortable and I'll go rustle something up?'

Richard directed Hannah to a room off the hall then set off into another part of the house.

Hannah was now in a room that was part business, part relaxation. A desk perched in the large bay window, with two comfortable sofas gazing at each other across a table in front of them. On the table were a pile of thick books. Hannah sat down and slipped the top one from the pile. It was a photographic history of the life of Winston Churchill. Beneath it she saw other subjects covered, all of them about some part of the country's history or someone very involved in it.

Richard returned with a tray.

'Tea, biscuits, cake,' he said. 'Milk and sugar?'

'Just milk,' Hannah said. 'And no, I'm not sweet enough already, I just don't have much of a sweet tooth.'

Richard poured the tea.

'So, the notes, then,' he said. 'What did you think?'

'They're threats!' Hannah said, the words jumping from her. 'To Bill! Have a look for yourself if you want. But that's what they are, threats. I can't really believe that they're real, that someone went to the time. It's completely beyond me.'

Richard picked up the notes and started to read them.

'Stop now or else,' he said. 'You exterminate vermin, not house them; One last warning; Keep Yorkshire Pure. Creative, aren't they?'

'That's a cracker, that one, isn't it?' Hannah said. 'Keep Yorkshire pure? Who on earth writes that, never mind thinks it!'

Richard kept reading, though stopped doing so aloud.

'That's the first time I've ever rummaged around in Bill's pockets,' Hannah said. 'Didn't feel nice at all. How did you know they were there?'

'He mentioned them on Friday,' Richard said. 'Showed me them.'

'Who do you think sent them?' Hannah asked.

'No idea,' Richard said. 'They're not signed, are they? Just words cut out from newspapers or whatever.'

'A few are written out by hand,' Hannah said and held one of them up. Then a thought crossed her mind. 'Have you been sent any?'

Richard didn't answer straight away and she picked up on that immediately.

'You have, haven't you? That's why you rang!'

Richard gave a nod.

'That was why we went for a drink together on Friday,' he said.

'And you didn't say anything? Why?'

'We both decided to ignore it,' Richard said, the notes in

his hand. 'I mean, just look at these! How can anyone be expected to take them seriously?'

'Why didn't you go to the police?'

'Because I've experienced this before, that's why,' Richard said.

Hannah was stunned.

'Really?'

'Long time ago, now, thankfully. I try to not think about it.'

'Why? What happened?'

'I went to the police and nothing happened. Nothing at all!'

'Surely something happened?'

Richard shook his head and sighed.

'They were just pieces of paper in the end. No forensic evidence on them, no way to trace them to the sender. A dead end.'

'Still, they were threats,' Hannah said. 'Where are the ones you've received, then?'

Richard said nothing for a moment then rose from his seat and walked over to his desk. He opened a drawer, pulled out an envelope, and returned to Hannah.

'Here,' he said, handing her the envelope.

Hannah opened the envelope, and pulling out the notes, read them.

'See?' Richard said. 'Nonsense on a few scraps of paper, that's all. And, like I said, I've been here before. Best to ignore them. Bill agreed. He didn't want to worry you, either.'

Hannah stared at the notes Richard had handed to her, resting them on the table with the ones she'd found in Bill's jacket pocket.

'What about the handwriting?' Richard asked.

'What about it?'

'Well, if these threats are local, there's a good chance we'll know the person who's been sending them. Not much help I know.'

Hannah's eyes widened.

'I'd not thought of that.'

She picked up the notes and shuffled through to the ones that were handwritten.

'It's just a scrawl,' she said. 'I mean, look at it, will you? Who writes like that? Reminds me of Daniel's school books! Honestly, the times we were called in about him for messing around or not doing his homework! He was a proper little bugger.'

'Do you think Bill would recognise the writing?' Richard asked.

'I doubt it.'

'Just another possibility, that's all. He doesn't like to worry you, does he? And he thought that these would do exactly that. I can only apologise for being party to this secretiveness. Perhaps not that sensible in hindsight.'

'No, probably not.'

'Bill's out baling hay, isn't he?'

'There for the day, what with the weather being so good.'

Richard checked his watch.

'Why don't we both go and see him, then?' he suggested.

Hannah rose to her feet.

'No, that's very kind, but I can talk to him myself about it.'

'All the same,' Richard said, 'I think it might be worth me having a chat with him, too, don't you think?' He picked up the notes, holding them between himself and Hannah. 'On reflection, now that we've spoken, if this is how strongly someone feels, then there's a very good chance that others feel the same as well, isn't there?'

'So?'

'So,' Richard said, 'it means we need to think things through a little more, that's all. There's no rush, now, is there? And, as I've always said, it's the project that's important—'

'—not the building, I know,' Hannah said. 'But his heart is set on it, you know that.'

'There are other buildings,' Richard said. 'He'll understand.'

Hannah wasn't sure. She'd come here concerned about a few silly notes and was now leaving with the thought of telling Bill he'd have to have a rethink.

'No, you're right,' she said. 'Perhaps it would be best if you came over with me. If you don't mind.'

'I wouldn't have offered if I did,' Richard said. 'Shall I just follow you down, then?'

'That'll be the easiest,' Hannah agreed.

Outside, Hannah walked over to her car when Richard caught up with her.

'Thank you for bringing this over to talk through with me,' he said. 'I'm sure we can work together to help Bill understand.'

'Two heads and all that, right?' Hannah said.

'Exactly,' Richard agreed. 'I'll see you there.'

CHAPTER SIX

A COUPLE OF HOURS LATER, WITH AFTERNOON NOW VERY much rolling on, Bill turned the tractor back up the field only to feel a jolt from the baler. The tractor kept rolling on, but the awful grinding sounds from behind him had Bill push the throttle back quickly to bring the vehicle to an abrupt stop. He swore under his breath. The day was still bright, which was good, but he really did want to be getting on.

Leaning forwards, Bill switched off the engine and it fell silent with a faint, soft rattle, almost as though it was simply falling asleep. Then, with an ache that could only come from sitting on an ancient metal seat cushioned with some old bits of carpet, he swung himself down from his perch, and much to his surprise, came face-to-face with two men in black balaclavas.

'And just who the bloody hell are you, then?' Bill asked, not exactly sure how to respond to this new and altogether bizarre interruption to his day. Why they were wearing bala-clavas he had no idea, but he found himself thinking that, with the sun as high as it was, and in such a clear sky, they must've been sweating like meat in an oven.

The men were standing behind the baler, both in jeans, dark jackets over shirts. And behind them, the spinney, making them difficult to see for a moment.

'This is a warning!' said the man closest to the baler. Of the two, he was the larger, Bill noticed, bulky like he had, at some point, played rugby, but over the years moved on from throwing a ball to chucking pints. His voice was a loud, gruff shout, northern to the point of sounding put on, and Bill wondered if he was trying to disguise it in some way.

'A warning?' Bill replied, not sure yet whether he was angry, annoyed, confused, or a volatile mix of all three. 'What are you on about? How can you two, standing there dressed like Halloween, be a warning? And about what, exactly?'

'The baler!' the other man said, pointing. He was smaller, squarer in build. 'That's the warning!'

'The baler?' Bill said. 'The baler's a warning? How's that, then? You're making no bloody sense!'

His anger growing now, Bill made to walk towards the men, but as he did so he spotted a huge lump of wood sticking out of his baler. It looked like an old fence post recently ripped out of the ground.

'Now, what the hell did you go and do that for?' he asked, his eyes flitting between the baler and the two strangers. 'Have you got a brain between you? No, don't answer that.'

'Like we said, it's a warning!' the first man said again, voice still loud and gruff and proper northern. 'You've had others. You've not listened. You need to listen!'

Bill though wasn't listening because he'd never been one for bullies. His attention had moved from the fence post and the two men to the front of his baler, where it connected to the rear of his tractor.

'See what you've done? You've busted the PTO shaft!'

'We've what?' the first man said.

'The power take-off!' Bill replied, jabbing a finger at where the damage was, his voice growing louder, gruffer, angrier. 'Looks like you snapped the bloody thing or sheared off the bolts with that stupid sodding fence post of yours! The hell were you thinking?' He turned round to face them both. 'No, don't answer that, because you can't, can you, either of you, whoever you are?'

The larger man walked over to Bill, towering over him. He stopped up short, though, when Bill, snapping round on his heels, met him halfway, unafraid.

'You've knackered it!' Bill roared. 'You've come into my field, uninvited, dressed like a couple of fat SAS failures, and buggered up my baler!'

'SAS what?'

'Those balaclavas!' Bill said. 'Who do you think you are, Andy sodding McNab?'

'Who's that, then?'

'You're joking, right?'

'We're not joking, this is a warning, like we said!'

Bill had had enough and before the large man in front of him could react, he reached up and grabbed the balaclava.

'Let's see who you are, shall we? Before I give you a bloody good hiding!'

Bill gave the balaclava a hard tug and felt it come loose. Then, as the face of his assailant was about to come into view something slammed into the back of his head with such force that he saw stars and then the ground coming up fast to crash into his face. Then darkness.

Now lying face down in the grass, Bill tried to work out just what the hell was going on. His head was ringing and as he tried to push himself up, his arms just gave way. Staying on the ground, he reached up to check his head. It was wet and sticky and when he brought his hand to his eyes for a closer look, his palm was slick with red.

Bill tried once again to push himself up, but as he did so his head swam and he was sure he was about to throw up. Above him, the air was filled with the sound of the two men arguing.

'What the hell have you done?'

'I ... er ...'

'What the bloody hell were you thinking? We were only supposed to warn him!'

I was only trying to help!'

'Help? How is what you just did helping anyone? We're here to warn him, remember? That's why we're here! I told you that! I was absolutely bloody clear on the fact!'

'Well, if you hadn't been so close to him...'

'Ah, so it's my fault now, is it?'

'No, that's not what I meant!'

'I didn't know he was going to try and grab my balaclava, did I?'

Bill was on his knees now and he tried to look round at the two men, but the movement made his head spin and his eyes were still blurry.

The two men continued to argue.

'You should've just told him what the warning was about as soon as we arrived! Then he'd have understood, wouldn't he?'

'Don't you try and weasel your way out of what you've just done! I mean, I just don't get why that would be the first thing that springs to mind, to twat him one across the head with a massive fence post!'

'Hey, none of this was my idea!'

'And what you just did, wasn't mine either!'

'I'm just saying that seeing as you spoke first then you should've come out with it and said!'

'There's a big difference between scaring someone, threatening them, and what you just did. And he knows anyway, doesn't he? He's had the letters!'

Bill tried to stand, gave up.

'What if he'd seen your face? What then? Then the cat would've really been out of the bag, wouldn't it?'

'I don't know if you noticed, but I caught the balaclava before he ripped it off!'

'I didn't mean to hit him so hard! It was an accident!'

'A fence post isn't an accident!'

'I panicked! He'll be fine! And I've gone and cut myself on that bloody baler of his in the process! Look!'

'You can buy new jeans.'

'Well, I'll have to, won't I? These are ruined! Bloody hell that hurts!'

Bill once again tried to stand. This time he managed to get to his feet, though doing so made his head feel woozy.

'Anyway, you can stop worrying. Look, he's standing up again, isn't he? He's fine!'

'Fine? How can he be fine? You hammered a fence post into the side of a pensioner's head and you call that fine?'

'Well, what was I supposed to do?'

'Not try and kill him, that's what! This is supposed to be just a warning, remember? And generally, people don't remember warnings if they're dead because some idiot's caved their head in with a fence post!'

Bill shook his head, his eyes focusing at last, then he turned to face the two men. Written warnings he could ignore, but this? Not a chance of it.

Right, you pair of bastards...

Bill ran at the men with all the fury of Hell in his eyes, fists up and ready. The men turned too late, wrapped up as they were in their argument about why they were there, what they had done.

Bill managed to swing a left at the smaller man. He caught him hard and sharp on the side of his chin, knocking him back with a yelp. Still with the element of surprise, Bill was then into the larger man, half falling into him with a spittle-filled roar. They both stumbled, Bill pushing on, slapping at the other, hammering him with his head, kicking him.

A shout from the smaller man burst into the moment and Bill turned to have another go.

The fence post caught Bill across the side of his skull with the dull, hollow crack of a ball scoring a direct hit at a coconut shy. If he'd been able to see inside his head at that very moment, he would have witnessed a starburst of fissures open across his skull as the force of the impact shattered bone. Then he tipped forwards into the open bale chamber.

Stars buzzed around Bill's head, pain lancing through his broken skull. Sharp metal jabbed into his face and body, drawing blood. He was stunned, couldn't move, and was now even more confused than when he'd first seen the two men as to exactly what was going on and why he was in the really painful centre of it.

Bill tried to push himself back out of the baler. He wanted to get back up onto his feet and have another go, but his shirt was caught on the knotters holding the twine and he couldn't get free. Or at least that's what he thought the problem was, because his body just wasn't responding anymore. He wanted to get up, knew that he had to, but for some reason, his arms, his legs, they just weren't listening to him. God, if Hannah saw him now, he thought, she'd play merry hell, that was for sure.

Voices again, though to Bill they sounded more distant now, as though he was trying to listen in on a conversation taking place in another room.

'I thought we just spoke about this?'

'He was going to kill us!'

'Kill us? He's an old man and he's been smashed over the head with a fence post by you once today as it is! Just what the hell is wrong with you?'

'I got him off you, didn't I?'

For a moment, the voices stopped. In the silence, and as Bill still tried to tell his body to move, he heard bird song and the far off bleat of sheep, and he thought that really, this was probably all just a misunderstanding, a joke gone wrong perhaps, and tomorrow he'd look back and laugh.

When the voices spoke again, they were much, much closer.

'I think you've killed him. And that's not going to help, is it?'

'What? I can't have!'

'He's not moving.'

'His eyes are open!'

'And that means he's alive, does it? Open eyes? Thank God you never went into medicine.'

'He's breathing still; look!'

More silence, and this time Bill wondered how he'd explain all of this to Hannah, the woman who had been with him through thick and thin, put up with him, loved him.

God, she really was something, and he'd tell her later, wouldn't he? Yes. Absolutely. He'd tell her just how much he loved her. Because he did. More than anyone had ever loved another ever before, he was sure of it.

'We'll go down for this, you know that, don't you?'

'What? It was an accident! It wasn't on purpose! It was self-defence!'

'You've smashed him over the head with a fence post; that is not an accident!'

'You know what I mean!'

A brief pause, a breath.

'You do have a point, though, when I think about it.'

'Really? You sure about that?'

'Yes.'

'What?'

'What you just said; it was an accident...'

This last silence was the longest of all and by now Bill was growing cold and sleepy. Perhaps Hannah would be along soon, he thought. She'd sort this out easily enough. She was good like that. No one messed with Hannah. He'd tried a few times, but soon realised that she was a force to be reckoned with. It was part of why he'd fallen for her in the first place, wasn't it?

Bill heard the clank of metal against metal.

'PTO wasn't bust. Just came loose. I've managed to fix it back on.'

'Why?'

'Like you said, remember? It was an accident...'

Bill caught the cough of the old Fergie's engine sparking to life. He tried again to move, only to then experience the oddest of sensations as his feet were lifted up and he was pushed further into the guts of the baler. Then, with his mind not so much full of worry for himself, but of his wife, of Hannah, of what she would say if something terrible happened to him, what she would do if the farm finally did manage to kill him—as she had always said that it might, what with the hours and the weather and the debt—the thrum from the Fergie's engine kicked up a notch, the baler clanked its way back to life, and Bill was dragged kicking and screaming into its jaws.

The last thing Bill saw was a heron coming to rest in the branches of a tree at the edge of the field. Well fancy that, he thought. Then an exquisite rasp of pain ripped through him, the heron once again took flight, and with it went his last breath.

Then darkness.

CHAPTER SEVEN

THE WALK FROM HAWES AND AWAY OVER TO HARDRAW, part of which was a very small section of the famous Pennine Way, was neither long nor arduous, being little more than a gentle stroll across fields and alongside the soft meandering of the River Ure. The water seemed to gossip with itself as it flowed on, bouncing over rocks and pebbles.

With Grace's dogs walked, Harry had then driven himself, Grace, and Smudge from her cottage in Carperby, a village down dale and over towards Leyburn, to his flat in Hawes. It was only on arrival that Grace had finally told him why they'd had to stop off: to grab his swimming stuff.

'But it's a waterfall,' Harry had said, confused.

'And you can't be visiting this one without a dip in the pool it falls into,' Grace had said. 'Trust me.'

'Why is it, those two words are always concerning?'

Grace's answer had been a simple smile and shrug.

Ben had been nowhere to be seen, probably staying over with Liz, Harry thought, smiling to himself about how much his brother's life had changed.

From Hawes marketplace, they'd walked down the hill and taken a left just after the doctor's surgery. Following the road a little way, they'd then cut across fields to be brought to the road once again, before crossing a bridge over the river and then, a little way farther on, heading back into the fields.

Smudge was never off the lead, not walking through fields with sheep and lambs in, but she already walked to heel well, Harry thought. Grace was helping him with the training, her own life as a gamekeeper giving her more than a little expertise in that area.

Harry had rescued the dog a few weeks ago from a puppy farm they'd stumbled upon during another investigation. With the proper jabs and checks from the vet, all was good. Harry had never really wanted a dog, but something had connected him with that little ball of black fur, and now he couldn't imagine life without her around. Actually, he could. For a start, he'd have more socks, seeing as the daft animal had taken to sneaking off with them to chew, the smellier the tastier, it seemed.

Harry loved the Dales, but then he knew now that it was impossible not to. Regardless of the weather, and the area certainly had more than its fair share of the best and the worst of it, the fells had a beauty to them that could, at the turning of a corner or the reaching of a brow of a hill, take his breath away. Here, though, was a bit of it that he'd never explored. There was no reason as to why, simply that his life thus far hadn't brought him out this way.

Harry noticed that the path they followed was one of ancient flagstones set into the soft bed of the fields in which they walked. Their surfaces were worn from years of use and he wondered at the numerous lives which had passed that way, those long-ago journeys still haunting the shadows which skulked under the small rocky escarpments lining some of their route.

Walking across the fields, Harry paused for a moment, breathing deep, his eyes casting back the way they'd come to the grey stone dwellings of Hawes, and the silent majesty of Wether Fell standing behind. Smudge stopped and sat down at his side.

'Not bad, is it?' said Grace.

'No, not bad at all,' Harry replied, reaching down and scratching Smudge's head. The dog licked his hand. 'Hard to believe I didn't actually want to come here, isn't it?'

'Not really,' Grace said. 'You get used to a place and leaving it is always hard, whether you like it or not.'

'Oh, I didn't mind leaving,' Harry said. 'I just didn't want to come here, to Yorkshire!'

Grace looked shocked, but Harry could see the laughter in her eyes.

'Well, you know what they say,' she said. 'It's grim up north. And, well, here you are, aren't you? Grimm, up north!'

'Here I am, indeed,' said Harry, then he turned and looked back along the path to their destination. 'And there's a pub at the end of this, is there?'

'The Green Dragon,' said Grace. 'You'll love it.'

Walking on, Harry and Grace made their way on into Hardraw, the path leading them behind a clutch of cottages stacked together as though sheltering from the promise of the worst of storms, and out onto a road. In front of them was a church, hiding behind huge trees, and to its right, the Green Dragon Inn.

Harry checked his watch.

'How can it be lunchtime already?'

'It isn't,' Grace said.

Harry showed her his watch to prove her wrong

'We've come to see Hardraw Force,' said Grace. 'So we'll be doing that and then we'll have a bite to eat. You need to earn it, first, I'm afraid.'

Harry wasn't exactly sure that he liked the sound of that.

Walking past the pub, Harry followed Grace as she turned down the side of the building then on through a small car park and into a café rich with the smell of fresh coffee and homemade cakes. A turnstile guarded the way leading onto Hardraw Force. They paid the fee and were through.

A few steps on from the cafe and Harry was astonished to find himself walking into the quiet gloom of a gorge cut into the fellside. Trees hung all around and the air was cool and a little damp, reminding him a little of being inside an old church.

Walking along a gravel path, they passed a stone band-stand and then onwards to follow a brook rushing past on their left. The water was clear, the stones beneath the surface stained the deep brown of peat and moorland. Where rocks and boulders stood to hinder the water's progress, great crests of white bubbled up, and the sound of it echoed around them.

'The waterfall's just up ahead,' Grace said. 'You ready for your Kevin Costner moment?'

'My what?'

'Robin Hood, Prince of Thieves.'

Harry remembered then Jadyn mentioning something about the film a few months ago, though he hadn't really been listening at the time, not enough to actually remember what it was Jadyn had been on about.

The waterfall came into view, a bright white spray

casting itself over the lip of the gorge a hundred feet above them, a watery horse's tail, laced with diamonds.

'Impressive, isn't it?' Grace said, leading Harry on a little further.

Harry followed, aware now that he was breathing in a faint, cool spray from the fall, only to then have his attention caught on the faint edges of a rainbow stretching its way through the air above them.

'Very,' he said, searching for something else to say, but coming up short. Words just didn't seem to do the place justice.

A few steps ahead of them Harry spotted a small, wooden gate across the path.

'No entry?'

Grace walked up to the gate, opened it, and walked through.

'Come on!'

'But the gate,' Harry said, staring at it, the sign's meaning more than clear enough for anyone to understand. 'You can't just go walking on through.'

'I think I just did,' Grace said.

Harry hesitated, looking back the way they'd come to see if anyone was following on behind, watching what they were up to. He turned back to Grace to see that she was now further along the path and closer to the edge of the pool into which the waterfall fell. Her rucksack was off and she was now barefoot, stripping down to her swimming costume. He looked down to see Smudge staring at Grace, clearly keen to follow.

'Come on,' Grace called over, with only her trousers to go. 'You'll love it, I promise.'

It wasn't the fact that he was a police officer and thus

eternally tied to following the rules that had given Harry pause. It was more that he could see good reason as to why the gate existed in the first place, as high above them the rim of the gorge hung over precariously, and the huge stones which littered the poolside were testament to its fragility.

'You've done this before, then?' Harry asked.

'Mucking about as a teenager, remember?' Grace said. 'We all used to come up here. It's a rite of passage, I suppose, to throw yourself in.'

Grace was now in her swimming costume and as yet Harry and Smudge were no further on than standing on the right side of the gate still.

'You'll notice I'm not a teenager,' Harry said.

'But you said yourself that you swam in Semerwater!' Grace said, laughter in her voice. 'So, get yourself over here quickly or I'll be going in on my own!'

Harry turned his attention from Grace back to the waterfall, the white tail of it hammering down into the clearly very deep and undoubtedly very cold pool below. He wouldn't have said he was afraid of going in as such, because he knew that was ridiculous, but he was unnerved by it. Something about the place was almost primaeval and staring too long into the gloom, which seemed to drape itself about them from the trees and the rocks, made him uneasy. Whether it was because the place itself was playing tricks with his mind, or that he was finding it difficult to accept that life could feel as good as this without something coming along to royally bugger it all up, Harry shivered.

A splash caught Harry's attention. Grace was at the pool's edge, already up to her knees.

Before he had a chance to think through exactly what he was doing, Harry swept through the gate, Smudge skipping along at his side, tossed his own bag onto the ground, and quickly changed. He didn't even bother with wrapping a towel around himself, instead, checking that no unfortunate stranger was about to pop their head around a rock or a tree, before he quickly whipped off his trousers and boxers and pulled on his swimming shorts.

Tucking the end of Smudge's lead under a hefty rock by his bag, Harry was quickly down at the water's edge with Grace, a few gingerly taken steps through huge boulders later. The sound of the waterfall was thunderous this close up, the pool clear, the bottom disappearing steeply into ominous darkness. Back at his bag, Smudge stared at them both, tail wagging.

Grace gave no warning, dropping low and sweeping into the water. Harry heard her breaths turn sharp as she swam out into the pool, the waterfall smashing down just a few metres away. Then Harry followed, giving no thought to the cold biting his skin as if it were a thing formed of a thousand ravenous, teethed fish. He waded in first, taking himself into deeper water with speed enough to cause a small wave, before finally tumbling forwards into the water with a splash.

Swimming out into the pool, Harry saw Grace smiling back at him, treading water as she applauded. His skin felt like he'd dived into a pool of needles, the pain a mix of burning and falling through ice. And his breath was short as he gasped between strokes.

'So, what do you think?' Grace asked, swimming over to join him.

'Bloody cold is what I think!' Harry answered, his voice harsh through chattering teeth.

'Good though, isn't it?' Grace asked. 'Wakes you up! And this is such an amazing place to have a quick swim.'

Harry was then acutely aware not just of where he was and what he was doing, but also of who he was with.

'You're smiling again, aren't you?' Grace asked.

'You're really getting the hang of this face, aren't you?' Harry replied.

'It's growing on me.'

Harry was about to say something about how no one in their right mind would want that, when a bright yelp and then monstrous splash split the moment in two.

'Smudge!' Harry roared, as the young dog, now in the water, swam out to join them, her lead dragging behind. 'You daft mutt! What are you doing!'

Smudge ignored Harry and continued to swim over, mouth seeming to grin at them as she paddled out.

'Doesn't like to be away from you, does she?' Grace observed, treading water with ease.

Smudge swam up to Harry and, once there, tried to climb up onto his shoulders.

'You bloody idiot!' Harry shouted, trying to get the dog off, but laughter was in his words. 'What are you doing? Get off! Come on, lass! Down! Get down!'

Smudge wasn't listening and instead just rested her front paws on Harry's head, as she sat on her owner's back, refusing to move and seemingly rather comfy.

Harry looked over to see Grace shaking her head and laughing. He then noticed that icy burning from his initial plunge into the water had subsided but that he was now starting to feel numb. There was a sluggishness to his movements as well as his blood was pulled deeper into his body and away from his limbs. And the weight of Smudge wasn't exactly helping either.

'Best we get back in,' Grace said. 'A dip's all well and

good, but unless you're used to it, this kind of cold will soon get you into trouble.'

She then kicked off back to shore and before Harry could set off to follow, Smudge leapt from his back and made chase.

Once out of the water, Harry felt a rush of endorphins flood his system, a mix of the water's cold and his own happiness at just how his life was turning out. Smudge shook herself dry then dashed about, tail wagging, clearly very happy with herself.

'Best you wrap a towel around you this time,' Grace said, nodding down the path, and Harry turned to see that at the gate a small group had gathered, staring not so much at the waterfall, but at the two idiots and their mad dog who had just gone for a swim beneath it.

Harry dressed as quickly as he could, aware of at least half a dozen pairs of eyes watching his every move. He heard a man's voice mutter something about his scars, shock threading the words together in a whisper.

Once done, Harry, with Smudge to heel, followed Grace back out through the gate and along the path towards the café. He was warming up now and as he went to ask Grace about the food at the pub, his phone buzzed in his pocket. It was in his hand and to his ear before he'd even realised what he was doing.

'Grimm.'

'Harry? It's Matt.'

Whatever cold Harry had experienced in the pool was now easily surpassed by the hacksaw-like chill he now felt at hearing the voice of his detective sergeant. Because if the reason for the call was important enough for Matt to interrupt Harry's day off, then whatever the news was, it was bound to be bad.

CHAPTER EIGHT

With Grace's help, Harry managed to persuade one of the pub owner's staff to give him a lift back into Hawes and to his own vehicle. Twenty or so minutes later, and with Smudge in Grace's care, he arrived at the location Matt had given him. The place was already buzzing with activity. In front of him lay a pretty patchwork of hay meadows, and once again Harry was faced with the truth that even in this, the most beautiful of places, awful things happened, lives were broken, people were hurt.

Harry was met at an open gate in the wall lining the road by PCSO James Metcalf. In his mid-twenties, Jim, as everyone knew him, was a busy lad. If he wasn't in uniform, he was out on the fells, helping his parents with the family farm in Burtersett, more often than not accompanied by his sheepdog, Fly.

A few metres along the road, Harry saw two vehicles parked up in a layby; a very clean, very expensive Range Rover, and an old hatchback that looked like it had not been washed since the day it left the car dealer's forecourt.

Harry turned into the gate, slowing his vehicle to a crawl and dropping his window into the door.

'Jim,' he nodded, a shiver racing through him then, an echo of the icy swim with Grace and Smudge.

'Hi, Boss,' Jim replied. 'Matt managed to get hold of you, then?'

The PCSO was armed with a clipboard and Harry could see that he was keeping a keen eye on the comings and goings of people at the scene of what had happened.

'He did,' Harry said. 'So, you're the Scene Guard, then?'

Jim gave a firm nod.

'Right then, what do we have?' Harry asked, looking over Jim's shoulder and into the green fields beyond. 'Who's here? What's happened?'

Harry could see an ambulance and police incident response vehicles. The grass of the field was short and he saw lines of bales drawn across it. A small group of trees were huddled together in the field.

'Everyone's here I think,' Jim said. 'Except for the scene of crime team, that is. But they're on their way.'

Harry frowned.

'Forensics? Matt said it looked like an accident.'

'It does, I mean it did,' Jim said. 'That's how it came in on the call, like, but we're not too sure.'

'Not too sure?' Harry said. 'Hardly the best reason to give for calling the SOC team, is it? Not the biggest fans of having their time wasted. Neither am I, for that matter.'

Harry was very aware that he sounded grumpy.

'Best you speak with Gordy about that,' Jim replied, then he pointed up into the field, towards the trees. 'She's over there with Matt, now.'

'Oh, I'll be doing exactly that,' Harry said. 'What about the rest of the team?'

Jim looked down at his clipboard.

'Liz is off today, and Jadyn is still on holiday. He's back tomorrow, though. Jen's over with Matt and Gordy.'

Liz Coates was the other PCSO on the team. Jadyn Okri was a police constable, Jenny Blades a detective constable. It was a small team, but pretty perfect all in all, Harry thought. He glanced over at the others.

'Can't see Jen,' he said.

'No, wait, that's right,' Jim said, shaking his head. 'She had to head off. Been a car accident over Aysgarth way. Sorry, should've said.'

Harry gave a grunt of acknowledgement then drove in through the gate. He parked up away from what was going on in the middle of the field, made sure he had his PPE on, and then headed off on foot.

The day was still and warm and Harry wondered what it would be like to have a job where days off weren't constantly under threat of being interrupted by work. Enjoying a full weekend, just relaxing without a worry, well that was something he wasn't sure he'd ever truly experienced.

A few minutes later he was walking up to an old tractor with a piece of farm machinery attached to the back of it, both of which were surrounded by strips of cordon tape. A figure broke away from what was happening and made their way over to meet him.

'Matt,' Harry said, using his Detective Sergeant's first name. That had been one of the numerous things he'd had to get used to when he'd moved up north from Somerset; everyone on his team using each other's first names. That level of familiarity just hadn't existed down south, or anywhere else in the force as far as he knew, but here, in Wensleydale, it was the norm. These people weren't just colleagues, they were friends, and they'd welcomed him warmly, as well as with copious mugs of tea, not to mention the cheese and cake. Harry was used to that now, even had a taste for the stuff, much to his constant surprise.

'Boss,' Matt said.

'How's Joan doing? Can't be long now.'

'It's not,' Matt said. 'Just a couple of months at the most I think, though I'm not very good with dates.'

'Well, you might want to get this one nice and clear in your head,' Harry said with a smile. 'The arrival of your first child's quite important.'

'It is that,' Matt said. 'Look, sorry about all this. But when you see what we have, you'll understand, I think.'

'I hope so,' said Harry. 'Jim's told me forensics are on the way. And I don't want to be the one telling Sowerby this was a wasted journey. She won't be too happy about that. Neither will I, for that matter.'

Harry's mind presented him then with the image of the pathologist, Rebecca Sowerby, and he quickly pushed it away again, preferring to deal with her in the flesh when she arrived.

'You won't be,' Matt said. 'Anyway, her mum's here and—'

'Margaret Shaw? She's here already?'

'She is that,' Matt said. 'And she agrees that making the call was the right thing to do.'

'So, we're consulting the district surgeon on police proce-dure now, are we?'

'I wouldn't say consulting, no,' Matt said. 'But you know what Margaret's like when she gets going. Hard to not be pushed along by her, if you know what I mean. She's a proper force of nature.'

'She is,' Harry said.

Again, Harry was aware of the grit and grumble in his own voice. Rebecca Sowerby's mother, Margaret Shaw, was the divisional surgeon. The team would've called her out to confirm the death of whoever was at the centre of what had happened. Harry liked her because she wasn't one for taking the long route round to getting to the point.

'The body was found just over an hour ago by the deceased's wife, Hannah Dinsdale,' Matt explained.

'Any relation?' Harry asked.

'To me? No,' Matt said. 'Dinsdale is just one of those names you'll find all over the Dales. A bit like Smith down south. Anyway, she's over in the ambulance.' Matt's eyes turned downwards and he shook his head. 'Poor woman, seeing that. Bloody awful.'

As yet, Harry wasn't fully up to speed with the details of what had happened, what it was that Mrs Dinsdale had found and he glanced over to see her sitting in the back of the ambulance. She was wrapped in a blue blanket, talking to a paramedic and Detective Inspector Gordanian Haig. The DI spotted Harry and gave a nod, signalling to him she'd catch up with him in a few minutes.

As for Mrs Dinsdale, even from where he was standing, Harry could see that she was in shock, her face pale as fresh pastry, hugging herself tightly. There also a man standing just a short distance away from her, on his phone, his back turned to Harry. He was wearing a green waxed jacket and Wellington boots, and even from here, Harry could see that neither had ever seen much in the way of rough weather and mud.

'Who's that, then?' Harry asked. 'Standing over there with Gordy and Mrs Dinsdale?'

'Richard Adams,' Matt said.

'Oh, him,' Harry said, recognising the man now. Harry recalled finding the man's son smoking a spliff down by Gayle Beck in his first couple of months in the Dales. He'd delivered the lad home and hadn't exactly received a welcome for it. As for Mr Adams himself, what Harry knew was that he was a businessman who'd moved to the area a few years ago and seemed to spend a lot of his time trying very hard to fit in while at the same time annoying everyone he met.

'He was with Hannah when she found her husband,' Matt explained.

'You know her, then?' Harry asked, noting Matt's use of the woman's first name.

'Around here, most folk know most folk, if you know what I mean,' said Matt. 'I don't know her well, like, just well enough to be friendly. Her husband, Bill, is, I mean, was, well known. Good farmer, always chatty. A generous man and well-liked.'

'Any family?'

'A son,' Matt said. 'Danny. We're trying to find him to let him know what's happened. Hannah said he was over this morning at the house, but that's the last that she saw him.'

Harry stared a while longer at Hannah and Mr Richard Adams. He had questions already, but there would be time enough to answer them. Now, though, he wanted to know exactly what they were dealing with.

'Come on then,' Harry said. 'Best you give me the guided tour.'

Matt said nothing more and turned back the way he'd

come, Harry following along at his side. As they drew closer, he saw Mrs Dinsdale look across towards him. Richard Adams did the same and raised a hand in a wave. Harry didn't return it.

At the cordon tape, Matt lifted it to allow Harry through.

'We've done what we can to preserve the scene,' he said. 'Never easy at the best of times, but at least the weather's being good to us. The paramedics arrived first so they had already been over to check the body, not that there was much point, really, as you'll soon see. And Hannah and Mr Adams as well, they've been over here, as you'd expect.'

Harry was already not liking what he was hearing. If this was a crime scene, then it was clear that the site had been disturbed considerably, and that would make identifying any evidence as to what had happened even more difficult.

'You ready for this?' Matt asked.

'Never,' Harry said, and ducked under the tape.

CHAPTER NINE

'Hello, Detective Chief Inspector!'

The voice, clear, bright and commanding came directly from Harry's right. Making her way towards him strode a woman in brown dungarees. She was wearing Wellington boots covered in patches usually used to repair inner tubes on bikes. Her green waxed jacket had seen better days, those days Harry estimated at being at least a decade ago, judging by the scuffs and rips in the old thing. One of the elbows was completely worn away and some attempt had been made at repairing it with black gaffer tape.

'Margaret,' Harry said.

'Thought I'd wait,' Margaret said.

'For me?' Harry asked.

'Oh, goodness no,' Margaret replied. 'You're far too young for me.'

'That's not what I—' Harry said but noticed a faint smile forming in the corner of Margaret's mouth.

'Rebecca will be here soon and I thought I might be able

to help her,' Margaret explained. 'At least pass on my observations personally. Always good to get it straight from the horse's mouth, wouldn't you say? Not that I look like a horse. Well, I suppose that depends which end you look at, doesn't it?' Margaret then tapped gently her own behind. 'Well upholstered round there, that's for sure, wouldn't you say?'

Harry had liked Margaret from the first moment he'd met her on his first case in the Dales. Her bluster and her somewhat dark sense of humour he found endearing. On the other hand, her daughter Rebecca had been considerably more difficult to get to know. But that relationship had warmed over the months and now Harry didn't feel so on edge at the promise of Rebecca's imminent arrival.

'What can you tell me, then?' Harry asked as the three of them closed the distance between themselves and the tractor just ahead. He could see now that the machinery at the back was a baler, not that he recognised it, just that it was a good guess helped by the line of bales leading up to it.

'Maybe you should just wait to have a look yourself,' Margaret said.

'But prepare yourself,' Matt advised. 'I've seen some awful stuff in my time, Boss, but this? Well, it's... I mean...'

The detective sergeant's voice died, breaking apart on the description he obviously couldn't bring himself to offer.

Harry moved away from Matt and Margaret and swung round to the right of the tractor and baler. He came full circle, doing his best to try and be open to picking up any little details that might be significant. The old rule was still the one he depended on most of all: look for something that should be there but isn't, or something that is, but shouldn't be. It was a mouthful, but it made sense.

Yet all he could make out was that the baler was attached to the tractor—an old grey thing and, Harry thought, surely better suited to being in a museum than out in the fields— and that both tractor and baler had come to a stop midway through turning the dried hay of the field about them into bales. The shaft connecting the baler to the tractor had snapped, though whether that had happened before or after the real reason they were all there he had no idea. Hopefully, forensics would be able to help with that.

Around and about the baler and tractor Harry was able to make out what looked to him like chips of wood, though from what he had no idea. Not something he would've expected, but perhaps a branch or two from one of the old trees at the edge of the field had somehow become caught up in the machinery, he thought.

With his first observations completed, and nothing really jumping out at him, Harry moved in closer, approaching the tractor from the front. Then, as the thought occurred to him that for Margaret to have confirmed death, there must surely be a body somewhere about, Harry's eyes, at last, fell on the remains of the victim.

'Good God,' Harry said, unable to disguise his shock, unable to take his eyes away from what he was now staring at, no matter how much he wanted to.

'Sometimes I wonder about that, you know?' Margaret said.

'About what? God?'

Margaret shrugged, her hands shoved firmly into her pockets. 'I've been a churchgoer on and off all my life, but when I see something like this?' She shook her head. 'Would any God of supposed infinite goodness allow something like this to happen? Just doesn't make sense to me at all. The great mystery of faith, I suppose.'

Harry had no answer to that, and right now didn't seem like the proper time to be holding a philosophical discussion on the nature of belief. Particularly with a surgeon who, in her free time, was also a member of the local church choir.

At first, it was a little difficult for Harry to make out exactly what it was that he was looking at. The baler was red and dusty and around it lay clumps of hay. Harry could make out a few spots of blood but nothing that showed him someone had died here. Close to the ground and attached to the underside of the baler was a cylinder covered in hundreds of wire spikes. Their job, Harry assumed, was to pick up the hay from the field and to churn it up into the baler compartment above. Here, through a range of mechanisms that he couldn't really make out, the hay was then shuffled along into the rest of the machine, that being a covered chamber, currently open, where the hay was compressed and tied in twine, before being deposited back out into the field.

In the righthand side of the compartment above the cylinder of wire spikes, Harry could see a pair of booted feet. They were almost comical to look at, sticking out like some practical joke left by a few young drunk farmers. The rest of the body was not visible, forcing Harry to walk around the baler and take a closer look inside the other chamber. And it was here where the true horror of what had happened was laid bare.

What had once been the living, breathing body of Mr Bill Dinsdale was now little more than a lump of broken, crushed meat and bone, oddly neat in many ways, Harry thought, as the poor man had been stitched into a hay bale.

Blood seeped out and onto the ground below. The internal mechanics of the baler had done to Bill what they would do to hay, crushing it and hacking it into a shape that it was never meant to achieve. Harry could see a good deal of Bill's body in the bale, but none of it seemed to be in the right place anymore, with a hand sticking out of the top, a shoulder at the rear, and most grisly of all, the smashed and minced remnants of the man's face at the front.

Harry stared for a moment at the body. This bleeding mashed up thing in front of him had once been a person, someone with a wife, a son, a life. And it had all come to a horrifyingly violent and terrible end. His job, the job of his whole team now, was to find out how. And if it wasn't an accident, then what actually happened? Because if someone was responsible for this, if someone had done this to Bill Dinsdale on purpose, then that was the kind of someone Harry wanted to be caught soon.

Harry gave a gentle nod to Bill, a silent agreement between himself and the dead to find out what had happened, then made his way back over to Matt and Margaret.

'You alright?' Matt asked.

'I've seen worse,' Harry said, 'but really only ever in theatre, if you know what I mean.'

'You don't talk about your time in the Paras much,' Matt said.

'No, I don't,' Harry replied, putting an end to that discussion before it even had begun.

'I've attended farm accidents before,' Matt said. 'We all have. But this really is something else.'

'Exactly my point,' Harry agreed. 'War is never kind to a human body, that's what war is. But you don't expect to see anything like that outside of it. And in a place like this? Somehow, that just makes it seem even worse.'

'And yet, here we are,' Margaret said. 'And on such a beautiful day, too.'

Harry turned to the district surgeon.

'So, Margaret, your view is that this wasn't an accident, then?'

'It's just an opinion,' Margaret said, 'and you'll all be onto the ins and outs of it soon enough, I'm sure. But yes, that's what I think having had a look around and at the body.'

'All opinions matter in a case like this,' Harry said.

'I know I'm just here to confirm death,' Margaret continued, 'and I wasn't really needed for that in this case, as you can see. But I'm sticking around to speak with Rebecca, like I said, just to share my thoughts with her. Also, I knew Bill.'

'What?' Harry was taken aback by this news. 'I'm... look, I'm really sorry. Maybe someone else should do this, then?'

Harry realised he'd reached out and had a hand on Margaret's arm, in a surprising attempt at comfort.

'Who?' Margaret said. 'Anyway, though I appreciate your concern, I'm fine. Death's something you come to terms with at my age. You have to or you'd go mad.'

'Even so,' Harry said, letting go of the district surgeon's arm.

'Even so, nothing,' Margaret replied. 'Bill was a good man and this, accident or no, needs to be got to the bottom of. And I can't help by buggering off for a cry, now, can I?'

'Of course,' Harry said. 'So, why do you think this could be anything other than an accident?'

Harry had his own ideas, but he was sounding Margaret out first.

'Well, you've seen where the body is,' Margaret said.

'And it's my opinion that there's just no way on earth that Bill simply fell in there by accident! And if he was going to end up anywhere at all, then it would be in the baler compartment itself, not where he is right now.'

'But that's where he is, isn't he?' Harry asked, looking back to the baler.

'Part of him is, yes,' Margaret said. 'But the rest of him is still above the pick-up.'

'That's the cylinder,' Matt explained. 'With the wires.'

'If he'd fallen onto the pick-up,' Margaret said, 'he'd have been ripped apart, bits of him would be everywhere. I mean all over the place.' Margaret spread her arms wide to emphasise the point she was making. 'It would've taken him apart like a blender then spread him around like mince.'

Well, that was a vivid description, Harry thought.

'And he's not just there, is he?' he asked.

'No, he most certainly is not!' Margaret said. 'I've seen accidents with balers before. If you're going to fall into one, then the bale chamber is where you'll do it, probably by getting caught up on some baler twine or something and getting dragged in. But only then if you're messing around with the thing while the engine is still running. Which, if you'll pardon my French, is the act of a bloody lunatic!'

'The engine must've been running, though, for him to end up where he is now,' Harry said, then he pointed at the shaft of metal hanging from the rear of the tractor which he could see had originally been attached to the baler. 'I'm assuming that's how the baler's powered by the tractor, and it's snapped clean off.'

'Which all goes back to the point I just made,' Margaret said. 'There's just no way he could have ended up where he is with the baler running.'

'Then how in God's name did he get there?' Matt asked. 'From what I knew of Bill, he wasn't one for cutting corners with stuff like this.' He looked to Harry and added, 'And don't be worrying about me; I knew of Bill, but I didn't know him. Anyway, that little Grey Fergie of his is in proper working order if you look at it, and the baler, too. They're both vintage bits of machinery, but they're well looked after, everything cleaned and oiled. This just doesn't make sense.'

'And what's with all the wood chips?' Harry asked.

'They're everywhere, aren't they?' Matt said. 'And I don't mean just on the ground either, I mean you can see splinters inside the baler itself.'

'Like something was shoved in there, you mean?' Harry asked.

'Wouldn't like to say,' Matt replied. 'That's a job for forensics. But possibly, yes, I suppose so.'

'A branch from a tree could've been lodged in there somehow,' Harry suggested. 'Maybe he was trying to unjam the machine?'

'Not with it still going, he wouldn't have been,' Margaret said. 'Not unless he was deliberately trying to do something extraordinarily stupid. Which I doubt.'

'Harry!'

Gordy's voice butted into the discussion and Harry turned to see the DI pointing through the spinney of trees to the other side of the field where two large and obvious white vans could be seen waiting to get into the field. Harry guessed that the driver of the first was talking with Jim, who would be busy writing down the necessary details on his clipboard.

'Speak of the devil,' Matt said.

'And she shall appear,' Margaret finished, though Harry noticed the flicker of a mischievous smile on Margaret's face.

Harry couldn't hide his smile, so he led them all away from the tractor, around the trees, and then back over to the other side of the cordon tape as the vans moved slowly into the field.

CHAPTER TEN

HARRY MET THE PATHOLOGIST OVER AT THE VANS, which were now parked up a good way from the area cordoned off by his team when they'd arrived on the scene.

'Nice day for it,' Rebecca said as she climbed out of her van to meet Harry. 'So, what are we dealing with?'

'What have you been told?'

'I'm not a fan of questions being answered with a question,' Rebecca said.

Harry gestured over at the field. 'Margaret... I mean your mother's here,' he said. 'Wanted to stay and have a word with you about it all I think.'

'Definitely dealing with a body, then,' Rebecca asked.

'I'm assuming you know that, otherwise, you wouldn't be here.'

'Fair point,' said Rebecca, as she finished pulling on all of her PPE, the white all-in-one suit she and the rest of her team wore bringing a sinister air to what should've been a pastoral scene, if it wasn't for the ambulance, police and the body. 'Though you do know we attend crime scenes that don't have bodies, don't you? We're not ghouls. We don't doggedly follow the Grim Reaper around as a matter of course!'

'Not what I was suggesting at all,' Harry said quickly, keenly aware of how sharp the pathologist could be.

'How disturbed is the crime scene?'

Rebecca was now at the rear of the van, guiding her team as they removed their equipment ready to head over to the tractor and baler and the grisly contents thankfully hidden from view. The photographer had already made his way over and was busy filling his camera's memory card.

'It looks okay, but it's hard to tell,' Harry said. 'From what I understand, the deceased's wife and a friend found him and called the ambulance, so I've no idea how much of the site has been messed about with. From what I can tell, the body hasn't been moved, but that's probably because, well, you'll see when you get there.'

Rebecca stared up at Harry, her eyes betraying her concern.

'Bad, then?'

'I've seen worse, but like I said to DS Dinsdale, never outside of soldiering,' Harry said.

'Best we get to it, then,' Rebecca said.

Harry stepped back and watched as the pathologist led her team up the field to the crime scene. On the way, Margaret joined her daughter and they stopped for a chat as the scene of crime team set themselves to work. It wasn't long before a white tent was set up over where the body was, to protect it as best as possible from the elements. And the weather could certainly change on a pin in the Dales, Harry thought.

'What next then, Boss?' Matt asked. 'Personally, I'm gasping for a mug of tea.'

Harry looked at his DS and saw merit in the idea.

'You know what, I think we all could do with one,' he said. 'And I'm pretty sure the SOC team will be grateful for one when they're done.'

'There's a new roadside café just away towards Hawes,' Matt said. 'One of those trailer ones. I could go and see if it's open?'

'On a Sunday?' Harry asked.

'Yorkshire, remember?' Matt said. 'There's always a need for tea!'

'Take Jim with you, then,' Harry said. 'You'll need two pairs of hands.'

'Anything to eat?' Matt asked.

Harry remembered then that he and Grace had been heading to the Green Dragon for a bite when the call had come in.

'Surprise me,' Harry said.

Matt laughed.

'You could be very sorry you said that.' Then, as he turned to leave, he said, 'So, what do you think?'

'About what happened?' Harry asked. 'Right now, I can't really say.'

Matt agreed and added, 'Hard to see how it was just an accident though, isn't it?'

'It is,' said Harry. 'We'll just have to wait and see what we get from forensics.'

'Margaret made some good points though,' Matt said. 'And I'm leaning towards that way of thinking.'

'Yeah, you're not the only one,' said Harry.

Harry then watched Matt head off to Jim before turning around to walk back up the field and over towards the ambulance. Over at the tractor and baler, the pale ghost-like figures of the SOC team were busying themselves with the job they'd been given, and Harry was put in mind of the kind of scene most people would only ever see on television or in the movies. There was something unnerving and chilling about the way the white-clad figures went about their work. As though the methodical nature of what they were doing added to the already sombre air.

Harry went up to the ambulance and was met just a few steps away from it by Detective Inspector Gordanian Haig.

'I hope we didn't drag you away from anything too important,' she said, her soft highland's accent adding a musical note to her words.

'If you'd have called a bit sooner you'd have saved me from going for a swim,' Harry said.

'A swim? Where?'

'Hardraw,' said Harry.

'The waterfall? Are you mad, man?'

Harry shrugged.

'It was Grace's idea.'

Gordy smiled, shook her head.

'Trust me, it wasn't funny,' Harry said. 'The water was so cold it burned!'

'That's not what I was smiling at,' Gordy said.

'Really? What, then?'

'If you don't know, then that's all the better, I think,' Gordy said. 'A good sign. Anyway, how's Smudge?'

'With Grace,' said Harry. 'When we were swimming, the daft animal jumped in after me and climbed onto my back! Nearly drowned me!'

Harry saw that Gordy was now fighting to keep her smile from breaking into a laugh.

'How're things here?' he asked.

'As you'd expect, I suppose,' said Gordy. 'Shock, disbelief, more shock. But then, no one can ever be prepared for anything like this, can they? The death of a loved one is one thing, but this? No, it's too much, for sure. An awful accident.'

'Hmmm,' said Harry.

Gordy looked at him now, concern in her eyes.

'You do know that by saying nothing you're actually saying quite a lot, don't you?'

'It doesn't look like an accident,' Harry said.

Gordy narrowed her eyes at Harry as though she hadn't heard him right.

'Not an accident? But the man's in a baler! How on earth could this be anything other than an awful accident?'

'That's what we have to find out, isn't it?' Harry said. 'I'm assuming you'll be looking after the family of the deceased?'

'I will,' Gordy said. 'There's a son, Daniel, as well, but as yet we've no word on his whereabouts.'

The detective inspector was also the family liaison officer and Harry could think of no one he'd ever worked with before who had been better at the job than Gordy. She had a firm, caring nature to her, cut through with a humour that was never misplaced and always welcome.

'He's local?'

'He is,' Gordy said. 'Hannah, that's Bill's wife, she said that she saw him this morning. She's tried to contact him but he's not answering his phone and, as yet, we've not managed to track him down.'

'That's a bit odd, isn't it?' Harry said.

'It is,' Gordy agreed.

'How was everything when you arrived? Were you first on the scene?'

'Paramedics were already here when we turned up,' Gordy said. 'Not by long, mind. They're excellent, by the way. Really on the ball with looking after their casualties.'

'Best I go and introduce myself then,' Harry said. Then added, 'Best you don't say anything about this being anything other than an accident. At the moment, that's just me thinking aloud. We'll need to wait on forensics, see what comes of that first before we know where we are.'

Harry left Gordy and walked on over to the paramedics. The first was a large, tall man whose face was mostly hidden by beard, and the other was a woman who was sitting with Bill's wife. They were both sporting tattoos creeping out from beneath rolled-up sleeves. Richard Adams was with them. Harry showed his ID, not that he needed to, but force of habit and all that.

'Any chance of a quick chat?'

The man turned to face Harry and direct him round to the side of the ambulance, at which point Harry noticed the large and quite astonishingly detailed tattoo of a spider that stretched across the man's throat.

Harry leaned in to double-check the man's name on his jacket. Standing closer to him now, Harry felt for a moment that he was in the presence of someone who was either directly descended from the Vikings, or who really, really wanted to be, and was doing everything in his power to prove it. Not just tall but broad, the man's beard was not so much simple facial hair as a work of art, trimmed and shaped so neatly it was impossible not to stare. And it was made all the more impressive by the polished baldness of his head.

'I won't keep you long,' Harry said.

'My name's Jack, by the way,' the man said, folding his

arms across his substantial chest. 'But most people call me Spider.'

'I'm sure they do,' Harry replied.

'I love spiders, you see,' Jack said. 'We both do.'

'Both?'

'Lauren and me,' said Jack and nodded over at the other paramedic. 'We met on the job, realised we both loved spiders, and here we are five years on! Amazing, right?'

'Very much so,' Harry agreed.

'And tattoos, obviously,' said Jack and pointed at the one on his neck. 'This was done from a photo of one of my own spiders, see? The detail's amazing.'

'I won't ask if it hurt,' Harry said. 'How is she?'

'Bit of a state, but doing okay, all things considered,' Jack explained. 'She'd found him and called the emergency services. Obviously, there was nothing we could do. I mean, you've seen him, too. Poor bloke. Horrible.'

'When was that, exactly?' Harry asked.

Jack checked his watch.

'We've been here probably forty minutes, at a guess?'

Harry looked over at Bill's wife, and at Mr Adams.

'They were both here?'

Jack gave a nod.

'Lucky he was with her, really,' he said. 'I don't think anyone would cope too well on their own faced with that.'

Harry silently agreed.

'Did you notice anything when you arrived?'

'How's that, then?'

Harry shrugged. 'Anything unusual or...?'

Harry's voice faded because really, when faced with someone killed by a baler, anything else unusual was probably going to be missed.

'Can't say that we did,' said Jack. 'We arrived, Lauren stayed with them, I went for a look-see over at the tractor, then your lot turned up a few minutes later.'

'Did you move anything or touch anything over at the crime scene?'

'So, it's definitely a crime scene, then, is it?' Jack asked. 'Not an accident?'

'Was the baler open when you arrived?' Harry asked, trying a different tack.

'It was,' said Jack. 'We didn't touch anything. There was no need. You saw that for yourself. And I was none too sure about the machinery anyway and didn't want anyone else getting hurt.'

'Sensible,' said Harry. 'Do you think they'd be okay to speak to me?'

'I should think so, yes,' said Jack. 'Now?'

'No time like the present,' Harry said then made his way back around at the rear of the ambulance.

'Just want to have a quick chat, if that's okay,' he said, looking to Mrs Dinsdale, who was still wrapped in a blanket.

'You sure that's necessary right now?' Mr Adams asked, even though Harry hadn't been speaking to him directly.

'Very much so,' Harry said.

'Hannah, she's had such a terrible shock,' Mr Adams continued. 'Could you not speak to her later? Wouldn't that be better for everyone?'

Harry thought for a moment, then said, 'That's a very good idea.'

Mr Adams seemed to puff himself up just a little at being listened to.

'I thought you would see sense!'

Harry ignored him and crouched down on his heels.

'Mrs Dinsdale?'

The woman looked up at him and in her eyes, Harry saw the shattered remnants of a life that had, only a few hours ago, been complete. He'd seen that look too many times before. This just never gets any bloody easier, does it? he thought.

'Firstly, I am deeply sorry for your loss.'

'Thank you,' Mrs Dinsdale said, her voice croaked and quiet.

'We will do everything we can to support you however we can. And I can already see you're in very good hands.'

Mrs Dinsdale just stared back at Harry.

'If it's okay,' Harry said, 'I'm just going to have a quick chat with Mr Adams here, and then I'd like to speak with you as well, if you don't mind?'

Mrs Dinsdale didn't answer, but her eyes widened just enough to tell Harry that just the thought of talking about what had happened was terrifying.

'It won't take long,' Harry said, doing his best to reassure her. 'Just a few questions, that's all. If we want to talk to you again, well, we can make arrangements for that later, can't we, I'm sure?'

Mrs Dinsdale gave a nod, wiping her eyes at the same time.

Harry was back up on his feet, eyes on Mr Richard Adams.

'After you,' he said, and then with an outstretched arm, directed the rather surprised-looking man back to where he'd just spoken with Jack, the paramedic.

CHAPTER ELEVEN

'This won't take long,' Harry said.

'That's not a problem,' Adams replied. 'I'm just concerned for Hannah, that's all, as I'm sure you understand.'

'You were with her, then, when she found her husband?' Harry asked.

'I was, yes,' said Adams. 'And I'm thankful that I was, because facing this on her own would've been terrible, I'm sure. Poor woman. Horrendous for her. Horrendous for everyone. Bill was an important member of the local community. He was a good man and will be missed greatly. A truly tragic accident.'

Harry noticed how Adams had a way of speaking that gave the impression everything he said was well-rehearsed.

'So, you were here first, then. No one else around?'

'No,' Adams said.

'Perhaps you can take me through it?' Harry asked, notebook at the ready. 'From when you arrived?'

'I'll do my best,' Adams said.

'Well, that's all I can ask, isn't it?' Harry said. 'It's also all I expect.'

Adams cleared his throat, took a deep breath like he was preparing himself for a terrible ordeal.

'We could see that something was wrong as soon as we arrived,' he said. 'The tractor, it wasn't moving. We couldn't see Bill anywhere.'

'And that was when you arrived, yes?'

'It was.'

'What did you do?'

'We went over to see what was wrong, of course,' Adams said. 'We called out for Bill, but there was no answer. We soon found out why.'

'What did you see?'

'What you've seen for yourself,' Adams said. 'The tractor, the baler, Bill...'

'Were there any other cars in the area when you arrived?'

'No,' Adams said.

'I understand that Mrs Dinsdale has a son.'

Adams rolled his eyes, shook his head, let out a breath through his nose.

'Yes, she has a son. Daniel.'

Harry jotted down the name, noting the hint of disdain in Adams' voice.

'Do you know where he is?'

'I haven't the faintest idea, no,' Adams replied, his tone cutting. 'But I know where he should be and that's right here, with his mother.'

'I'm just trying to work out the order of things, that's all,' Harry said. 'You're here and Hannah's son isn't and I just wondered if you knew where he was, if she or you or anyone else has managed to contact him about what's happened to his father? From what I understand, he's local?'

'He is, yes,' Adams said. 'Works with his parents on the farm after being away for quite a few years. But I understand that your team is currently trying to locate him?'

Harry wasn't sure if there was a dig in what Adams had just said or not, so he moved quickly on so as not to give it enough time for him to think about it.

'Can I ask, please,' he continued, 'where you were before you came to the field?'

'At home,' Adams said. 'Where else would I be? It's a Sunday after all, and I usually try to keep it quiet, spend it with family, that kind of thing. Go to church if the mood takes me. Not really my thing, but sometimes, it sort of fits, doesn't it?'

'And where was Mrs Dinsdale?'

'How you do mean, where was she?' answered Adams.

'As you arrived here together I'm assuming that she was with you before you came here. Did she visit you?' Harry asked. 'And if so, can you tell me why? Or did you meet her? Which again leads me to ask, why?'

'I'm sure Hannah will be able to tell you more when she's able to,' Adams said. 'However, yes, she arrived at my house a few hours ago. She wanted to speak to me about something and to ask if I wouldn't mind then speaking to Bill about it, too. So, we drove over here together. Those are our cars on the road over there.'

Harry didn't know what to make of what he was being told. For a start, Mr Richard Adams really didn't look or feel like the kind of person either Bill or Hannah would have much to do with.

'Do you know Bill well?'

'I knew him well enough, yes, of course,' answered Adams. 'On a social-professional level, that is, if you know what I mean.'

'I don't.'

'Rotary,' said Adams.

'What is?'

'We're members,' Adams said. 'The Rotary Club? It's a national organisation, I'm sure you've heard of it.'

'Oh, that,' Harry said.

Harry had never been the biggest fan of clubs of any kind. Particularly not ones that always seemed to revolve around businessmen with lots of money, desperate to show everyone else just how much of it they had and what they were doing with it. And all behind the guise of raising money for good causes, which they clearly did, and Harry had a quick word with himself to rein in his grump, which was even affecting his unspoken thoughts.

'You should join,' Adams said, his face brightening with a smile.

'Good God, no!' Harry replied, the words out before he'd had a chance to stop them. 'I mean, it's just not my kind of thing, if you know what I mean.'

'I'm not sure that I do,' Adams said. 'It's not like the Free Masons, if that's what you're worried about.'

No, he wasn't worried about that, Harry thought, but the small number of run-ins he'd had with that particular organisation was also another reason that put him off joining any kind of large club. That, and the funny hats.

Harry was losing track now of what point he'd been trying to get to.

'So, Hannah visited you and then you both came to the field to speak with Bill,' he said, just going over things again to remind himself as much as anything. 'I assume that it was important?'

'Just a little bit of personal business, that's all,' Adams said. 'Nothing that important, really.'

'Doesn't sound like it wasn't important,' Harry replied. 'Not if Hannah came out to see you about it and then you both drove over here to see Bill to continue the discussion. I mean, it must have been important enough for you to do that, mustn't it?'

'Bill has a bit of a reputation,' Adams said. 'Some of his ideas are a little out there, you see, and not everyone is as supportive of them as he would wish. I am, of course, and Hannah was concerned and thought I would be good to speak to. Bill can be a bit of a handful, I think, but in the best of ways.'

'And you're the one to help handle him?'

'I'm always happy to help another member of the Rotary,' Adams said. 'That's what it's all about really. Mutual support.'

Harry, not really sure now where the conversation was going, went to ask another question when Gordy hurried around the side of the ambulance. She was on her radio with urgent worry in her eyes.

'Gordy? What is it?'

'It's Matt!' Gordy said, walking on past Harry at a pace and over towards the field's gate. 'I mean, it's Jen, there's been an accident! Matt and Jim are on their way now.'

Harry was confused.

'What accident? I thought Jen was attending one?'

'She was, I mean she is,' said Gordy, pausing from rushing on to answer Harry. 'But there was a hit and run and Jen was the one who was hit!'

Gordy's words hit Harry with the force of a train wreck and he left Mr Adams and the conversation behind him and chased after her.

'What do you mean Jen was hit? Where? What happened? Bloody well slow down and tell me what's going on!'

Gordy stopped.

'I don't have any other details,' she said. 'I'll let you know more when I get there.'

Gordy turned back towards the gate, breaking into a jog.

'No, you bloody well won't!' Harry shouted, catching up quickly with the detective inspector. 'You're staying here and I'm going!'

'No, it's not a problem at all.'

Gordy halted at the gate.

'I'm not asking, I'm telling!' Harry growled. 'Get in touch with her parents and let them know what's happened, and keep me up-to-date with whatever's going on here, understand? Including finding out where Hannah's son is.' Harry looked over at Mr Adams. 'And tell him that I want to continue my little chat with him tomorrow.'

'You should stay here,' Gordy said. 'This is a crime scene. You're the ranking officer and—'

Harry cut the detective inspector off.

'Don't go telling me what I should or shouldn't do! I know exactly what I am and where I should be!'

Harry's words were sharper than he probably meant them to come out, that much was obvious from the narrowed eyes Gordy was using to stare at him. He also trusted that the DI would let him off this once. Then he was running, searching in his jacket pocket for his keys as he did so.

'Harry!'

Harry reached the gate, turning at Gordy's shout of his name.

'What now?'

'Don't drive like an idiot, you hear?' the DI shouted. 'Matt will be doing that for the both of you, I'm sure.'

Harry gave a nod, raced the last few metres over to his vehicle, and was gone.

CHAPTER TWELVE

THE JOURNEY FROM THE CRIME SCENE OVER TO JEN AND whatever had happened to her went by in a blur. Harry's chats with Jim, Matt, and Margaret, with Rebecca and Gordy and the delightful Mr Richard Adams, were forgotten for now, though the tattoo of the spider on the paramedic's neck would probably haunt him forever.

All that mattered right there and then was that at the end of this journey one of his team had been involved in an accident. How bad it was, whether she was injured or not, and if so, how badly, Harry hadn't the faintest idea, but a hit-and-run was never going to be good. How it had actually happened and who was responsible he'd worry about after, but first, he needed to be there for Jen.

Matt and Jim would arrive before him for sure, and he had every confidence in them not just as police officers but friends. And that in itself was something he still wasn't completely used to, the whole blurring of lines between colleague and friend. But it didn't change the fact that he needed to be there as soon as he could.

Having left the field and followed the lane along to the end, Harry came out at the hamlet of Worton, a place so small that you could blink and miss it. Oddly though, it did have a house which had, many years ago, been a pub, and insisted on still looking like one whether the owners wanted it to or not. Here, Harry took a left and pulled out onto the main road, heading away from Bainbridge, its beautiful village green and historic Roman fort, and on towards Leyburn. Bainbridge also had stocks on the green, a form of punishment that Harry couldn't really condone. On the other hand, he'd met a good number of criminals for whom a stint in the stocks, being pelted with anything rotten and squishy from the vegetable aisle at Sainsbury's, would do the world of good. Not necessarily for them, perhaps, but certainly for the people, for their victims.

The road was clear and he sped on, the landscape around him barely registering. Soon he was climbing out of the valley and up into Aysgarth, a village Harry hadn't really taken much notice of as yet during his time up north. It was a place he always passed through rather than a destination. Jen's accident was out the other side of the village so he sped on, the road heading past Aysgarth Falls and back down again towards the valley floor, carved into the landscape over thousands of years by the river Ure.

Harry was working hard to not think the worst, refusing to accept that Jen would be in a bad way. But not knowing was almost worse than knowing, so he pushed all thought from his mind and focused on the road ahead.

After a straight, flat section lined with the emerald green of Dales pastures, the road hooked a left into the shadow of trees and, a few seconds later, Harry saw flashing lights.

Slowing down, he spotted two cars, one upturned on its roof, two ambulances, and two incident response vehicles, one of which he assumed was Jen's, the other belonging to Matt and Jim.

Jim was out on the road directing traffic around the accident, not that there was much to direct. The vehicles which had been involved in the original incident, for which Jen had been called, were still on the road and to one side of a sharp right over a bridge. As for Jen, Harry couldn't see her yet, just the vehicle she had driven over in, which was in one piece.

Harry eased off the accelerator, slowed down, and pulled his vehicle to a stop. Jumping out, he was over to the scene in a few strides.

'Matt?' Harry shouted. 'Matt! Where the bloody hell are you? Matt!'

'Over here!' came a voice from one of the ambulances, followed by a sharp whistle.

Harry jogged over just as the other ambulance pulled away, lights flashing. So, that was the other accident being dealt with, Harry thought, but what about Jen? Was she okay? What the hell had happened?

Harry stared in through the open door of the ambulance to see Jen lying on the gurney. Lights blinked at him as he tried to make out just how bad it was, but it was hard to tell beyond the wires, the medical equipment, and her blood-soaked uniform. Matt was with her, along with two paramedics.

Harry went to speak, but no words came, the shock of what he was seeing squeezing his throat to a tight choke.

'She's okay,' said Matt, but Harry could see from the pale face of his friend and colleague that she was anything but.

'She clearly isn't!' Harry said, his gruff voice axe-sharp. 'So don't you try and bullshit me, Matt! What the hell happened? What? And where's the other vehicle? The one that hit her?'

Matt made to respond but wasn't given a chance.

'What details do we have? We need officers on this now! We need them on the road and we need them finding the bastard who did this, you hear me? I want—'

Harry saw Matt give a nod to the paramedics, realised just how loudly he was shouting, and cut himself short. He then stood back as the detective sergeant made his way out of the ambulance, leaving Jen behind in obvious good care.

'What the hell are they waiting for?' Harry asked, looking over Matt's shoulder, his voice an angry hiss through clenched teeth. 'Shouldn't they be heading off to hospital with her right now? What's the delay? Even I can see that she needs urgent attention, and it's a good few years, to say the least since I had to medivac someone with injuries!'

Harry was raging but he still allowed himself to be led away from the ambulance just a few paces.

'They're keeping her stable,' Matt said, his voice calm and firm. 'Air ambulance is on its way.'

'Air ambulance? What?' Harry clenched and unclenched his fists. 'Bloody hell, Matt! Why didn't you tell me?'

'You didn't really give me a chance.'

'Is she okay? I mean, I can see that she's not, but what have they said?'

Air ambulance: it was both the best and the worst news in two words, Harry thought. It meant that Jen would be at hospital within only a few minutes of being picked up, and that was a relief. But it also meant that her injuries were potentially very serious, even more so than those of the drivers in the accident she'd been sent to attend to in the first place. And no, Harry thought, that wasn't irony, that was just life being an unfair bastard, as it so often was. There was the chance that it was all just a precaution, but even so, it was a massive jump in what he'd been expecting to roll into when he'd arrived.

'She was first on scene at the original incident,' Matt explained. 'Had it all in hand from what I've been told, which is no surprise, is it? The drivers of the two vehicles were okay, just a few cuts and bruises, like, nowt serious at all. Amazing really, all things considered.'

Harry glanced over at the two cars.

'Even the person driving that one on its roof?'

'Hard to believe I know, but yes,' Matt said. 'Bit shook up but that's about it. Probably more worried about the insurance.'

'Lucky,' Harry said. 'And then someone hit Jen?'

Matt took a deep breath and let it back out slowly before speaking again.

'She had the two drivers away from their vehicles, had given them a check over herself, made sure they were comfortable and safe while they all waited for the ambulance to arrive, which it did soon after. She'd gone over for a chat with the paramedics and was then just walking back out into the road to direct traffic, when—'

A thrumming sound filled the air, cutting Matt off. Harry glanced up, looking for the helicopter, remembering doing the same in theatre, battle-weary, bloodied, and gasping for a brew. Then the bright yellow of the helicopter was right there and coming down in the field directly over from the ambulance holding Jen.

Matt said no more as they both jogged over to the ambulance, the paramedics already on with transporting Jen on the gurney over to where the helicopter had now settled.

'Anything we can do?' Harry asked.

'Yeah, stand back, if you could!' one of the paramedics replied, a firm kindness in his voice that had Harry doing as he was told.

A couple of minutes later, watching Jen get lifted into the helicopter, Harry's gaze drifted over to the two cars on the road. Jim was there, too, carefully guiding an SUV past what had happened and on over the bridge.

From where he was standing, Harry could see that the corner leading onto the bridge was more than obvious to any oncoming driver, as the ambulance would have been as well. So how the hell had they not seen it? What on earth had happened for Jen to be hit by a car while attending a traffic accident? Harry quickly ran through the options that to his mind would potentially explain what had happened.

It could be a drunk driver, he thought. Yes, it was only the afternoon, but that didn't stop some folk from having a good go at pickling themselves when there was still a good deal of the day left to live through. A quick trip to a pub chain open early enough to serve breakfast and you'd find people enjoying a full English with what was often not their first pint of the day. The thing was, Harry thought, if someone was pissed enough to not notice they'd hit someone, then there would be every chance they'd be found in their own vehicle incident a little further on, wrapped around a tree or upside down in a field. But there had been no reports of anything like that, had there?

Another thought, and one more common nowadays, Harry thought, was someone on their phone behind the wheel; texting a friend, checking emails, flicking through whatever pointless social media accounts they had, hell, even taking a bloody selfie! But again, Harry wasn't so sure. Where the accident had happened, any sharp reactions on the part of the driver would have more than likely had them slamming into the bridge. Looking up from a phone at the point an accident happened wasn't the kind of thing that generally resulted in anything other than blind panic.

The helicopter was in the air now and Jen was on her way, the paramedics making their way back to their ambulance.

With no conclusions as to how the accident had happened, Harry pulled himself out of his thoughts and spoke with Matt.

'So, someone hit Jen while she was doing her job, and then immediately buggered off,' he said, a chill wind catching him as it whipped its way through the trees and along the road. But it was nothing to the ice in Harry's veins now, and the burning rage in his guts. He started to make his way over to the paramedics, Matt alongside, and gave a wave over to Jim. 'From which direction?'

Matt pointed back up the way Harry had driven down on his way over from the fields by Askrigg.

'Aysgarth way,' the detective sergeant said.

'Then they'd have seen all of this, wouldn't they?' Harry said, sweeping his arms out to take in the whole area where the accident had occurred. 'The road's clear and nothing is obscuring the view, is there? Not a bloody thing!'

'And yet they still hit her,' said Matt, his voice quiet, though Harry detected something darker in it, a hint at the rage the man was feeling, and an emotion he obviously wasn't used to. Unlike Harry, who'd spent decades keeping his at bay and who was very close to just letting it break free right now.

'Deliberate carelessness, that's what it is,' Harry said then, as they drew close to the ambulance, his voice quieter, darker. 'Whoever it was, they came through here hard and fast, and they didn't have the time or the inclination to stop. Hitting Jen? It just didn't matter.'

'How do you mean?' Matt asked.

'I mean,' Harry said, 'that wherever they were going, or whatever they were leaving, that was clearly their number one priority. Hitting Jen just didn't figure in their minds at all, did it? And they'd have heard the impact as well seen it.' Harry looked up the road, then back across the bridge. 'Did anyone see what happened other than Jen?'

'The two casualties now on their way to hospital,' Matt said. 'And the paramedics who've taken them. Jim's grabbed some quick statements from them all and contact details so we can follow up.'

'Well, that's something,' Harry said.

A voice interrupted Harry and Matt's discussion.

'Er, excuse me?'

Harry and Matt turned to find themselves staring into the face of one of the paramedics who had been attending to Jen. Just a young man, Harry thought, his own dark eyes staring now into the bright, fox-keen face of the paramedic.

'Yes?' Harry said.

The paramedic held out his hand. In it was a key.

'She gave me this,' he said. 'And told me to give it to someone when they turned up. I'm assuming she meant you.'

The paramedic tipped the key into Harry's hand.

'She was speaking, then?' Harry asked.

The paramedic gave a nod.

'She was in a lot of pain,' he said. 'We gave her something to help with it. Didn't speak much after that. At all, actually. Means it was working anyway, doesn't it, the pain killer?'

'And Jen gave you this?' Harry asked, ignoring the paramedic's rambling. 'Why?'

The paramedic shrugged.

'All she said was that I had to give you the key and to tell you to check on Steve.'

Harry frowned.

'Me specifically?'

'You're DCI Grimm, right? She mentioned your, er...' The paramedic circled his own face with a finger.

'Yes, I'm Grimm,' Harry said. 'But just who the bloody hell is Steve?'

'Boyfriend, maybe?' the paramedic suggested.

Harry looked at Matt.

'Jen ever mentioned a Steve to you?'

'Not that I can remember,' Matt said. 'She's quite a private lass, though, isn't she?'

'So, who is he, then, and why on earth do I need to check up on him?' Harry asked. 'You know where Jen lives?'

'Yes, over in Middleham,' said Matt.

'You have an address?'

'We all have her address,' Matt said. 'And each other's. Just look under contacts on your phone. I can show you how, if you want?'

Harry said nothing, clenched his jaws and shoved the key into his pocket.

'There's nowt to worry yourself with here,' Matt said, gesturing over at the upturned vehicles. 'You go off and do as Jen asks. And you'll be off to the hospital after, no doubt, so let us know how she is, won't you?'

'You do know I'm in charge here, right?' Harry asked. 'DCI, remember?'

'Obviously,' Matt said.

A few moments later, Harry was back in his vehicle and heading down dale to Middleham.

CHAPTER THIRTEEN

Having followed Matt's directions, Harry concluded that next time it would just be easier to have the detective sergeant with him. He'd managed to find his way to Middleham, which wasn't too difficult seeing as he'd been there before when he'd bought himself an old egg poacher from a little antiques shop. It was at this point that everything then went a little bit wrong and Matt's directions became vague, to say the least. He'd given them begrudgingly, admonishing Harry for having neither a vehicle with sat-nav nor the patience to use it on his phone. Regardless, where Harry was now, he was pretty sure that Jen didn't live here at all, not least because directly in front of him was a ruined castle.

On arriving in Middleham, Harry had driven on into the small marketplace. The centre was a cobbled island and Harry wondered just how treacherous the place became on a harsh winter's night, a hard frost turning the cobbles to black glassy domes. Around the cobbles and facing in, were numerous grand-looking buildings and Harry had the impression of walking onto a film set of how people imagined the Dales to be. Except that, quite wonderfully, this was actually what it was like.

He'd noted a number of pubs and decided he'd have a word with Grace later to see if she fancied coming over here for a meal some time. It was close to where her dad lived anyway, over in Redmire, so she would probably have a good idea as to which was the best pub in town. From the centre of town, Harry had then made his way down some very narrow streets indeed, done a few about-turns, explored a few more even narrower streets, until finally he'd given up and just parked outside the castle.

As ruins went, it was a thing of rough beauty, Harry thought. It was a building that had clearly been a grand residence in its day and yet somehow had become magical in its decay, almost as though the damage gave it character. There were stories to be told in those walls, Harry thought, because as he knew better than most, scars were the teller of tales.

Turning his back on the castle, and leaving his vehicle behind, Harry walked down to the main road. Turning left would only take him out of Middleham, so he headed right, into town. Then, going over Matt's directions, he took a left soon after, wondering then how he'd missed it, to begin with, and end up where he had. He walked along this road a way, the older, historic dwellings giving way to more modern buildings, until he was at last at the estate where Jen lived.

Harry checked the key to remind himself of the house number. Then on he went along a road, around a large patch of grass, and to Jen's house.

In front of the house was a lawn, neatly edged. He went to the door, slipped in the key, and pushed on in.

Inside, the house was as neat as the small lawn at the front. Nothing was out of place, though that wasn't really difficult, Harry thought, considering just how little there was in the way of clutter. Jen, Harry could see, was someone who had a place for everything and clearly made sure that everything was in its place. A rack under the stairs was stacked neatly with running shoes, running equipment, a couple of rucksacks. There were photos on the wall, not stuck up haphazard, but neat and orderly, a gallery of goodness knew how many events that the detective constable had entered.

Harry then thought about why he was actually there, to check on Steve. He scratched his head, looking about the place. Steve? Just who the hell was Steve? Well, Harry thought, it was pretty bloody clear from what he'd seen of the house so far that Steve was absolutely not a secret boyfriend. Because no bloke Harry had ever known could exist in something this ordered, neat, and tidy. He wished he could himself, and he'd tried, but it had never quite worked out in the same way.

Harry went through to the kitchen. He was still none the wiser as to who or what Steve was, though he was mightily impressed with Jen's fantastic fridge, and how every work surface was completely clear. He then moved through to the lounge. Here, the walls contained a continuation of the gallery from the hall and the more Harry looked at the photos the more irritated he felt with himself about his own dwindling interest in trying to keep fit. It was clear from what he saw, and what he knew of Jen anyway, that she didn't have that problem at all. Maybe he could persuade her to help him a bit more? No, better still, to help the whole team!

Harry was just imagining Matt's face at being given a

fitness plan when a movement caught his eye. He snapped round on his heel, expecting to see either someone standing over in the door or a cat. Neither were there to welcome him. Then he saw the movement again, this time realising it was from over on the large and very comfortable-looking sofa up against the wall. It was covered in cushions and for a second or two, Harry was half convinced that he'd been seeing things. Then the movement came again and he realised that no, he wasn't seeing things at all, and that the who and the what of Steve was there right in front of him.

'Bloody hell, Jen!'

The lizard was, to Harry's eyes, at least four feet long, from the tip of its nose to the end of its tail. He'd not noticed it when he'd come into the lounge because against the cushions it was fairly well camouflaged, particularly when it was sat so still.

Harry wasn't really sure what to do. He'd never checked up on a lizard before. He had no idea what exactly it was that he was checking for. Then he saw on the wooden floor over by French windows, opening out onto a neat and tidy back garden, a small bowl of water, almost empty. Harry picked it up, topped it up in the kitchen, then placed it back down. As he did so, Steve the lizard slid off the sofa and padded slowly across the floor to the water for a drink.

Stepping back to allow Steve past, Harry couldn't resist and reached out a hand to touch the creature. Steve stopped what he was doing and looked up at Harry, staring into his face. Harry gave Steve's head a scratch, then Steve, clearly done now with Harry, went back to his water.

Moving back out into the hall, Harry glanced upstairs. His next port of call was to get back in his car and to head over to the hospital in Northallerton to check up on Jen, so it would be sensible, then, to take in a few things from home, a book perhaps, some clean clothes. But checking up on Steve was one thing. Looking through someone's wardrobe for a comfortable sweater, well, that was a big no.

Harry pulled out his phone and made a call. And exactly half an hour later, there was a knock at the door.

'Thanks,' Harry said, opening it, allowing Grace in. Over her shoulder he saw Smudge in the window of her car, staring at them both.

'So, one of your team owns a lizard called Steve, then,' said Grace.

'He's in the lounge,' said Harry. 'Probably lying on the sofa again. Bloody difficult to see, he is.'

Grace popped her head into the lounge then looked up the stairs.

'I'll be five minutes,' she said, then was gone.

Harry went back through to the lounge. Steve was nowhere to be seen. Harry had a moment of panic, worrying then that Steve could, when he wanted to, move lightning quick. And that he had, when the front door had been opened to let in Grace, done a runner. The thought of having to do a search for a lizard in the Dales didn't really fill Harry with glee. Neither did the idea of having to share the news with Jen. But then a movement had caught his eye and he'd spotted Steve, or at least the end of his tail, slinking behind a soft chair in the corner of the room.

Harry stood at the French windows looking out into the day. He'd gone from a freezing cold dip in Hardraw to seeing a violent death in a field, a shocking accident involving one of his staff, and now, to cap it all, a massive lizard that could, very easily, hide in plain sight.

Grace was at the door.

'This should do,' she said, a small suitcase in her hand.

'You found that as well?' Harry asked.

'The case? No, that's mine. I've grabbed her some clothes, some stuff from the bathroom, and a couple of books from her bedside cabinet that looked like she was reading.'

'Thanks,' Harry said, though instead of looking at Grace directly, he was staring into the middle distance.

'You okay?' Grace asked.

'The lizard,' Harry said. 'I mean, it was there, right in front of me, and I just couldn't see it. Didn't even notice it!'

'It's well camouflaged, like you said,' said Grace.

'Yes, but it's not just that, is it?' Harry said.

'How do you mean?'

'I wasn't looking for a lizard so I didn't see one,' said Harry.

'I'm not following you,' said Grace.

Harry wasn't so sure he was following himself either, but his brief meeting with Steve had made him think over the last few hours, the crime scene in the field, the accident.

'I'm missing something,' Harry said. 'I just know it. Something's right there in front of me, probably really bloody obvious, too, like Steve back there, but because I don't know what it is, I can't see it.'

'I can see how that would be a problem,' said Grace. She handed Harry the suitcase. 'Want me to come with you?'

'To the hospital?' said Harry. 'No, there's no point in that. And what would we do with Smudge? Head back to yours and I'll see you later.'

'You sure?' Grace asked.

'Absolutely,' Harry said.

Outside, and pulling the door closed on Jen's house,

Harry again thought about Steve, about the field, and about Jen. But no matter how hard he thought, he just couldn't see clearly, not yet anyway.

But he would, Harry thought. Of that, he was absolutely bloody certain.

HAVING MADE his way over to see Jen, Harry had not been able to do much other than leave with her parents the bag of her things. Jen herself was unconscious and wired to so many machines that really there had been little point in him staying.

'You met Steve, then?' Jen's dad had said, a man just the other side of fifty by the looks of things, Harry had thought, and as wiry and fit-looking as was his daughter. 'Elusive little bugger, isn't he? Don't know what she sees in him, but there you go. And between you and me, she's brought worse home in the past, if you know what I mean. That's our Jen: one of a kind, that's for sure.'

'She is that,' Harry had said, and then gone on to reassure them both as best he could that he and the team would do everything they could to find those responsible for what had happened.

'And thanks for bringing her things over,' Jen's mum had then said. She was very much like her husband and daughter, another runner, Harry thought. He could see Jen in the woman's eyes, a sharp keenness in them, like those of a hawk. 'I hope it didn't take you too long to find it all.'

Harry spotted the hidden thoughts in those words and said, 'Grace, my, er... she came over, sorted it all out for Jen, brought over one of her bags to use as well.'

'Grace one of the team, is she?' asked Jen's mum. 'Jen's not mentioned her.'

'No, she's not one of the team,' Harry said. 'She's my, er...'

Harry was struck then by something strange: what to call Grace. Was she his girlfriend? He supposed she was, but they'd never said anything official as such. And that word—girlfriend—it just seemed too young, didn't it, for what they were? Teenagers had girlfriends and boyfriends. But middle-aged men and the women mad enough to see something in them, perhaps not. Partner, then; was that it? No, couldn't be, Harry thought. An awful word. Anyway, they hadn't been seeing each other for very long, and the word partner simply felt too serious for something so new. The confusion over this lasted all the way home and Harry came to no conclusion at all.

Later that evening, Grace popped over to Harry's to drop off Smudge with her rightful owner. Harry had been so wrapped up in what had happened to Jen that he'd forgotten to call in on his way home from the hospital.

'You can stay, you know,' Harry suggested, doing his best to stifle a yawn. 'It's no bother. No, what I mean is, that'd be great. But, you know, if you have to go, then ...'

Grace laughed.

'You'd be no use to me! You're exhausted!'

Harry stood back, doing his best to look shocked at what she was clearly implying.

'I'm fine!' he said. 'Better than fine! Fit as pins and raring to go!'

But Grace was having none of it.

'I've an early start anyway,' she said and planted a soft

kiss on his rough cheek. 'I'll give you a call tomorrow. Plus, I need to keep an eye on Jess, don't I? Those little pups are certainly keeping her busy.'

And with that, his girlfriend, his partner, Grace... was gone.

Harry slipped back into his flat, Smudge at his feet. As for his brother Ben, he was, as was becoming increasingly common, staying over with Liz, and Harry wondered how long it would be before they'd look to getting a place of their own.

Harry made his way into the lounge and slumped down on the sofa, resting his head back and closing his eyes. Smudge jumped up beside him and rested her head on Harry's lap. Harry scratched the dog behind the ear and thought back over the day.

As days went, it had certainly been one to remember, though not necessarily for the right reasons. With what had happened to Jen taking him away from the scene over by Askrigg, he was still mulling over his thoughts on that and not really coming up with much.

There had been a message on his phone earlier, from Detective Inspector Haig, but she'd not been able to give any more detail beyond what he already knew. It was an odd one though, he thought, that was for sure. How Bill Dinsdale had ended up in that baler, Harry didn't know, but thinking about what Margaret had said when they'd walked around it, had certainly made him suspicious. Yes, farm accidents happened because farming was dangerous. But this just didn't smell right to Harry. Something about it was off. And those wood splinters still bothered him, too, the perfect example of something that was there that he was pretty sure shouldn't have been. And he knew that, on their origin, could easily hinge where things would move next.

Yawning again, Harry eased himself forward to pull himself out of the sofa. He fancied spending a few moments staring into the fridge, willing it to provide him with a drink and a snack. But as he rose to his feet, his phone rang.

CHAPTER FOURTEEN

'Grimm,' Harry said, shaking his head at his inability to not answer the damned phone just once for a change.

'Sorry, I know it's late,' came the reply. 'I shouldn't have called. Don't know what I was thinking.'

'Sowerby?' Harry said, recognising the pathologist's voice, a yawn breaking free as he spoke.

'Yes,' Sowerby said. 'I thought, seeing as you had to rush off earlier, that you'd probably want to hear what we've found so far? I hadn't realised it was so late. I'll call you first thing tomorrow. Sorry.'

'No,' Harry said, quickly jumping in before the line went dead. 'Now's good.'

'You sure?'

Harry rubbed his eyes, pushing the weariness back into them, but it just pushed its way out again as another yawn.

'I'm sure, I'm sure,' he said.

'So, how are things?' Sowerby asked. 'I heard one of your

team was in an accident. That was why you had to head off, wasn't it?'

'She's in hospital,' Harry said. 'Hit and run.'

'Really? That's horrific!'

'Yes, it is. She was attending another traffic incident when it happened, would you believe?'

'What? That's, well, it's not worse, but it also is. I'm so sorry, Harry. If there's anything I can do...'

Harry was a little taken aback by Sowerby's use of his first name so didn't answer.

'So, you were ringing about today,' he said, keen to hurry the conversation along.

'God, yes, sorry,' Sowerby said. 'The baler.'

The image of what Harry had seen a few hours ago in the otherwise quiet and simple beauty of a Dales meadow crashed into his mind, bright and vivid and bloody.

'It looked bad,' he said. 'Sometimes, no, a lot of the time, actually, I don't know how you folk do your job.'

'I wonder that myself,' Sowerby said. 'Anyway, I can confirm the obvious for a start.'

'Dead, then?'

'Very much so. And despite what we see on television, I can't actually give you an exact time of death, but it was clearly only a few hours earlier, probably late morning, maybe early afternoon. But I'm putting my money on early afternoon.'

'Why's that, then?' Harry asked.

'Stomach contents,' Sowerby replied. 'The deceased—'

'Bill Dinsdale,' said Harry.

'Yes, well, he'd had his lunch. Cheese and pickle sandwich, a pork pie, as well. There was some apple in there, too.'

'Yeah, that's not breakfast, is it? So, how did he get in the baler?'

'With a great deal of difficulty,' Sowerby said. 'And not all by himself, either.'

'He couldn't have fallen in, then?'

'The injuries would have been different and he probably wouldn't have ended up where he was,' Sowerby said. 'Also, no, I just don't see how he could have fallen in. At all. The angles are all wrong for a start, the height of the baler. It's just not something you fall into. He could've been dragged into it, I think, but from what we've seen, it doesn't look like that happened.'

Harry remembered what Sowerby's mum, Margaret the district surgeon, had said.

'You agree with your mum, then.'

'Sometimes, yes,' Sowerby said. 'By which I mean all of the time, when it comes to work, anyway. But we still looked at everything, where the body was, injuries in relation to what caused them and how—that kind of thing. But there was something else, too.'

'Was there?' Harry asked. 'What?' Then he added, 'You mean you've already done the autopsy? On a Sunday?'

'Didn't have much else to do,' Sowerby said. 'Sometimes it's better to just get on with things, isn't it? And tomorrow will be busy anyway.'

Harry understood. This kind of work messed with the way of life most people wanted—nine-to-five, the weekends free.

'The body was a bit of a mess,' Sowerby explained, 'but some of the injuries don't match up to what we would have expected.'

'In what way?'

'Blunt force trauma,' Sowerby said. 'Skull fractures from something hard and heavy.'

Harry wasn't so sure, not after having seen the body himself.

'You sure about that?' he said and regretted it immediately.

'Of course, I'm bloody well sure!' Sowerby snapped back.

'Look, no, that's not what I meant,' Harry said, backtracking quickly. 'Came out wrong.'

'Happens a lot, doesn't it?'

Silence took over for a moment and Harry hoped they could get back to what they'd been talking about without focusing too much on his considerable lack of tact. Sowerby knew her stuff, that much he was very sure about, having worked with her a good number of times now. But there was still an edge to her, particularly if what she was saying was questioned. He was the same though, wasn't he? he thought.

'The injuries from the baler, well there's lots of crush injuries, that kind of thing, broken bones, all from being pulled through the machine. Add to that lots of penetration wounds, deep cuts, burns, too, from the baler twine as it was pulled tight, what with everything getting tangled as he went in deeper.'

Sowerby was painting a very grim picture indeed, Harry thought. Bill Dinsdale's last moments on Earth had been the stuff of nightmares, a horror movie brought to life.

'However, there are impact wounds on the skull, like I said. And I would be confident in saying that they occurred before the deceased entered the baler.'

At this, Harry clenched his jaw, breathed hard and deep.

'So, let me see if I have this right,' Harry said, 'because it sounds to me like what you're saying is that our victim, old

Mr Dinsdale, was twatted hard on the bonce before being shoved headfirst into the baler,' he said.

'I'm simply giving you my observations and findings,' Sowerby said. 'But yes, that's a fair conclusion.'

Harry shook his head. So, it was a murder they were dealing with then, or at least that's what it looked like. But then again, it still struck him as a little over the top as a way to kill someone. There was something off about the whole thing, he thought. Setting out to kill someone with a baler required forethought. Plus, why do it in the first place? He'd dealt with some rough crime scenes and awful deaths in his time, and those were usually carried out both as punishment and warning.

Harry had witnessed the worst humanity could do to its own. No matter how hard he tried the memories stuck with him, scars he carried deep inside as obvious to him as the ones on the rest of his body, his face. The worst of them had involved everything from boiling cooking oil to chainsaws, drills, and woodchippers. Being dragged into one of those thanks to a rope around your ankles and your hands behind your back was no way to go, but it was certainly effective, both in the death it meted out and the terror it sent to one's enemies. But a baler? Really? Harry wasn't buying it. Exactly what he wasn't buying, he wasn't sure, but he would be. And soon.

'What about all those splinters of wood?' Harry asked. 'They were all over the place. I thought it might be from a branch or something?'

'They were in the baler as well,' Sowerby said. 'And we found further wood splinters around and embedded in the fractures in the skull.'

'Sounds to me like whatever was used to knock Bill unconscious went into the baler with him,' Harry said.

'It certainly looks that way,' Sowerby said. 'And for his sake, I hope that he was.'

Harry silently agreed.

'Analysis of the fragments identified the wood preservative creosote.'

'Not a branch, then,' Harry said. 'More like a fence post.'

'Perhaps carried to the crime scene,' Sowerby said.

'Anything else?' Harry asked.

'We've found a small amount of blood on the baler,' Sowerby said. 'It doesn't belong to the victim. And there are some threads of material. We'll have those analysed as soon as we can.'

'So, there's DNA, then?'

'There is, yes, but it's only of any use if we have someone to match it to, isn't it?'

Harry heard paper being shuffled.

'Other than that,' Sowerby continued, 'it's impossible to tell how many people were in the field before we all turned up, so we have nothing to offer with regards to imprints, anything like that.'

'Fair enough,' Harry said. 'But that's a good deal to go on, anyway. Thanks.'

'I'd say it was a pleasure,' Sowerby said, 'but I don't think that really ever fits a conversation like this, do you?'

'I appreciate the thought,' said Harry.

'Well, if I find anything else, I'll let you know,' Sowerby said. 'Photographs and a report will be to you tomorrow or the day after.'

And with that, they finished the call and Harry was left in silence.

When Harry finally rested his head on his pillow and closed his eyes to the world, he did his best to block out the day he'd just lived through. But Bill Dinsdale, dead and in a freezer somewhere now, had other ideas, as the last thing Harry saw before sleep took over was the old man's face staring at him through twisted metal, and the lurid orange of baler twine pulling his skin into a bleeding, weeping knot.

CHAPTER FIFTEEN

WHEN MONDAY CAME ROUND, HARRY WASN'T SURE HOW best to greet it. A bloody good kick up the arse sprung to mind, he thought, but that probably wasn't for the best. So, breakfast done, and with no Grace around as a distraction, Harry took Smudge out for an early morning walk, then made his way along to the Hawes Community Centre.

Arriving before the rest of the team, he unlocked the door and headed in, Smudge settling down in a bed he'd bought for the dog a few weeks ago. And the dog was very much making the most of it, Harry noticed, as it snuggled down, clearly aware that when Jim turned up, so did his dog Fly, which meant very little rest for either of them.

Kettle on, Harry popped a tea bag into the enormous pint mug Matt had bought him a few months ago from a caving café over in Ingleton, when a knock came at the door. Harry turned to see the silhouette of a man standing there in the half-light.

'Morning,' Harry said, checking his watch to see that it wasn't even seven-thirty yet. 'Can I help?'

The man stepped into the room.

'Ah, Mr Adams!' Harry said, unable to disguise the surprise and disappointment in his voice at recognising the man.

'You suggested yesterday that I should pop in if I could spare the time,' Mr Adams said.

'I did?' said Harry, thinking back. 'Yes, you're right, I did. And, well, here you are, nice and early.'

'This was the only time I could find to spare I'm afraid. Early, yes, but I hope I'm not too early?'

The kettle clicked off.

'Tea?' Harry asked, avoiding the question because yes, the man was early, but there was nothing he could do about that now.

'Do you have Earl Grey?'

Harry's laugh was immediate and loud.

'I very much doubt it!'

'Then no. But thank you.'

Harry made himself a mug of tea then guided Mr Adams back out of the office, bringing a glass of water for the man in case the conversation went on just long enough for him to require it. He left Smudge behind, the dog lying on her back in her bed, dead to the world.

'We've a few other rooms here,' Harry explained, opening the door to one as he spoke. 'Good for interviews, confidential chats, that kind of thing. Another for evidence storage. It's quite the Tardis back here. Hard to believe when you look at the place from the outside.'

'I'm sorry, but I don't watch Doctor Who,' said Mr Adams.

'Neither do I,' said Harry. 'I was just...' but Mr Adams was already in the room so Harry followed and shut the door.

In front of them was a table with two chairs on either side.

'Take a seat if you would,' Harry said, sitting himself down.

With Mr Adams now sitting opposite, Harry reached over and placed the glass of water in front of the man then took a sip from his tea. The liquid was just shy of being hot enough to scald: perfect.

'Needs a biscuit,' Harry said, putting the mug down on the table. Or cake, he thought, maybe even some cheese, regardless of it being so early in the day. Though he was quite sure his detective sergeant would tell him, *'There's no such thing as too early for cheese.'*

'No, I've just had breakfast, thank you,' Adams said, then he tapped his stomach. 'Need to keep those pounds off.'

If someone had brought him a nice new packet of Chocolate Digestives, Harry had a feeling he would've consumed the lot and to hell with trying to be healthy.

'So, where were we?' Harry asked, taking out his notebook and flipping through to his notes from the previous day.

'Have you managed to contact Danny?' Adams asked.

'Daniel?' Harry asked, trying to place the name. 'Bill and Hannah's son?'

'Yes,' Adams said. 'Daniel. Unless there's another one I'm not aware of?'

'Right now, I'm not actually sure,' said Harry. 'I was called away yesterday, as you know, and I'm sure there will be plenty of updates for me this morning once I have the team together for our Monday meeting.'

'It's rather a small team though, isn't it?' Adams said. 'Must be challenging.'

'It can be,' Harry replied. 'Policing has changed a lot over the years, as you know.'

'And you cover a very large area.'

'We do,' Harry said, not exactly sure where this was all going. It certainly wasn't going anywhere near the incident in the field the day before. 'It's not easy, but the team here, well, they're the best I've worked with, if I'm honest. Though I'd be grateful if you didn't tell them that. Don't want it going to their heads.'

Harry wasn't really sure that Mr Adams was listening as he then asked, 'Do you have much support in the community?'

This chat was turning into an interview, Harry thought, and not the right way round, either.

'As far as I know, we do, yes,' Harry said, struggling to get back in control. 'Now, about yesterday, Bill Dinsdale...'

'You see, this is why I really think you should come to one of our Rotary meetings,' Mr Adams said, ignoring Harry's attempt to get back to the reason he'd wanted Mr Adams to pop in in the first place. 'It could prove to be very beneficial.'

Harry wasn't sure what to say in return, so he said nothing and waited for the other man to speak some more. It was clear from his body language that he was going to. He had the air about him, Harry thought, of a man used to speaking in public or at the very least in front of people in meetings, of being listened to.

'Everyone there, well, they're local business people, you see, community leaders, that kind of thing. It's exactly where you should be, don't you think, forging good and close working relationships with just those same people?'

Harry didn't want to think about being anywhere near it,

but now that he was being forced to, he wondered if the man had a point.

'And you said that Bill Dinsdale, he was a member, correct?'

Adams gave a firm nod.

'This thing that you said Hannah came over to see you about, before you went to the field to talk with Bill, was that to do with the Rotary?'

For the first time, Mr Adams was quiet.

'No. Well, not as such, but I think I need to leave that for Hannah to talk to you about,' he said.

'And why's that, then?' Harry said, leaning forwards a little, making himself look just that little bit bigger. 'If you think it has anything to do with Bill's death, then don't you think you should tell me?'

'What do you mean? Bill's death was an accident!'

The man had a point, thought Harry. His own chat with the pathologist the night before had made him think otherwise, but that needed to be discussed first with the team and then with Hannah. The last thing he needed right now was Mr Adams here heading off into the great unknown and blabbing on. Information was a sensitive thing and how it was dealt with and shared was a careful business. One wrong statement, one misplaced piece of information, and everyone was under scrutiny. Even worse, the press would be all over it, vultures hungry for fresh meat.

Harry changed tack, ignoring what he'd just said.

'Is there anything you can tell me, anything you might think important, before I speak with Mrs Dinsdale?' Harry asked.

Adams shook his head. 'I do not think it appropriate for

me to talk about anything which may be deemed personal to the DinsDales. I'm sure you understand?'

'No, I'm not sure that I do,' Harry said, taking a long, slow drink from his mug of tea.

Mr Adams leaned back in his chair and folded his arms across his chest, resting his chin in his right hand for a moment.

'Look, what I can tell you is that the reason Hannah came over, well, it was to do with a property purchase,' he said. He then leaned forward, his forearms on the table, hands clasped together. 'Bill's personal history is a very interesting one and it's all tied up with that. Bill was a little bit political you see. And I think that got on a few people's nerves. Yes, he was very well-loved, but still, now and again, I was given the impression he could be a bit, shall we say, preachy?'

'And what do you mean by a little political?' Harry asked. 'Or preachy? In what way? Because that's a pretty broad statement, isn't it? I mean, I'm a little political. Preachy not so much, but I worry about things. I'm sure you do, too.'

'Of course,' Adams said.

'The environment, for example,' Harry continued. 'That worries me greatly. I also have a bit of a problem with anyone who actually wants to be in government or to sit on a council, that kind of thing, do you know what I mean? People who thirst for a little bit of power and control. As good a reason as I can think of for them to not have it.'

Harry could see that Adams was a little uncomfortable now. Good, he thought.

'Other things bother me, too, like why is it that pubs and restaurants serve food on slabs of slate or wooden platters? I don't know about you, but I want my food on a plate and I absolutely don't want my chips to arrive in a little wire basket on the side!'

Adams was shuffling in his chair now, on the spot and out of his comfort zone.

'But we were talking about Bill, not me, weren't we? So, what was it, exactly, about Bill?'

'I don't think it's really for me to say,' Adams said. 'I've always maintained that issues such as religion and politics, for example, they're personal. So, I suggest you speak to Hannah about it when you can. Though I'm fairly sure that she won't be in any fit state to talk about it for a good while yet.'

Harry could see that he was going to get no further with Mr Adams and sat back in his chair. There was no point pressing, not right now. And just because one door was shut, that didn't mean another wouldn't open. He'd be sending Gordy off to see Hannah that morning and she was very good at opening doors, very good indeed. That Scottish accent of hers, it was like a secret weapon.

'When's the next meeting of this Rotary, then?' Harry asked, looking to draw the chat to a close. 'Might make sense for me to come along, like you said.'

Mr Adams looked almost surprised, Harry thought. He'd have to see if he could do something else at some point to have the same effect, to keep the man on edge a little, break through that steely shield of confidence he wore so well.

'It's this week, actually,' said Adams. 'Tuesday evening, seven-thirty. I can give you the details if you wish?'

'That would be very useful,' Harry said, and pushed himself away from the table and then up onto his feet. 'If you could just write them down for me now, that would be great.'

Harry flipped his notebook to the back, revealed a clean

page, and handed Mr Adams his pencil, who then jotted down a reminder of the time and an address.

'Is there a dress code at all?' Harry asked. 'Special handshake?'

'As I said yesterday,' Adams said, 'we are not, and we never shall be, the Free Masons.'

A few minutes later, and as he was seeing Mr Adams off the premises, Harry remembered something from the day before.

'You were on the phone,' he said. 'When I saw you in the field yesterday, I mean.'

'Yes, that was a call to Mr Turner,' Adams replied.

'And he is?'

'The chair of the Rotary,' Adams said. 'Thought it best to let him know about what had happened, so that we can all support Hannah. And Danny, obviously.'

'Fair enough,' Harry said.

Back in the main office, the rest of the team had now all arrived.

'Wondered where you'd gone,' Matt said, approaching Harry. 'I mean, your dog was here, but you weren't, not that Smudge seemed to miss you too much.'

Harry looked over to see his dog on her back again, but this time in the corner of the room and with Fly standing over her. Both animals were wagging their tails and baring teeth playfully.

'Mr Adams came in for a chat,' Harry explained.

'Early.'

'Very.'

'Useful?'

Harry shrugged. 'I'll see how tomorrow evening goes before I answer that.'

'How's that, then?' Matt asked.

Harry told him.

'Don't they wear funny hats?' Matt said. 'And have a weird handshake?'

'Rotary, Matt,' Harry said. 'Not Free Masons. Apparently, it's a lot different. Bill Dinsdale was a member.'

'I'm not seeing the connection,' Matt said.

'Neither am I,' Harry said.

A laugh bounced over from the other side of the room and Harry looked over to see the ever-beaming face of Jadyn, back from his holiday.

'I hate to say this,' Matt said as the young police constable now made his way over, 'but I think he's come back even more keen than when he went away.'

'That's not actually possible,' Harry said.

Jadyn came to a halt in front of Harry.

'I'm back, Boss! Did you miss me?'

'You've been away? Really? Can't say I noticed that you'd gone, if I'm honest,' Harry said, with a wink to Matt.

'Then you won't be getting your present, will you?'

At this, Harry frowned.

'Present?' he said. 'You bought me a present?'

'Don't look so worried!' Jadyn said. 'And I didn't just buy something for you, either, I bought something for everyone. Here!'

Jadyn held out a bag, which was obviously rather heavy from the way the straps were cutting into the constable's hand.

Harry hesitated before taking it. He wasn't used to getting presents at the best of times, and most definitely not at all from the people he worked with and managed. No, that was a lie. He remembered one Christmas a while ago now when he'd come into the office one morning to find a parcel waiting for him on his desk, all wrapped up with ribbons. Beautiful it was. To this day he still remembered the moment he'd opened it, the smell, and the investigation that had followed. Right now, he had some hope, at least, that Jadyn's gift wasn't going to be so gruesome or lead to the lad being put away for the rest of his life like the sender of that particular gift had been.

Jadyn shook the bag.

Harry took it and, with a concerned look at Matt, opened it.

CHAPTER SIXTEEN

'CIDER?' HARRY SAID, THE BAG OPEN, AND IN HIS HAND A cardboard container holding four bottles of the stuff.

Jadyn grinned and nodded.

'You see, we were down in somewhere called Cheddar,' he said, attempting an explanation. 'Me and the family, that is. We usually try and get away together. There's a lot of us, like, what with my two sisters and older brother, my uncles, grandparents. I thought it was pretty funny that they'd named the place after the cheese, but anyway, it's Somerset, isn't it? Cheddar, I mean? And I remembered that was where you were from before you came here, so I thought I'd bring you something to remind you of it.'

Harry lifted one of the bottles, saw the ABV was over seven percent, and slipped it back in with the others.

'Cheddar wasn't named after the cheese,' Harry said. 'It's the other way around.'

'That doesn't make any sense at all,' Jadyn said, shaking his head. 'The cheese is proper famous, isn't it? Anyway, it was after I'd bought those that I then realised I didn't know if you liked cider or not. But there you go, I hope you do. Like cider, I mean.'

'I do, actually,' Harry said. 'Haven't had any since coming up here. Doesn't really seem to be much of a thing in the Dales.'

'No, not really,' Matt said. 'Not exactly awash with orchards up here. Though my old gran, she used to have a few plum trees. I remember picking them for her as a kid, and she'd make this amazing plum jam!'

'Very thoughtful of you,' Harry said, resting the bag on a table behind him. 'You shouldn't have.'

'You've not tried them yet,' Jadyn said. 'Might taste like piss!' The constable's face froze in shock at what he'd just said to his commanding officer. 'No, I mean, you might not like them! But that's okay, if you don't because you can just give them back, and...'

Harry said, 'Don't worry, I'm sure they'll taste great.'

Jadyn smiled then turned back to the rest of the team as Gordy came over.

'If you want to head off to see Jen, I can run this,' she said.

'Thanks,' Harry said, 'but visiting times aren't till later anyway.'

'Anna will be visiting her as well, this afternoon I think,' Gordy said. 'I spoke to her last night. She was really concerned, not just about Jen, either, but about you, about all of us, actually. Kind of in her nature, I think, if you know what I mean.'

'How is she?' Harry asked.

Anna was the vicar over in Askrigg. She and Gordy had been a couple for a good few months now and things seemed to be going well for them. Harry had noticed how Gordy seemed more settled again, which was good.

There had been the faintest threat of her wanting to leave, to head back home, as she called it, to the Highlands of Scotland. But now, with a new romance blossoming, that seemed to no longer be on the cards. For now, at least. Harry was pleased about that. The last thing he needed was to lose someone like Gordy to a bunch of coppers from Police Scotland. Not that he had any personal beef with them, just that he'd been to Scotland himself. He'd experienced the midges and the rain, the disturbing obsession with Irn Bru, and firmly believed that Gordy would be wasted up there. And, if she stayed there too long, probably in more ways than one.

'She's great,' Gordy said. 'Busy, but that's the job. It's a bit all-consuming I think.'

'Like this one, then,' Matt said.

Gordy nodded in agreement.

'Most days she's out visiting, popping in to see how people are, doing the shopping for those who can't, just being someone to talk to, anything to help, really. Weekends are as busy as weekdays and evenings are filled with meetings, Bible studies, chats with people wanting to get married, all kinds of stuff to be honest. She's helped farmers deliver lambs, driven people to hospital, and once she even had to go and have a chat with a ghost!'

Harry saw Matt's eyes nearly pop out of his head.

'What, an exorcism?' he said. 'You're joking, right?'

'Church of England isn't really into any of that stuff,' Gordy said, 'but she knew the family was worried. So, she went over, sat up all night in this supposedly haunted room, and just chatted, threw in a few prayers and a Bible story or two, I think, and then that was that.'

'That was that?' Matt said. 'How can sitting in a haunted room be "that was that"? What happened? Did she see anything?'

Gordy looked at Harry, gave a wink, then turned back to Matt and said, 'Well, next time you see her, you'll have to ask her yourself!'

'Do you get to see her much?' Harry asked. 'Anna, I mean.'

'As much as I can but not as much as I'd like to,' Gordy said, but there was a flicker of a smile on her face. 'Which is a good sign, I think, don't you?'

'I do,' Harry said. 'A very good sign indeed. Right, shall we crack on, then?'

Matt leaned in and said, 'Best give them a five-minute warning.'

'What? Why?'

'Just enough time to get another brew on.'

'Good point.'

Five minutes later, Harry was standing up facing the rest of team, who were all sitting in front of him, nursing freshly brewed mugs of tea. Matt had grumbled a little that there was no cake but had then promised everyone he'd rectify that later and make sure there was enough in before the day was out to last them a few days. Under a table, Fly and Smudge were curled up, fast asleep.

'Right then,' Harry began, noticing then that just on the periphery of his senses, an ache was beginning in his head, the sharp stab of a pain promising worse to come. 'We've two things to be going on with; yesterday's events in the field over by Askrigg, and Jen.'

Movement caught Harry's eye and he watched Jadyn stand, and without any announcement whatsoever, walk over to a board on the wall behind Harry, wipe it clean, and pull out a pack of drywipe pens.

Harry turned to raise a single eyebrow at the police constable.

'All ready when you are, Boss!' Jadyn said, waggling a pen at Harry.

'Well, that's good to know, thank you,' Harry said, and turned back to the team. 'So, let's start with Bill Dinsdale.'

'Horrible way to go,' Jim said. 'Farm accidents are never anything other than horrendous.'

Harry decided to not pick up on what Jim had said about it being an accident; that would all become clear soon enough.

'I'm over to see Hannah, his widow, today,' Gordy said. 'She was in a rough way yesterday, and I made sure there were friends around to be with her. The shock of it all was almost too much.'

Harry was glad to hear that Gordy was already on it with Bill's wife.

'Understandable,' he said. 'What about her son, Daniel?'

'Danny?' Gordy said. 'No word from him yet and no one's seen him since the day before yesterday.'

'Bit odd,' Harry said. 'He needs to be found, not just to let him know what's happened to his father, either, but to be there with his mum.'

'It is strange, though,' said Jim, looking over at Gordy, 'him not being around, isn't it? Good way to look guilty if you ask me.'

'No jumping to conclusions,' Harry said.

'Jim has a point though, doesn't he?' Gordy said. 'Danny was over to his mum's in the morning. Apparently, they had a bit of an argument and then he left.'

'Argument?' Harry said. 'What about?'

'They're farmers, remember?' Gordy said, 'So the list is a long one, I suspect. Debt, for sure. Prices going up and down, how to run the place, changes. Hannah didn't say much about it, but I'm going to see if I can get a bit more out of her today.'

'We definitely need to find this Danny, then,' Harry said. 'Anything else from Hannah? Any other family?'

'No,' said Gordy. 'They're not a normal Dales family, really.'

'How do you mean?'

'Not from round here is what she means,' Liz said. 'I don't know much about it, but I don't think Bill's local, is he?'

'With a name like Dinsdale?' Harry said, looking then at Matt. 'Didn't you say that it's like the Dales version of Smith?'

'It's a good name, is Dinsdale,' said Matt. 'A strong name. Solid. Dependable.' No one laughed, much to Matt's very obvious disappointment. 'Well, anyway, I think his parents came over here during the war. I don't know much about it. Actually, I think that's all I know. But yes, Liz is right on that.'

Harry remembered his chat with Richard Adams earlier, him mentioning that Bill's past was an interesting one.

'Gordy, you think you can find out a bit more on all that?'

'I'll do my best.'

'Mr Adams mentioned something about a property purchase as well. It's why Hannah was with him in the first place. I tried to get to the bottom of it all, but he's a bit wriggly, if you know what I mean?'

'I do,' Gordy said. 'I'll see what I can dig up.'

'If Hannah can provide further details on that, at least we

can get that end of things all neat and tidy, can't we? Oh, and he mentioned something about Bill being political. No idea why, but worth looking into that, too.' He turned to Jim. 'Did we get anything from any of the neighbours?'

'Not really, no,' Jim replied. 'Mainly because there aren't any. Those we spoke to in the few houses around there saw nowt out of the ordinary. They'd seen Bill heading to the fields in his tractor, a few cars, but that was it.'

'Any details on the cars?'

Jim shook his head.

'Not very helpful really, I know. Sorry about that.'

Harry decided then that it was a good time to share what he'd learned from the pathologist during her phone call the night before. The team sat quietly as he went through the points he'd discussed with Rebecca, behind him Jadyn's ferocious penwork on the board squeaking away. Their quiet acceptance that this was no longer just an accident was admirable.

'So, someone knocked him out and then shoved him in the baler?' Matt said. 'But... but that's crazy! Who the hell would do that? And why? It doesn't make any sense!'

'The how's just as much of an issue,' said Jim. 'My dad has a baler just like Bill's. Refuses to get a new one because the old one still works, though only because he's constantly tinkering with it.'

'What do you mean?' Harry asked.

'If Bill was near the baler, checking it over, then the tractor would be off, wouldn't it?' Jim explained. 'The engine wouldn't be running. That's just good practice. Safety and all that.'

'People make mistakes, take shortcuts,' suggested Harry. 'You know that as well as anyone.'

Jim shook his head.

'No, not with a baler or anything like that they don't,' he said. 'Bill certainly wouldn't anyway. You don't go fiddling around with what's going on inside if it's all still moving! You'll lose an arm and that's just for starters. That's how folk get killed.'

Liz said, 'And they have been too, right? There's been a lot of accidents with balers over the years, all over the country.'

'I was chatting with Dad about it last night,' Jim said. 'You see, Dad knew Bill, but then everyone knows everyone round here, pretty much, don't they? Anyway, he was saying that Bill was even more of a stickler for doing things properly than he is apparently. Always double and triple-checking everything. Not one for cutting corners or being lax about safety, was Bill.'

Harry was quiet, for a moment, thinking about what had been said.

'Trouble is, Sowerby's findings don't lead to that conclusion, do they?' he said then. 'I think it was all probably meant to, you know, have us thinking that old Bill was involved in a horrifying and tragic accident. But I also think what we can all see now quite clearly is that something else went on. And, even though this might seem impossible considering what happened, something much worse. Because this being an accident, that's one thing. This being deliberate?'

Harry shook his head.

'Bill, he wasn't a small bloke either,' said Matt. 'I wouldn't have tried lifting him, that's for sure.'

'How do you mean?' asked Liz.

'I mean,' said Matt, 'that as we all know, it's not easy to lift a fully grown man. We've all dealt with drunks, people who've been in accidents. They're a bugger to shift if they're in no fit state to help.'

'And?'

'And,' Matt said, 'if old Bill has been thumped on his head by a fence post or whatever, then I'm assuming he's on the ground unconscious, yes? Which means whoever did it now has to pick him up, carry him, and throw him into the baler, don't they? And that's a tough job for two people, let alone one.'

'We don't know how many were down there with Bill,' Harry said. 'But your point's a good one.'

Harry winced then, the sharp pain in his head stabbing forward harder than before.

'You okay?' Matt asked.

Harry waved away the question, focusing on the meeting.

'Right now, we've bugger all to go on,' he said. 'Suspects wise, I suppose we've the currently missing son, Danny, and that's it. What I do know is that something about this doesn't smell right, like it's not going to be that simple, if you know what I mean. Plus, we need to share this with the deceased's wife. And that's not easy.'

'I'll do that this morning,' Gordy said, raising her hand. 'As I said, I've already arranged to head over and check up on her. She's going to need a lot of support through this.'

'You sure you're happy to do that?' Harry asked, steeling himself to head out after the meeting with Gordy.

'Absolutely,' Gordy said. 'We've spoken, so there's that trust there already. And I'll see if she's heard from her son, maybe find out a little bit more about the family, that kind of thing, see if I can find out why she was with Adams.'

'And I'll head back over to the field,' said Jim. 'Have a

look round. I know the SOC team have done their thing, but you never know, right?'

'Whereas lucky me over here, I've landed myself with attending a meeting of the Rotary Club tomorrow evening,' Harry said, ignoring the faint laughs from those in front of him. 'Now, onto what happened with Jen. Matt?'

The detective sergeant stood up and took Harry's place.

'All we know right now is that Jen was attending the scene of a traffic incident when she was hit by a car. Who it was that was driving it, what make or model the car was, we've no idea. Not yet, anyway. So, this is going to be a back-to-basics approach. We know where they must have come from and the direction they were headed. Someone some-where must've seen something. There has to be footage on a security camera somewhere, right? Maybe a dash-cam picked them out, and that's what we need to find. And it's not like we have the biggest team to be going on with either, not now that we have two major incidents to be looking into.'

'I'll see if I can get some additional help pulled in,' Gordy said. 'It's good experience for officers to get out of the likes of Harrogate or wherever, and to find out how things work over this way. Can't promise anything, though. If something big comes up elsewhere, that's where resources will go. And there's a good chance they'll view literally anything as big when compared with something up here.'

'Worth a try anyway,' Harry said. 'I think we all know what we're on with, yes? Gordy, you'll make that call and head over to see Hannah, see if you can find out more about why Danny was around, what they talked about, this prop-erty thing. And you'll need to tell her that this has all moved on from it being an accident, if you know what I mean?'

'I do,' Gordy said.

'Jim,' Harry continued, 'once you're done over at the field, and if there's nothing else to be had from the neighbours, join Matt in pushing on with finding out who hit Jen. Liz, you head off with Matt as well and I'll join you once I'm back from seeing Jen. And I think that's it.'

'I'm going to call her parents in a minute,' Liz said. 'They might have a bit of news on how she's doing.'

'Boss?'

Harry turned to see Jadyn staring at him.

'Yes?'

'What about me?'

'What about you?'

'I mean, what task am I on with?' Jadyn asked.

Harry was about to send him off with Matt when another idea came to mind.

'This Rotary Club,' he said. 'Can you find out a bit more about it for me? Who runs it, membership, that kind of thing. After that, join Matt if you can.'

Jadyn's face lit up.

'On it, Boss. No problem.'

'Good,' Harry said. 'Then let's get shifting. I'm away to the hospital now and I'll let you all know how Jen is. Any updates, just let me know.'

'What about Swift?' Gordy asked.

The mention of Harry's favourite Detective Superintendent, Graham Swift, only served to increase the pain in his head.

'He might be useful,' said Gordy. 'And he needs to know about Jen.'

'You call him, then,' Harry said, and before Gordy could complain, he was out the door looking for fresh air to clear his head.

Outside, Jadyn dashed past. Harry called him over, an idea crossing his mind.

'You free tomorrow evening at all, Constable Okri?'

'I think so,' Jadyn replied. 'Why?'

Harry smiled.

CHAPTER SEVENTEEN

FEELING A LITTLE GUILTY ABOUT ROPING CONSTABLE Okri into going to the Rotary Club meeting the following night, Harry now found that his headache was not only getting worse, but seemingly pushing its way out of his skull through his eyes. He'd had migraines, yes, but this wasn't one. A migraine was pain and sickness and needing to lie down in a dark room. This felt like his brain was full of knives and they were all trying to escape at the very same time. He had no idea what had brought it on but was very much wishing it would bugger off sharpish. And being told after the meeting by DI Haig that Detective Superintendent Swift would be calling him later in the day wasn't helping either.

Having closed the meeting and dismissed the team, Harry had then taken a quick look through the Action Book for the week ahead. It wasn't exactly rammed with time-critical tasks, and he was fairly confident the jobs in there would be picked up as the week progressed. The team had an amazing ability to manage the book together, no one ever really taking charge of it as such, and it just ran along, nice and smoothly.

Liz joined Harry outside.

'I've just spoken with Jen's parents,' she said. 'Other than asking me at least half a dozen times to thank you for taking a few things over for their daughter, they haven't heard much else on how she's doing.'

'So, she's still out for the count?'

'She's stirred a few times,' Liz said. 'Her mum told me that she's tried to speak a couple of times as well, but I guess she's just on so many pain killers and whatnot that she's completely out of it.'

'Probably for the best,' said Harry. 'How bad is it?'

'Not as bad as it looked, I think,' Liz said. 'Concussion, mainly.'

'There was a lot of blood.'

'Cuts and grazes,' Liz said. 'Looked worse than it was. Like when we were kids, that's what her mum said, how there would be loads of blood after someone fell over or off a bike, all that screaming, then when it was cleaned up, not much to see for it.'

Harry pushed back against the images flashing by in his mind of Jen in the back of the ambulance.

'I can't believe we have so little to go on,' Liz said.

Harry said nothing, then heard the door to the community centre swinging open behind them. Then Matt was standing at his side.

Harry rubbed his temples. He needed paracetamol.

'I've just checked and there's a report of a speeding car come in, so we can go and see what we have on that. Might be that we can get a few more details.'

'Cameras is what we need,' Harry said.

'This is Wensleydale!' Liz laughed. 'The closest thing we have to CCTV is the camera outside the Penny Garth Café at the top of town.'

Matt shook his head.

'And the only thing that ever seems to catch is fat, middle-aged motorcyclists eating bacon butties, and the queue outside the chippy!'

'Oh, I don't know,' said Liz. 'You're forgetting sheep, tractors, and the fancy-dress parade for Hawes Gala.'

'This was down dale anyway,' Harry said, dismissing the subject, the pain of his head twisting his voice into an angrier snarl than he'd meant it to be. 'So, not much bloody use to us right now, is it? Anything else?'

Matt and Liz were quiet.

'Well,' Harry said, voice calm and measured again, 'best you both bugger off and see what you can find. We have Bill Dinsdale's death to get to the bottom of, which is a task in itself, plus some reckless bastard out there put our Jen in hospital!' Just talking about what had happened was bringing a boiling pit of lava to his stomach and Harry clenched his fists just enough to keep himself calm. 'So, we'd best find them and soon, because I for one can't be having Jen returning to work knowing they're still out there. None of us can. Understood?'

'Absolutely,' Matt said. 'And you're off over to see Jen, yes?'

Harry gave a nod.

'If she's awake, she might remember something about what happened. And any small detail could help.'

'What about Smudge?' Liz asked.

Harry glanced down to see that his new furry best friend was sitting to heel and staring up at him.

'I'm still getting used to having a dog around,' he said, scratching his head.

'And a team that'll always help out with dog sitting,' Liz grinned, crouching down to tickle the dog under its chin. 'Looks like I'll have to take her, then, doesn't it?'

Almost as if she had understood what Liz had just said, Smudge slumped down onto the ground and flipped over for tummy rub.

Matt looked over at Harry and asked, 'You alright? You look pale.'

'It's nothing,' Harry said. 'Headache, that's all.'

'And I'm guessing you've not taken anything for it yet, right? Honestly, sometimes...'

Matt huffed, shook his head, and nipped back inside the community centre, returning a moment later with a box of paracetamol. Harry took two and sunk them with the glass of water Matt had also brought with him.

'Thanks,' said Harry. 'It was a busy day yesterday, that's all. And I wasn't expecting the lizard.'

Liz laughed at this.

'You met Steve, then?'

Harry flashed his eyes at this.

'You know of Steve?'

'Know of? I've looked after him a fair few times when Jen's been away or whatever. He's a sweetheart, isn't he?'

'A sweetheart?' Harry said. 'He's a lizard! And a bloody big one at that! How did no one tell me of this before?'

'No one knew of it before,' said Matt. 'Well, no one other than Liz, here, it seems.'

'How's that even possible?' Harry asked. 'It's a massive lizard! In her house! How does anyone keep that a secret?'

'You'd be amazed at what folk can keep a secret if they

want to,' Liz said. 'Anyway, she's not had him that long. It was a rescue, I think.'

And that was the truth of it right there, Harry thought: folk keeping secrets, and something told him that whatever had happened to old Bill Dinsdale, secrets were being kept there, too. Harry did not, under any circumstances, like secrets.

A few minutes later, having seen Matt and Liz off into the day, Harry gave himself a few moments more in the fresh air. Not just to help soothe his aching head, but to clear it a little, too. The team were all well on now with what needed to be done, doing follow up work from the day before, trying to find where on earth Bill and Hannah's son Danny had gone, knocking on doors to see if anyone had noticed anything suspicious. Harry found it impossible to believe that the killing of someone by a baler was an event that would just happen in isolation. Surely, a ripple of what had happened would reach someone somewhere, he thought, and remind them of something they'd seen or heard?

Leaving the community centre, Harry walked down the lane, past the pet shop on the left, and into Hawes market-place. The place was quiet, he noticed, but then it was a Monday and sometimes even Dales folk weren't too fond of the start of a new week. Above him, the sky was a pale blue, matching the cool breeze that ghosted through the town.

A few steps later and Harry climbed into his vehicle, slipping the key into the ignition. His headache was starting to ease off, he noticed, but then a sharp knock came at his window and sent a fresh stab of pain through his brain.

Harry turned to see a man staring at him from the other side of the window, the size of him blocking out any light trying to get through.

Harry sent the window down into the door.

'Dave,' he said with a nod.

'Harry,' the big man replied.

From his first day in the Dales, Dave Calvert had seemingly set himself to being a friend of Harry's, regardless of whether Harry wanted one or not. He wasn't always around, thanks to his work taking him offshore, but when he was around, he'd always look in on Harry and see how things were.

'What you up to, then?' Harry asked. 'Didn't think you were back till next weekend.'

'Bit of a change round at work,' Dave replied. 'How are things, then?'

Harry told him about Jen but said nothing about Bill Dinsdale. News about that would get around soon enough, but there was no point hurrying it along.

'That's bloody horrendous!' Dave said. 'And she's in hospital? Anything I can do to help? Just name it.'

'No, we're good,' Harry said. 'I'm off to see her now, actually.'

'I can join you if you want?'

That was Dave through and through, Harry thought, always willing to help out.

'Best I go alone,' Harry said. 'Not sure how she is exactly and I'll be looking to ask about yesterday as well. Don't want to overwhelm her.'

'No, fair enough,' Dave said. 'What about a pint, then? You free this week? Tomorrow evening suit?'

Harry went to say yes then remembered his earlier chat with Richard Adams.

'Can't do tomorrow,' he said.

'Grace over, is she?' Dave asked. 'Things going well, then?'

'Yes, they are and no she isn't,' Harry explained. 'I'm off to the Rotary Club.'

Harry saw Dave's eyes widen.

'Rotary? You? You're having a laugh, aren't you?'

Harry shook his head.

'It's just a fact-finding thing,' he said, cautious to not touch on what had happened over by Askrigg. 'Relationship building and whatnot.'

'And who put that idea into your head, then? That Swift bloke?'

'No, that was Richard Adams,' Harry said.

At this, Dave stood up and scratched his head, his forehead creased.

'Did he, now?'

'He did.'

'And you're sure you're alright? None of this sounds very Harry Grimm to me. The Rotary? Who'd 've thought it?'

Harry laughed.

'I'm fine, honestly. It's all part of the job, that's all. You know much about the Rotary?'

'Yes, but it's not my scene, if I'm honest,' Dave said. 'I've a few friends in it, and I know plenty of others involved. They do a lot of good, that's for sure, raising money and such like, and at least they're not the Masons, which is always a good sign, isn't it?'

'Couldn't agree more.'

'I think it's that I'm not really one for joining clubs and organisations,' Dave said. 'Then ending up with jobs to do at the weekend, having to mix with people I've nowt in common with, being forced to socialise with them... It's just not me.'

'Nor me,' Harry said. 'But for the greater good, right?'

Dave gave that statement a thoughtful nod.

'I'll give you a call then,' he said, standing back up and stepping away from Harry's vehicle. 'Give my best to Jen and if there's anything you need, just let me know.'

'I will,' Harry said.

Dave strode off into the day.

'Right then,' Harry said, and he turned the key, sparked the engine to life, and headed off to see Jen.

CHAPTER EIGHTEEN

When Gordy arrived at Bill and Hannah Dinsdale's farm, the first thing that struck her was the neatness of the place. She'd visited plenty of Dales' farms as part of the job and they were a mix of the well-kept and the rundown. Some farmers, beaten down by the life they lived could find things getting away with them, family moving away perhaps, buildings not being maintained, machinery unrepaired. Others fared better against the ever-present storm of the farming life, but only just.

The Dinsdale's farm, however, was a thing of almost resplendent beauty, she thought, as she pulled into the farmyard. And for a moment she was put in mind of how the Dales were often presented on television, a place of sepia tones and nostalgia, those long-ago days people hankered for, regardless of the fact that they'd never really existed at all.

Parking up, Gordy climbed out, took a deep breath. The yard was cobbled and clean, an old water pump to her left, well-oiled and standing sentry-like over a water trough. The barns which surrounded the yard stared blindly inwards through shuttered windows and Gordy saw not a single loose or missing tile. Another barn stood just a little away, stacked so neatly with new bales of hay Gordy half suspected a spirit level had been used.

Up by the farmhouse itself rested a Land Rover, though not the usual Defender seen on the roads. This was older, though how old, Gordy hadn't the faintest idea. She had some recollection of these models being described as a Series something or other, but what series she didn't know. The pale blue paint shone clean and bright, the cream white of the wheels just the same. Walking past it and over to the front door of the house, she saw that the interior of the vehicle was perhaps even cleaner, the black vinyl seats, the footwells, all clean and swept free of dirt and dust. No small achievement considering its life.

Gordy knocked at the door, waited for a moment, then knocked again, harder this time, a knock that said she wasn't going anywhere until it was answered.

Stepping back, she thought back to the previous day, the horror that had been waiting for them in the field. As the family liaison officer, her concern now was for the relatives of the deceased. Danny, the son, was still missing. This was a concern, not just from the perspective of needing to ensure the family were provided with adequate support, but also that it brought with it a natural air of suspicion.

The door opened.

'Mrs Dinsdale?' Gordy said, as from the inky gloom on the other side of the door, a woman stepped forwards.

Hannah said nothing, just stared, her eyes bloodshot and sunk deep into shadow.

'Can I come in?' Gordy asked, stepping forwards just enough.

She wasn't one for pressing, but her job was to help and support, and on these occasions, there was usually a need just to lead a little.

Hannah blinked, shuddered a little as though a cold chill had just raked her skin, then stepped back into the house.

Gordy followed, closing the door behind her.

Inside, the house was as neat as the yard at its feet, though grey light and shadow draped itself from the walls, curtains closed, no lights on.

Hannah, still quiet, turned on her heels and shuffled off along the hallway and through another door. Gordy followed and found herself in the kitchen. The room was dated, the units and furniture proudly 1970s, but everything was clean to the point of being well preserved. It was as though she had stepped into a museum.

'Tea?'

'Only if you're having one yourself,' Gordy said, sitting herself down at the dining table in the middle of the room.

Hannah didn't answer, just filled the kettle then placed it on the stove, a white Aga sitting against the far wall. It was pushing out a heat that Gordy had felt as soon as she'd entered.

No words were spoken, the quiet held at bay only by the gradually increasing excitement of the kettle as it came to a boil. When it did, the whistle was sharp and shrill and Hannah allowed it to go on just a little too long as she made her way slowly towards it to take it from the heat.

Lifting the kettle, Hannah carried it over to the sink and poured some of the water into a teapot. She then swilled the hot water around a little before emptying it and dropping in a few teabags. She poured in the rest of the water and carried the teapot over to the table, placing it on a cast-iron trivet.

'I'll get the mugs,' Gordy said, and walked over to the draining board by the sink. This was a kitchen without a dishwasher. She then took some milk from the fridge and sat down once again.

Hannah sat down, the movement one of deflation, as though the very life of her was being sucked out of her body as Gordy watched.

Gordy poured out two mugs of tea.

'Sorry, no biscuits,' Hannah said. 'Monday's my baking day. Usually up early. Not today though. Not today.'

Gordy allowed Hannah a moment of quiet, just to get used to having her in the house. She wasn't a stranger, but neither was she a close friend. And with the news she had to deliver, she needed to make sure that Mrs Dinsdale was able to take it in.

'I miss him,' Hannah said, breaking the silence. 'Everything is so quiet, you know? But it's a quietness that's deafening, if that makes sense. It's everywhere; in the house, outside, it's inside my head. I can't get away from it, even when I'm asleep.'

'It makes complete sense,' Gordy said. 'What happened, it was and is terrible.'

'I keep expecting him to just walk through the door or to hear his voice. I know he's no longer here, but at the same time, I just can't accept it.'

Gordy lifted her mug to her mouth, allowing Hannah the space just to speak, no interruptions.

'He went off so happy, you know? It's one of his favourite jobs, just rolling along in his tractor, turning the hay over, baling. Makes him so happy. And it was such a beautiful day, too, wasn't it? And so's today, by the looks of things. Not that I've been out in it yet.'

Hannah fell quiet again. Gordy waited to see if she was going to say something else, but when nothing was forthcoming, she took a deep breath and leaned forward.

'Mrs Dinsdale—Hannah—as you know, I'm here in my capacity as the family liaison officer, to support you as best I can at this time. However, I do have something important I need to tell you.'

At this, Hannah raised her eyes to Gordy, the tiredness in them cut through with the deepest sorrow.

'Important?' she said. 'What do you mean, exactly? Is there something I don't know? Is it Daniel? Have you found him? Honestly, the last thing I need now is for him to go wandering off! From the day he arrived, he was wayward, and he's not changed! I need him here!'

Gordy knew that with news such as this, there was little point in beating around the bush. She also thought the comment about Danny was a little strange, but she'd check on that in a few minutes.

'We think that someone else may have been involved in your husband's death,' Gordy said.

'What?'

Hannah's voice was a sharp whisper of shock and disbelief.

'Evidence has come to light which gives us reason to believe this was not an accident.'

'Not an accident?' Hannah spoke each word slowly and deliberately as though they didn't belong in her mouth in the first place. 'How can you say that? It makes no sense! I saw him! I saw what happened to my poor Bill! And so did you, didn't you? All wrapped and tied up and a mess? Not an accident? How could it be anything else? He was there on his own! No one was with him! This doesn't make sense!'

'It's a lot to take in, I know,' Gordy said. 'And I'm sorry that I have no more that I can tell you at this time. But as soon as I do, I will share it with you.'

Hannah was on her feet.

'Not an accident? You can't just leave it at that! How was it not an accident? He was dead in a baler!'

'It's probably best if you stay seated for now,' Gordy said, but Hannah wasn't listening.

'Then someone did this to him, that's what you're saying, isn't it? That someone killed my Bill? Murdered him?'

'Please, Mrs Dinsdale,' Gordy said, on her feet herself now, hoping to guide the woman back to her seat. 'I've told you all I can at this time. We are investigating a number of different lines of enquiry and will obviously keep you up to date with things as they develop.'

'But who'd kill him?' Hannah asked. 'Who would kill my Bill? He was a good man! A good man! He didn't have any enemies!'

Gordy noticed then how Hannah went to say something else but stopped, as though the words were caught in her throat. And she looked oddly concerned, a thought unspoken perhaps, prodding at her mind.

Gordy rested a hand on Hannah's arm and eased her slowly back to her chair. Hannah resisted.

'All he wanted to do was run the farm and help others when he had the time, you know that don't you?'

'Tell me about Bill,' Gordy said.

'How long have you got?'

'Long enough,' Gordy replied, a gentle smile on her face.

'Generous and kind, that's what he was,' Hannah said. 'It's not like we've ever had much, but he'd still give to charity, donate to causes he believed in, anything really to give someone a helping hand.'

'We need more people like that,' Gordy said.

Hannah gave a nod of agreement. 'He was always saying how he had to give a helping hand because of how he and his parents had been helped all those years ago.'

At last, Gordy sensed Hannah's resistance give a little and she was able to gently guide her back into her chair.

'I just don't understand what you're telling me because it doesn't make any sense! It's not true! It can't be!'

Gordy waited a moment, giving Hannah a little time with her grief, then asked, 'Is there anything you can think of over the past few days or weeks that seemed a little strange?'

'Strange? How do you mean, strange? Bill wasn't a strange man! No, he was as straight as they come, honest and good to the point where you'd sometimes just want to slap him for it!' Her eyes widened. 'I didn't, I mean, I'm not a violent person, and neither was Bill, but you know what I mean, don't you? Strange? What kind of question is that? This is the Dales and we're Dales folk! Strange doesn't come into it!'

Gordy was quiet for a moment, trying to work out a way to help Hannah think a little differently about the days leading up to the death of her husband, and about the as-yet undiscussed meeting with Richard Adams. However, with how Hannah was, Gordy wanted to take it easy and let her get around to those things of her own accord. She would only prod and poke if absolutely necessary.

'Is there anything that's changed? Maybe Bill's behaviour? Or perhaps you saw him with someone you didn't know? Was, is, everything okay with the farm?'

Hannah rolled her eyes.

'Farming's a hard life, you know.'

'I've no doubt,' said Gordy, having dealt with the aftermath of too many situations where mounting debt and falling prices took its toll on farmers and their families, sometimes with the most tragic of results. She didn't want to say too much, to come across like she was prying, but she was also aware that she needed to say just enough to see if anything came to the surface in Hannah's mind, no matter how small or seemingly insignificant. 'Was debt ever an issue?'

'Debt?' Hannah barked the word with a cold, disbelieving laugh. 'Never been in debt in his life, hasn't Bill. I know that's hard to believe, but that's how he lives. Obviously, we had all the Government subsidies, same help as anyone else, but he's careful, is Bill. Astute.'

Gordy noticed Hannah was now talking about her husband as though he was still here.

'He's a man as careful with his money as he is generous,' Hannah continued. 'Not a penny missed or lost and not a single one wasted, neither.'

'Well, if you do think of anything,' Gordy said, when Hannah, head shaking, cut in.

'There is something. It's why I was there with Richard in the first place. We'd gone to speak with Bill about it.'

'Speak about what?'

Gordy saw a flicker of concern dance across Hannah's eyes.

'The threats,' Hannah said.

CHAPTER NINETEEN

GORDY ALLOWED HANNAH TO EXPLAIN.

'Richard rang me yesterday, told me about these notes he and Bill had been sent. I didn't know anything about any of it. I went over to chat with him about it and then we went to see Bill. Then all of that was just forgotten when we found Bill in the baler...'

Hannah choked on the memory.

'These threats,' Gordy said. 'What were they about?'

'He wasn't exactly political, you know,' Hannah said. 'But he always had this urge to do what was right. It was a little annoying sometimes.'

Gordy remembered what Harry had said about Bill being political. And now they were onto the meeting with Mr Adams, too. Good.

'Can you explain a bit more?'

'I think he just wanted everyone to be helped in the same way he'd been helped, that's all,' Hannah said through a smile tainted by her sorrow. 'You know they came over in the war, don't you?'

'Who did?'

'Bill and his parents.'

Gordy shook her head.

'They were refugees. Changed their names to fit in, worked hard, saved up, bought this place with what they had, not just from working here, mind, but with what they brought with them.'

'That's impressive,' said Gordy.

'He was always quiet about it,' said Hannah, animated now as she talked about Bill, her affection shining through. 'I think it was a terrible time for him. Traumatic, running from home, running for their lives, from Nazi Germany.'

'A Jewish family?'

Hannah gave a nod.

'You know, I don't even know his real name? How completely mad is that? I don't think that he even knew it himself. I mean obviously, he did, but he never mentioned it. He was five when they arrived, nineteen forty-one, I think it was. Changed their names as soon as they arrived, I believe.'

'How did they get here?' Gordy asked.

'Well now, that was the Quakers,' Hannah said. 'You know, the ones who sit around all quiet at church or whatever it is they call it. Meeting Room, I think. Not like the Methodists in the chapels who are always bellowing out hymns, whether they can sing them well or not! Bill loved that, the hymns. Anyway, the Quakers, they helped them with something called a guarantee, I think.'

'I can't remember this being covered in history at school,' said Gordy.

'I think what they did was buy something, this guarantee or whatever it was, to ensure that the person coming into the country from wherever, like Germany, wasn't then a financial burden, on the government, like. Don't think they wanted people coming over who they'd then have to pay to look after, not with the war on.'

'And Bill and his parents, they ended up in the Dales?'

'They did,' said Hannah. 'People ended up all over and they ended up here. Worked on the farms around and about. I think his dad had been a music teacher originally, but there was no call for that over here at the time, was there? Can't remember what he said his mum had done back home. Anyway, they just turned their hands to what they could, and the country needed people to work the land, didn't it? So that's what they did.'

'That's quite the story,' said Gordy. 'But I don't see what the connection is, between that and whatever it is that you found.'

'He was always saying how he wanted to help others like they'd been helped,' Hannah said. 'I knew he had some grand scheme bubbling away in that head of his, though he never said much. Then, a few months back, he told me about it.'

'Told you about what?'

'Hawes Chapel!' Hannah said.

Gordy was confused.

'Hawes Chapel? I don't understand.'

'He'd saved up enough already,' Hannah said, 'which is why he only told me then, if that makes sense? He didn't want to unless it was definitely something he could do. I knew he'd sold off a couple of the barns and a small bit of land. I thought it was all to do with just farm management stuff, you know? Maybe put some of the money away and use the rest to replace some of that old machinery, and it was about time, too, that's for sure!'

Gordy was working hard to keep up with what Hannah was telling her. It wasn't easy.

'So, he had enough for his part in it, what with Richard being involved as well, but not so much that myself and Danny would be any the worse off.'

'Mr Adams?'

Hannah nodded.

'Richard, yes. They know each other through Rotary, you see. They'd not gone ahead with it until Bill gave it the go-ahead, because it was his idea. And he wanted me involved as well, once he was happy with everything. And I was, so we did!'

'Did what?'

'Bought the chapel!' said Hannah. 'Can you believe it?'

'You mean he bought it from the church?'

Hannah shook her head.

'No, the church sold it years ago. Became an art gallery for a while, but no surprise that didn't work out. Then it was just vacant. I think it was repossessed by the banks. I'm not really sure.'

'But why buy it in the first place?'

'To give something back,' Hannah said. 'That's what he was always talking about. How he had to do something, like how something was done for him and his mum and dad.'

'How would a chapel do that?'

'Shelter,' Hannah said. 'Food, a bed, the things those poor souls need getting washed up on our beaches, that's how. Not just them, either, but the homeless, people needing a place to stay while they sort themselves out. I'll be honest, it wasn't all completely thought through, but that was the main thrust of it.'

Gordy was quiet for a moment. It was a lot to take in.

'These notes, then,' she said. 'You said that they were threats?'

At this, Hannah's face fell.

'I don't think there's much in it, if I'm honest. And Bill obviously wasn't too worried about them, otherwise, he'd have mentioned them to me, wouldn't he? Though, thinking about it, maybe he didn't mention them because he didn't want me to worry. That was Bill, that was, always putting others first.'

'What is it that they actually say?'

'I can show you,' Hannah said and reached over to a drawer to hand Gordy an envelope.

Gordy emptied the envelope. The top note was written in letters and words cut from magazines and newspapers.

'We were going to speak to Bill about them yesterday,' said Hannah, as Gordy made her way through the notes. 'Richard and me, that's why we were down at the field in the first place. Richard is Bill's partner in this, as I've said, doing this project with the chapel.'

'And you didn't think to mention them?'

'Why would I?' Hannah asked. 'There's a bit of a difference between those stupid little notes and my husband being killed in a baler, isn't there? Yesterday it was an accident, that's all it was! My Bill, killed in a baler! Why would I even think that it was done on purpose? I wouldn't, would I? Because that's not normal! At all! And now you're here telling me it's something else? It's too much to take in.'

Gordy allowed Hannah a moment to calm down.

'I still don't believe it,' Hannah said, then pointed at the notes. 'And those are nothing more than someone with nothing better to do, I'm sure. Someone sad and bored and a little pathetic if you ask me. Who hides behind something like that? Why not just come out and say it, face-to-face?'

'And I assume what they're asking him to stop is the plan for the chapel?'

'There's always going to be folk who don't agree with what you're doing, even when it's good, and Bill wouldn't have worried about any of that.'

Gordy placed the notes on the table and rested a hand on them.

'Whoever did that to Bill yesterday,' she said. 'These notes? They could be from them.'

Hannah was silent and Gordy could see the maelstrom of emotions she was going through wild in her eyes.

'Are there any more?' Gordy asked.

'No, at least, I don't know of any. Only the ones Richard received, but I don't have those.'

Gordy removed a plastic evidence bag from her pocket. She always carried a few on her person, just in case. She slipped the notes inside. Yes, she'd handled them, but that wouldn't matter too much, because if there was anything of importance here, then forensics would find it. And someone would be needing to speak to Mr Richard Adams as well now.

'What are you doing with them?'

'These are evidence,' Gordy said. 'We need to have them analysed.'

'Yes, of course.'

'Does your son know anything of this?'

'Daniel? Of course not! He doesn't even know about the plans for the farm, the chapel, any of it! And before you ask, it's because Bill didn't want to have him involved and complicating everything. He wouldn't understand, you see.'

'You mentioned Daniel earlier,' Gordy said. 'Something about him being wayward from the day he arrived.'

'Well, it's the truth of it!' Hannah said.

'In what way? Did he get into trouble?'

'Always wandering off, he was,' Hannah said. 'Was arrested once, would you believe? God, the shame of it! But he was only a foolish teenager.'

'Foolish in what way? What had he done?'

'He nicked some fireworks!' Hannah said, shaking her head. 'Bangers I think they were, from the newsagent. He was fifteen. Didn't half scare him, though, getting arrested, doing a bit of community service. He calmed down some after that, for a while anyway, and then he left home, as they all do, eventually, don't they?'

Hardly a master criminal, Gordy thought, then asked, 'What did you mean by *from the day he arrived*?'

'He's adopted,' Hannah said like it was a fact that everyone should know. 'We, well, we couldn't have kids, you see. So, we adopted Daniel. Bill liked that, too, helping to give a child a home, a family.'

Gordy asked, 'Have you spoken with Daniel or seen him since yesterday?'

'No,' Hannah said. 'I haven't. I've no idea where he is.'

'Can you give me his address?'

'Yes,' Hannah said, 'here! Well, it's supposed to be here, but he basically moved in with an old mate of his months' ago. Probably found us a bit boring, which is fair enough, isn't it? Different generation and all that, not like he's young himself, mind. When I saw you at the door, I thought you were here to tell me something about him, not Bill, not this!'

'When did you last see Daniel?'

'Yesterday morning,' Hannah said. 'He came round,

helped himself to some toast, as usual, then he ended up all upset about the farm.'

'Upset?'

Hannah gave a nod, hugging herself now as though cold.

'It's a long story,' she said, leaning back in her chair. 'He's our only son. Been away since university really. He came back two years ago to help. He's never properly understood it. I mean, he loves the farm, but he's always at us to do something different with it. His trouble is that where we see roots, a home, he sees pound signs. Money.'

Gordy looked back at the notes on the table, then at Hannah.

'And you're sure Daniel knew nothing?'

'Bill only wanted to tell him once everything was sorted,' Hannah said.

'And why was that?'

'Because he'd only want to try and change our minds. Because everything here, when we go, well, it's his, isn't it?'

'Everything?'

Hannah gave a slow, sad nod.

'The house, the farm. Everything.'

CHAPTER TWENTY

When Jim arrived at the field where Bill Dinsdale had been found in the baler, there was little to indicate the horror the place had witnessed not even twenty-four hours before. Cordon tape pinned to thin, plastic poles stuck into the ground, surrounded the area where the tractor and baler had been, both of which had since been taken by the SOC team to go over in the minutest of detail.

Parking up outside the field, and leaving Fly asleep in his vehicle, Jim slipped in through the gate, closing it behind him because old habits die hard, and no farmer would leave a gate open unless there was good reason to do so.

Jim made his way slowly across the field and over to the crime scene. Drawing closer he saw darker patches among the mown grass where the victim's blood had soaked into the ground. There were wooden splinters as well, scattered about, and the remnants of a failed hay bale, last in an unfinished line of its otherwise perfect brothers.

Circling the cordon tape, Jim didn't really know what he was looking for, though he remembered some advice Harry had given him a good while ago now, though he'd mentioned it numerous times after. And that was to always be on the lookout for something that wasn't there but should've been, and also the exact opposite of that.

Looking around him, Jim felt pretty sure that he wasn't about to find anything of use, but there was nothing wrong with being thorough and having another look. Things could always be missed.

From the crime scene, he widened his search, moving outwards in a spiral, eyes to the ground, occasionally looking up should a sound catch his attention, be that a passing car or the call of a bird. And those moments reminded him of the stark beauty of the place in which he lived, the green fells sweeping up both in front of him and behind, great, sleeping giants, their blankets the patchwork of fields and moors.

Eventually, Jim circled back round to the gate, the search fruitless, but then, as he approached his vehicle, he noticed something, and it wasn't just the fact that Fly was staring at him through the driver's window, his nose squashed up hard against the glass, leaving behind a lovely wet smudge.

Above the wall lining the road, stood a high fence, taking the height of the barrier between the field and the road from four to at least six feet in height, perhaps higher. Jim and his dad had done the same in various fields on their own farm because sheep were natural escapologists. The walls were strong, that was true, but not always high enough to discourage a determined ewe or tup that took a fancy to whatever was on the other side.

They could easily scale a drystone wall and in the process usually knock the thing down, particularly if the rest of the flock followed suit. So, a length of wire fencing hung above a wall on the end of fence posts worked well to convince them otherwise. The fence itself was in good order except that where Jim was now standing, a post was missing. And it wasn't through neglect, that much was clear from the rest of the fence, the way the walls were so well maintained.

Jim walked over for a closer look. Leaning over the wall he could see that a post or two were loose, as happens when exposed to the Dales weather and determined sheep. However, only one post was missing, and right next to it, a few of the stones from the top of the wall were now on the other side in the field, pushed in somehow.

Remembering the day before, the baler, Jim drew the only conclusion he could; there was a good chance that the missing fence post was the source of the wood splinters they'd found on the ground and in the baler itself. And that meant that whoever had been involved with what had happened to Bill had stood right where he was now and reached over to yank the post free of the fence.

Jim stood back and pulled out his phone to call Harry when he saw something on the fence by the missing post. It was a scrap of material flapping in the morning breeze. He stepped closer for a better look as a fresh gust of cool wind swept in, sending the scrap fluttering like a trapped bird. Aware then that the material could easily come loose, he turned back to his vehicle, found an evidence bag, and carefully pulled the scrap loose, slipping the open bag over it before pinching the outside with his fingers to pull it free. On closer inspection, he saw that the material was fairly thick and looked like it had been pulled from a checked overshirt or jacket of some kind.

Jim pulled out his phone and called Harry.

No answer, straight to voicemail, so he left a message and climbed into his vehicle.

Slipping his key into the ignition, Jim went to start the engine when there was a knock at his window. Staring at him was the face of a woman he'd spoken to yesterday, a resident of one of the houses which lay scattered around the area close to the field in which Bill had died. Behind her stood her horse, a huge brown and white animal, its hair sleek over its well-muscled frame.

She lived in what had been, until a few years ago now, a barn on one of the neighbouring farms, no doubt sold off by the farmer to clear a debt or two. Jim knew that some people complained about it happening, but his view was a little more pragmatic. Many of the farms didn't need the number of barns they were lumbered with and maintaining them was often a cost they couldn't afford. And yet they were expected to keep them in a good state of repair regardless of their usefulness.

Jim wound down his window.

'Can I help?'

'I'm not sure,' the woman said. 'This might seem a little strange, but I thought I should mention it.'

'Mention what?'

'Actually, I only remembered it when I saw you here just now, so I thought I'd come over. It's probably nothing.'

'What's probably nothing?'

The woman turned around and pointed far off across the fields.

'That barn over there,' she said.

Jim leaned out of his window to see where the woman was pointing.

'Which one?' he asked. 'There's a few.'

'You see the one over there on the left? The small one with the little enclosure in front of it?'

Jim gave a nod.

'Well, not that one, or the next one along on the right, but that next field, you see? The one there? It's bigger than the other two and there's a few sheep in front of it? Don't ask me what they are. Sheep all look the same to me.'

Sheep didn't all look the same by any means, Jim thought, but right now, that wasn't really important, though it did niggle the farmer in his DNA.

'So, something about that barn, then?' Jim said.

'Well, of course, something about the barn!' the woman said. 'And I just thought you should know in case you could do something about it?'

'About what?' Jim asked.

'The barn!' the woman replied.

Jim was confused and offered a smile and a nod.

'Perhaps you can tell me what it is exactly about the barn that I need to do something about?'

The woman's eyes widened a little.

'I've not told you, have I?'

'No,' Jim said. 'You haven't. Is this to do with yesterday at all?'

The woman laughed and at the sound her horse nodded its huge head, letting out a breath that caused its mouth to vibrate.

'There was a man there early this morning,' the woman said.

'A man,' Jim said.

'Yes, and he was in the barn and, well...' The woman leaned in conspiratorially. '... he looked suspicious.'

'In what way?' Jim asked, pulling out his notebook.

'In a suspicious way!' the woman said. 'You know, furtive.'

'Can you tell me anything else?' Jim asked, concerned now that this was just wasting time when what he really needed to do was get the evidence he'd just found over to forensics.

The woman stood thoughtful for a moment, reaching up to stroke the head of her horse.

'We've been out for a good few hours you see, me and Sunrise here. I called him that because he was born as the sun rose. It's a good name, isn't it? Suits him I think.'

'The barn,' Jim said.

'We passed by it at about six, maybe six-thirty,' the woman said. 'Heard something inside, but it didn't sound like sheep. Those ones there now, I think they must've been away down the field a bit. Anyway, as we were passing by, we heard this sound, like I said, and then this man came out. Looked a bit rough, too, if you don't mind me saying so.'

'Did you recognise him?' Jim asked.

The woman frowned.

'Now that you ask, yes, I think I did, but I don't know where from. Funny how that happens, isn't it? How you recognise someone but you've just no idea how or why and then there they are, in a soap on TV or an advert about shampoo or something! But I don't think he's off the telly.'

'You said he looked rough,' Jim said. 'Can you elaborate on that?'

When the woman spoke again, her voice was almost a whisper, as though she was either letting Jim in on a secret, or saying something that she didn't want others to hear.

'I think he'd slept in the barn,' she said. 'And he was stumbling, like he was drunk or hungover or something. Oh, and he was on his phone, too. So, I don't think he can be homeless, can he? Because homeless people don't have phones, do they?'

Jim ignored the last comment and asked, 'Can you remember what he was wearing?'

'Jeans,' the woman said. 'A dark jacket, maybe? Can't really say. He stumbled off and I had no desire to follow.'

Jim glanced back towards the barn the woman had mentioned, checking through the information he had.

'Is there anything else?'

'No,' the woman said, shaking her head. 'It's probably nothing, but like I said, I saw you here and thought there was no harm in mentioning.'

A few minutes later, and having taken the contact details of the woman, Jim was making his way across the field, Fly to heel. This wouldn't take long, he was sure, and it was best to check now, while he was in the area.

At the barn, he had a quick scout around to see if he could see anything, but all that he found were sheep droppings and horseshoe marks in the ground. Then he made his way over to the barn itself, and at the door, gave Fly the command to stay, before entering.

Inside, the barn was a gloomy but warm and dry place, and the air was rich with the scent of hay and sheep. Dust motes swirled about in sunlight cutting across the space from gaps in the shuttered windows, transparent blades of faint gold.

Jim had a look around, not really sure what he was looking for because all he saw in front of him was a barn used by animals for shelter. Whoever it was the woman had seen, there was no trace of them here, so with a shrug, he turned to leave.

A dull thunk from the ground by his foot stopped him.

He glanced down and saw, half-hidden by what he had taken to be little more than a large pile of hay and straw, but revealed now by his foot, the corner of what looked to be a large wooden trunk.

Jim brushed away the hay and straw then, after quickly pulling on some disposable gloves, opened the trunk.

Five minutes later, Jim called Harry.

CHAPTER TWENTY-ONE

MATT'S KNUCKLES WERE WHITE. AT HIS FEET, HARRY'S new dog, Smudge, was fast asleep, curled up in a ball and snuggled up on an old jacket of his.

'You okay, there?' Liz asked, as she tore down a narrow lane, their patrol car bouncing along almost as though it was enjoying itself.

'Oh, yes, I'm absolutely fine and dandy!' Matt said, not quite able to bring himself to take his attention away from the road ahead to look at Liz as he spoke. 'Never felt better!'

Liz slowed down, dropped a gear, brought the car around a sharp bend with the ease of someone who could drive the lane blindfolded and in reverse, then accelerated out of it again.

'You don't look exactly relaxed.'

'Don't you worry about me,' Matt said. 'You just focus on your driving.'

'I always focus on my driving.'

'If you say so.'

Liz said, 'Relax, have a Werther's!'

Matt was pretty sure that he and Liz had very, very different views as to what he meant by being focused. He was also sure that a caramel sweet popped into his mouth wasn't going to help any.

At last, Liz again slowed down, took a right, and kept her speed at something that meant Matt could blink again.

'Caldbergh,' Matt said. Then added under his breath, 'At last.'

Smudge must have noticed the change in pace as she sat up then and rested her head on his legs. He gave her soft, dark head a little scratch. Harry had done well, here, Matt thought. Smudge was a bonny dog, as Gordy would say, with eyes on her that could melt the coldest of iron hearts.

'Never actually been here before,' Liz said, as they drove around a right bend, shaded by trees, then along past a house on their right before easing left into the village itself.

Passing along a short lane, with a small number of large houses on either side of it, Liz brought them to a stop.

'It's a place you need a reason to come to, if you know what I mean,' Matt said. 'The road doesn't go anywhere, just splits off down a couple of lanes that fade off into the fells beyond.'

'It's nice though,' said Liz, looking around.

'Holiday cottages mainly, I think,' Matt said. 'It's a sign of the times, I know, and it brings money in, but sometimes, I do wonder if we'll get to a point where the Dales are just holiday cottages and nowt else, some huge leisure park for those slightly better off than the rest of us.'

Liz stared over at Matt, shaking her head.

'Bit doom and gloom for you, isn't it?'

'You know what I mean though, right?' Matt said. 'And all it does is just push up prices, displace locals...'

Matt's voice died off.

'What's got into you this morning?' Liz asked.

'Oh, just ignore me,' Matt said. 'Just being a grumpy old man.' He looked at the houses around them, found himself thinking of Joan, of their soon-to-arrive new family member. 'Imagine living in one of these though, eh? Would be wonderful, wouldn't it?'

'Ah, so that's it, then,' Liz said.

'What's it?'

'It's only natural, I'm sure,' Liz said.

'What is? What are you on about?'

'It's lovely actually, that you're bothered.'

Matt was confused. What did Liz know that he didn't?

'Enlighten me.'

'Think about it,' Liz said. 'You and Joan, you've a wee one on the way, right? You've lived in your house for years now, just the two of you, and it's seemed more than fine, I'm sure.'

'It's a lovely little place,' Matt said, smiling.

'Of course it is,' Liz said. 'And now you're thinking, with a baby on the way, that maybe it's not big enough, or you want more garden, yes?'

Matt frowned.

'Am I?'

He didn't like this feeling at all, the thought that someone knew him better than he knew himself, particularly someone so much younger.

Liz laughed, but the sound was affectionate, not cruel.

'You're going to be a dad,' Liz said. 'You've been looking after Joan all these years, right? Helping her with her illness, the wheelchair, everything. And now something new is coming along, something you both want, but you're wondering how you're going to cope. You want my advice?'

'You sure about that?' Matt asked.

'Of course I am!' Liz said. 'Just relax. You'll be fine. Great even. Being a dad, it's not about big houses and large gardens and having the best car in the school car park. None of that matters.' She poked him in the shoulder. 'What matters is you. And though you probably don't think it right now because you're so worried, you'll be a fantastic dad. You just will. It's obvious.'

'It is?'

Liz shook her head, rolled her eyes.

'Come on,' she said, 'out we get.'

Matt followed Liz and climbed out of the car, leaving Smudge behind, not that she seemed at all bothered.

'It's this house,' he said, making his way over the road.

Liz followed and they were soon at the front door. To one side were a couple of boxes, about the size of a few packs of A4 paper. They were well-taped up.

Matt knocked and noticed a rumble in his stomach.

'What was that?' asked Liz.

'I'm hungry,' said Matt. 'It's coming up to lunch.'

Liz checked her watch.

'It's only eleven,' she said.

'Exactly,' said Matt. 'So, it's pre-lunch anyway, isn't it? We'll swing by Leyburn when we're done here. There's a bakery does the most amazing pork pies with this thick slice of black pudding on top. Heaven in pastry!'

The door was opened by possibly the most ginger-haired man Matt had ever seen. His hair, though short, was almost orange, and his beard, also short, was much the same. It was impressive, Matt thought, and made the man a little difficult to put an age to. His eyes, the laughter lines, put him at maybe fifty, but that hair, there was no grey in it at all. The lucky sod, Matt thought.

'Mr Heath?'

'Yes?'

Matt introduced them both.

'This will be about that absolute idiot, yes?'

'The car you mean?' Matt asked.

'Of course, the car! Bloody hell, a death wish I'm sure! Come in! Oh, and can you bring those with you as well, please?'

Mr Heath pointed at the two boxes.

Matt bent down to pick up the boxes only to discover on doing so they were a little heavier than he'd expected.

'Just leave them at the bottom of the stairs,' Mr Heath said.

Matt allowed Liz over the threshold first and followed close behind, doing his best to make it look like the boxes weren't about to pull his arms off.

The house was best described as large, Matt thought, placing the boxes over by the stairs. Everywhere he looked things just looked bigger than what he was used to. The doors seemed to have been built to accommodate people at least eight feet tall with ease. The high ceilings gave him the sensation of walking into a church, their footsteps echoing as they walked. The staircase led up from the hall in a great, oaken sweep, the wood a deep brown and polished to a shine. The walls were decorated with large paintings and in the corner by the front door stood the largest pottery vase Matt had ever seen. It was filled with walking sticks.

Mr Heath led them through to a lounge containing a fire-place Matt was sure he could almost stand up in.

'Lovely place,' Liz said.

'Thank you,' said Mr Heath. 'It's Mum's, actually. Dad's gone, died a couple of years ago. I was visiting all the time, just to keep an eye on her, then visits just grew longer and longer, and now here I am. Rented my own place out. Can't say I miss it. I'm rambling. Sorry.'

'And your mum is here?' Matt asked.

'Upstairs,' Mr Heath said. 'The boxes are hers. More bloody books! Honestly, I wish she'd just stop buying the things. It's like a library up there. But will she listen? Of course, she won't! Boxes come in, boxes go out, and on it goes. Still, keeps her busy, doesn't it?'

'I'm sure it does, yes,' said Matt, with no idea at all what Mr Heath was talking about.

'She's into dealing in books, you see,' Mr Heath then explained. 'Started as a hobby but it's taken over. Rare copies, first prints, folio editions. And, would you believe it, she's making good money from it, too. But then she always was a reader. And so was Dad, bless him. University lecturers, you see? Retired here. She's seventy-eight, but you wouldn't know it. Coffee?'

Matt glanced at Liz who gave him the smallest of smiles back. Yes, he thought, she'd noticed it as well; Mr Heath was a man who could talk.

'So, Mr Heath,' Matt said, 'about this car...'

'No coffee, then?'

'No, we're fine, thank you,' Matt said, spotting Liz's subtle shake of her head.

'It's good coffee. The best. I'm in coffee, you see? That's what I do. Source it, import it, single-origin stuff, all fair trade. That's why there was no problem with my moving here to be with Mum. I can work from anywhere, unless I'm visiting a producer, of course.'

'Yes, of course,' said Liz. 'And were you going somewhere when you saw the car?'

Matt was impressed. It was a great example of how to get someone back on track with what they were supposed to be talking about.

'To see a producer? No, of course not,' Mr Heath said. 'I never fly anywhere on a Sunday if I can help it. Not because I'm religious, just because I have to set rules and boundaries and what's the point of a rule or a boundary if you break it?'

'Quite,' said Liz.

'I was, however, on my way back from a little warehouse I rent over in Leyburn. I had one close to my other house, obviously, but moving here, well, I was lucky to be able to find one I think, but I did, and it's where I store my stock. Not that it's there for long as it's all about freshness, isn't it? And—'

'Where did you see the vehicle in question?' Matt asked, lacking Liz's subtlety and butting in.

'That was at the junction, just this side of Wensley,' Mr Heath said. 'I had indicated, you see, and in good time, too, because I'm a very careful driver. And then, there he was, just racing towards me, and on my side of the road, too! Madness!'

'On your side of the road?' Liz asked.

'Coming right at me!' Mr Heath said. 'Overtaking right at a junction! Goodness knows what speed he was doing. A hundred maybe? Definitely not sixty.'

And not a hundred either, Matt thought, not unless the driver was trying to kill himself at the approaching corner. He knew the road as well as anyone, and that kind of speed would have you off before you even had a chance to turn the wheel and attempt the bend.

'You said the driver was a he,' Matt said.

'No woman would be foolish enough to drive that fast,' Mr Heath said.

Matt thought about his earlier journey over with Liz and wasn't so sure.

'I didn't get a good look at him,' Mr Heath said, 'but yes, I'm sure it was a man. Big, too.'

'Can you remember anything about the car at all?' Liz asked. 'Anything else about the driver?'

Mr Heath, for the first time since Matt and Liz had arrived, stopped talking and rested his chin in his hand, deep in thought.

'The car was black,' he said at last. 'Yes, definitely black. Don't ask me what make though. I'm not a car person at all.

'Was it an estate, a saloon, a hatchback?' Matt asked.

'It had a boot,' Mr Heath said.

'A saloon then,' said Matt. 'And what time was this?'

'Late afternoon I think,' Mr Heath said. 'And they were arguing.'

Matt looked up.

'Who were?'

'The driver and his passenger of course,' Mr Heath replied. 'I think that's probably why he was speeding. They were really yelling at each other, arms flailing about. It's amazing they didn't crash into me or anyone else!'

Matt checked his notes.

'So, we have a black saloon, male driver, one passenger—'

'I don't know if it was a man or a woman,' Mr Heath said, interrupting. 'But they were definitely arguing.'

'And they were arguing when they passed you at the junction to Coverdale and Carlton?'

'Yes, that's the one, isn't it? Yes, that's where it was, right there! Madness!'

Matt rose to his feet. He didn't want to stay any longer than he had to, not with someone who had Mr Heath's ability to talk.

'This has been very useful,' Matt said, making his way from the lounge and out into the hall, Liz quickly coming up behind him. He noticed that the boxes at the bottom of the stairs had been opened, the contents half emptied. 'If we need to talk to you again, we have your details.'

'Was there an accident, then?' Mr Heath asked. 'Because I wouldn't have been at all surprised.'

'Like I said,' Matt repeated, 'if we need to talk to you again, we know where you are.'

Realising that sounded a little more threatening and sinister than he'd meant it to, Matt quickly led himself and Liz out of the house and back to their car. Inside, Smudge was stretched out on the back seat.

'She's not so much big as long, is she?' Liz said as they both climbed in. 'Useful, then, Mr Heath, you think?'

Matt clipped himself in.

'Hard to say,' Matt shrugged.

Liz started the engine.

'Where now, then?'

Matt raised a finger.

'What?'

'You hear that?'

Liz frowned.

'What?'

'A pie,' Matt said. 'Calling my name.'

Liz shook her head.

'Leyburn, then!'

As Liz clipped herself in, Matt thought back over what they'd learned from Mr Heath, which wasn't much, but at least they now knew there had been two in the car. That they had been arguing, now that was an interesting observation. The journey from where Jen had been hit to where Mr Heath had seen the speeding car was about ten minutes, give or take. So, had they been arguing since hitting Jen, maybe even because of it? Or had they been arguing before that, which was why they'd smashed into a police officer, too distracted to be fully aware of the road? Or was it, Matt thought, that the argument had nothing to do with Jen at all and everything to do with the speed they were doing and a need to get away from something fast. And if that was the case, then just what was it that they were running from?

Liz turned the car around, but when they came back past Mr Heath's house, the man was standing in the road, waving his arms. Matt wound down his window.

'Mr Heath?'

'Something else!' Mr Heath said. 'There was something else. The wing mirror!'

'What about it?'

'It wasn't there,' Mr Heath said. 'Passenger side. No wing mirror. I remember now because I thought to myself at the time that not having a wing mirror was very dangerous and how the driver was just asking for trouble, you know, with the speed he was doing, and a missing mirror.'

'You're sure about that?'

'Of course,' Mr Heath said, a firm nod to support his statement. 'No wing mirror on the passenger side. And I'm very surprised he had one on the driver's side as well after coming so close to me when he whizzed past!'

Matt thanked Mr Heath and Liz eased out onto the road and back out towards the main road.

'So, I'm guessing we're not going to Leyburn, then,' Liz said.

'No, we're not,' said Matt.

CHAPTER TWENTY-TWO

Harry placed his phone back in his pocket and climbed out of his vehicle. Jim's call was certainly interesting. The PCSO had described to him the contents of the box he'd found in the barn. It looked as though someone, identity as yet unknown, was using the barn as a little hideaway. For what reason, he didn't know, but Jim was now on with finding out which farm owned the barn, the box now on its way back to the office for further examination.

Harry was just about to head into the hospital when a voice called out his name. He came to a dead stop, knowing there was no way to pretend he'd not heard it. Turning, he waited for Detective Superintendent Graham Swift to close the distance between them.

'Sir,' Grimm said, as his boss came to stand in front of him.

'DCI Grimm,' Swift said. 'DI Haig passed on the message that I would meet you here, yes?'

'She said you were going to give me a call.'

'That's right, that's what I said,' Swift replied. 'My apologies.'

Harry was taken aback. When had Swift ever apologised to him? Never, that was when, he thought, and that, rightly or wrongly, made him immediately suspicious.

'Not a problem,' said Harry.

'I thought it best that I just come here as soon as I could,' Swift said. 'DI Haig mentioned you were on your way over to see Officer Blades, so I cancelled what I had in my diary and came over as soon as I could. I understand that she's already had some visitors, her parents, a vicar as well, so that's a good sign, I'm sure.'

'It certainly is,' Harry said, remembering that Gordy had mentioned that Anna was going to pop over. 'A very good sign indeed.'

'And how are you?' Swift asked. 'And the rest of the team? Something like this, it can have a huge impact. And what with what happened to your predecessor, DCI Alderson...'

Harry had never met the person he'd been sent to temporarily replace a year ago. That the man had ended up taking his own life was tragic and terrible and it had affected the team deeply for sure.

'We're working on finding those responsible,' Harry said, deciding against sharing his own more personal feelings with his superior officer. 'Not much to go on, if I'm honest, but it's early days.'

'A hit-and-run,' Swift said, shaking his head, though Harry saw more in the man's face than mere concern. There was anger there, too, burning just hot enough to show itself in his eyes.

'Indeed, sir,' Harry said. 'Shall we go in?'

Once in the hospital, Harry led them to where Jen was resting, and after a quick chat with a nurse at the reception to the ward, was happy to discover that Jen wasn't just awake but chatting happily and doing very well.

The ward was quiet, Harry noticed, in a way that only a hospital ward can ever be, with the background hum of the hospital itself playing like some ominous orchestral soundtrack to the lives passing through its doors. Beeps and hisses and hushed voices mingled, twisting around them as they headed through to Jen's bed.

Harry wasn't surprised to find Jen's parents at her bedside and he introduced Swift as soon as they arrived. He was also pleased to see Jen looking considerably better than the last time he'd seen her. Since then, his mind had only worked to make that memory even worse, chucking in a few extra bucketfuls of blood for good measure

'You have my deepest sympathy,' Swift said, shaking their hands. 'And I can assure you that we are doing everything we can to find those responsible, and that we have the best team on it you could ever wish for.'

By now Harry was beginning to wonder just who this was, because it sure as hell didn't sound like the Swift he knew.

After a quick chat, Jen's parents stood up.

'We'll give you a bit of space,' Mr Blades said. 'Could do with a coffee anyway. Shall we say twenty minutes?'

'That's plenty long enough,' Harry said, then winked at Jen. 'Doubt she can stand the two of us here for that long really, if I'm honest.'

With that, Mr and Mrs Blades headed off and Harry and Swift took a seat each.

'No grapes?' Jen said.

Harry was puzzled.

'Grapes,' Jen said. 'I'm in hospital. And no one's yet to bring me any grapes.'

'I can get some if you want?' Swift offered.

Jen shook her head and smiled, Harry could see that she was putting on a brave face, pain just showing itself as she winced a little. He admired that.

'It's a stupid question I know,' Harry said, 'but how are you feeling?'

'Sore,' Jen replied. 'Like I've been in a fight with a rhino. How's Steve?'

'Oh, Steve's fine,' Harry said. 'Had him long?'

'Just a few months. Lovely, isn't he? You know, he joins me on the sofa in the evening sometimes to watch the telly. Big fan of Gogglebox.'

Harry had nothing to add to that.

'I've been told I was very lucky,' Jen said.

At this, Swift huffed.

'Lucky? How can you be lucky? You were hit by a car while on duty! In my book, that just doesn't count as being lucky!'

'It was actually just the wing mirror,' Jen said. 'Clipped me as it went past. Apparently, I span around like a spinning top.'

'You mean you remember?'

Jen shook her head painfully once again.

'Not a thing really. One of the paramedics from the other accident popped in earlier to see how I was. They just heard this screech of tyres and turned to see me spin round then fall to the ground. Sounds very dramatic, doesn't it?'

'But how did they know it was a wing mirror?' Harry asked, confused now, trying to think back to when he'd turned up at the scene, when he'd spoken with the para-medics himself.

'You didn't find it, then?'

Harry and Swift did a double-take.

'You mean it came off on impact?'

Jen rubbed her head, tried to sit up, gave up.

'Well, I don't remember,' she said. 'To be honest, I don't remember any of it at all. I remember being out on the road, directing traffic, waiting for the ambulance to turn up and deal with the accident I was attending. That's all as clear as day.'

'Then what?'

'I remember a flash of something,' Jen said. 'Like properly blinding it was, the car hitting me I suppose, at the same time as this tremendous bang sound. Like a door being slammed. I guess that was when I was hit. Next thing I know, I'm here.' She waved weakly. 'Hello...'

Harry's mind was racing now.

'So, how do you know about the wing mirror, then?' he asked.

'Like I said, one of the paramedics came round to check up on me. Off duty, too, which was nice. They arrived to deal with one accident and ended up having two on their hands. Called another ambulance, then from what I understand, I was flown here, wasn't I?'

Harry clenched his fist, suspicion starting to twist his gut.

'At the accident, then, you didn't actually meet the paramedics?'

Jen shook her head.

'They arrived just after I'd been hit I think. Lucky, really.'

'When was this?'

'When was what?'

'When this paramedic came to see you?'

'About an hour ago maybe,' Jen said. 'Left just before my parents arrived.'

'And this paramedic, he told you about the wing mirror?'

'He asked if anyone had mentioned it to me. I said no because no one had. He then said that I should get it back and keep it as a souvenir. Then he left.'

'But this is the first time I've heard about a wing mirror,' Harry said. 'Nothing was found at the site, Jen. The paramedics didn't say anything to us at all.'

'Are you sure?' Jen asked.

'I was there,' said Harry. 'And so were Matt and Jim. No one mentioned a wing mirror.'

Harry was on his feet.

'Sir? A moment, if you please?'

'What's up?' Jen asked. 'What did I say?'

Harry led Swift away from Jen's bed and around a corner out of earshot.

'I don't think it was a paramedic,' Harry said. 'That was the driver of the car checking up on things: the wing mirror.'

'That's a hell of a jump to make, but I agree,' Swift said. 'And whoever they are, they're worried about it. My guess is that they didn't notice they'd lost it until it was too late in the day. I'm also guessing that they haven't gone looking for it yet because they're worried it's an active crime scene.'

'Last thing they'd want to do is turn up and walk into one of us.'

Harry's phone was buzzing in his pocket. He pulled it out, saw Matt was calling.

'I suggest you head off now,' said Swift. 'I'll get onto

hospital security. Whoever they are, the cameras will have them. I'll get a description from Jen, too. That should help.'

Harry left the ward, answered his phone.

'Harry, it's Matt!'

'What's up?'

'Liz and me, we're on our way over to where Jen was hit. We've good reason to believe that the car that hit her lost its wing mirror in the process.'

'I know,' Harry said.

'You do?' said Matt. 'How?'

Harry ignored the question.

'You need to be aware that the driver could well be on their own way as well. So, be careful. Call Jim, Jadyn, and Gordy now and get them to head over as well. Any developments, anything at all, you let me know. I'll see you there.'

Harry killed the call on the run. It buzzed at him again.

'What now?'

Gordy's voice was on the other end.

'I think I have something,' she said.

'Good!' Harry said. 'Now hang up because Matt's trying to call you!'

'Matt? Why?'

Harry didn't answer, hung up, and raced on out of the hospital.

CHAPTER TWENTY-THREE

Harry arrived at the bottom of Temple Bank, sped over the bridge, and parked up. The rest of his team were already on site, having parked along the side of the road, a little further along, their whereabouts clearly marked with numerous bright orange cones. He made his way back to the bridge to find Liz, Matt, and Gordy doing a very careful search of the field. They were standing in a line, just a couple of metres apart, and walking very slowly from one side of the field to the other. They were halfway down, having already covered the area from the road to where they were now. But Jim and Jadyn were nowhere to be seen.

Harry gave a shout and a wave. The line stopped and three faces turned.

'Jim and Jadyn?' he called.

'River!' Matt called back.

Harry walked on a little further towards the bridge, the grey stone hidden beneath the dappled shadows of the trees.

'Jim?' Harry called. 'Jadyn?'

No answer.

Harry tried again, then he heard splashing. Looking down, he saw Police Constable Jadyn Okri and PCSO James Metcalf emerging from the dank darkness beneath the bridge. They were both sodden and dirty.

'Having fun, then?'

'Not really, no,' Jadyn said.

'The water's lovely,' Jim said. 'You coming to join us?'

Harry didn't have to think long about his answer.

'You look as though you're doing just fine without me for now. Find anything?'

Jim and Jadyn were both now out from under the bridge and a bit further down the river. A splash of sunlight was on them and Harry guessed they would be thankful for its warmth.

'Plenty,' Jim said, 'but I don't think we're really looking for an old Wellington boot, a lemonade bottle, the snapped end from a fishing rod, or this.'

Jim then held something up for Harry to see.

'Looks to me like a school bag,' Harry said. 'Or what's left of one.'

'That's because it is,' Jim said. 'Probably shoved out of the school bus skylight.'

'Seriously?'

'I did that journey myself, remember?' Jim said. 'Seven years, down dale and back up again. Used to get pretty wild at times. Bus driver was a saint for putting up with us, that's for sure.'

'So, no wing mirror, then?'

'No sign of it at all,' said Jim with a shrug.

Jadyn climbed up the bank from the river, slipping a couple of times as he made his way upwards.

'I think we need to have a look around here,' he said,

standing now in the trees and attempting to wipe mud off his hands on some damp grass. 'But we need all of us I think. More pairs of eyes and all that.'

Harry agreed.

'I'll check how the others are doing,' he said.

Back at the field, he saw that Matt, Liz, and Gordy were already making their way over back towards the road. When they arrived it was clear that the search had come to nothing.

'Maybe they arrived before us,' Matt said.

'Even if they did, they wouldn't have had time to do a search,' said Harry. 'I say we keep looking. And as you've found nowt in the field or the river, then we need to look through the woods.'

Matt shook his head.

'It's too large an area,' he said. 'We need more bodies.'

'That we do,' Harry agreed. 'And we've been telling the government that for years. But, as far as I know, they're still pretending to be deaf, so we'd best make the best of what we have, hadn't we?'

Harry led the way, jumping over the wall to join Jim and Jadyn. With the team together he lined everyone up along the wall, the river to their right, Jadyn walking along its edge, and at the far left of the woods, Gordy. She'd been giving him that *we need to talk* look ever since he'd arrived, but that would have to wait.

'Nice and slow,' Harry said, but was interrupted by Jim.

'Wait a minute,' he said and jumped back over the wall. When he came he had six long sticks in his arms and handed them out.

'Beating sticks,' he said. 'Left in there from shooting season. Always worth having a stick to hand, I reckon.'

'And what's a beating stick?' Harry asked.

'Beaters use them,' Jim said, as though what he was saying was beyond blatantly obvious.

'For what, exactly?' Harry asked. 'And don't say beating; that much I guessed.'

'On a driven shoot, pheasant or partridge or grouse, you have beaters. They line up and walk towards the standing guns. There's usually a couple of dogs as well.'

'They walk towards the guns?' Harry said, unable to disguise his disbelief.

'They have to make a lot of noise,' Jim explained.

'What, like, I'm over here so don't bloody shoot me?'

Jim shook his head in mock disappointment at Harry's answer.

'There's lots of shouting, calling out, whistling, that kind of thing. Sticks are useful for knocking bushes or whatever. Also, you're usually pretty knackered by the end of the day, so a stick is good to lean on as well.'

Harry lifted his stick.

'Good idea,' he said to Jim. 'Well done.'

Jim's face broke into a beaming smile.

'Right then, come on,' Harry said. 'And slowly, remember? I'll set the pace. Don't move past me.'

An hour or so later, the team had swept up as far as they could go and back down the other side of the river.

'Not a dicky bird,' Matt said, leaning up against the wall. 'Wherever that wing mirror is, it's gone, that's for sure.'

Harry had to agree and leaned up against the wall beside Matt.

'I'm going to have another look in the river,' Jadyn said. 'Just to make sure.'

Gordy, Jim, and Liz headed off for another sweep of the field.

'We should join them,' said Matt.

'What about Jadyn?'

'Oh, I think he's fine, don't you?'

Harry pushed himself away from the wall as a yawn struck, forcing his head back onto his shoulders. When he opened his eyes, he was looking up into the trees.

'I know this is just a few trees by a road bridge and a river,' he said, 'but even this is pretty beautiful, isn't it?'

'It is,' Matt said. 'That's the Dales for you though, isn't it?'

Harry was about to tell Matt about his and Grace's swim at Hardraw Force, when something caught his eye.

'Matt?'

'Boss?'

Harry lifted his stick to point up into the tree.

'What's that? Just up there?'

Matt looked to where Harry was pointing.

'Can't see anything,' he said.

'By that branch,' Harry said. 'The one that looks like the tree has a broken arm. There's something there, isn't there?'

'You sure?' Matt said, then, 'No, you're right, I see it now. But if you're thinking of having me climb up there...'

Harry was already at the tree.

'Wait a minute, Boss,' Matt said. 'Maybe we should get one of the—'

His voice died when he saw the look Harry gave him.

'You were going to say one of the younger ones, weren't you?'

Matt said nothing, didn't need to.

'I'll take that as a yes.'

Harry turned back to the tree and hauled himself up. Leaving the ground, he was aware then of how his brain's memory of climbing trees wasn't exactly matched by the memory of his muscles. They certainly wanted to get him there, that was true, but the effort wasn't just hard, it was painful. Pulling himself up to the next branch, it was as though his joints were being yanked apart. He remembered then doing some climbing training back in his army days. Out on the crags, that had been fun. Scary, but fun. And it had struck him as a sport he wouldn't have minded getting into. Now though, it seemed that a humble tree was about as close to scaling vertical heights as he would ever get or would ever actually want to.

'And just what the hell do you think you're doing?'

Harry heard Gordy's voice below him, her disbelief loud and clear.

'Get down, man!' she called up. 'You'll do yourself a mischief!'

'I'm fine,' Harry hissed through gritted teeth.

'Well, you soon won't be,' Gordy called up.

Harry looked down and saw that the rest of the team were now all together and staring up at him.

'I thought you were doing another sweep of the field?'

'We were,' Liz called up. 'But this is a bit more fun.'

Harry turned his attention back to the tree. The sooner he was up to see whatever was up there, just over an arm's reach away, then the sooner he could be back down on the ground. He pushed on, his legs shaking a little, his arms burning now.

'Get yourself down!' Gordy called again. 'We can't be having you in hospital as well!'

Then Harry was there and in front of him was the object that had caught his eye. How it had ended up there was surely a miracle, as was the fact that it had been wedged so neatly between a couple of branches. With a yank, he managed to loosen it.

'Get a jacket,' he called down. 'Open it. I'm going to drop this. It's too big to carry.'

A moment later, Matt called up, 'Ready, Boss!'

Harry looked down, took aim, and let go of what he'd found. It hit the jacket dead centre.

'Good shot!' Jadyn called out.

Harry, with great relief, climbed back down the tree.

'Well?' he said.

Matt lifted the object up for everyone to see.

'Wing mirror,' he said. 'Black.'

'Now all we have to do is find the car,' Harry said.

CHAPTER TWENTY-FOUR

As Mondays went, it had been a busy day. It was a rare thing to have the team together at the office with the afternoon closing out, but there they all were, including the two dogs.

Harry was sitting at a table, nursing a mug of tea, Smudge at his side, though the dog seemed to be fairly insistent that really where she was supposed to be sitting was on his lap.

Matt crashed in through the door, unable to control his enthusiasm for what he was delivering.

'Reckon we all deserve these!' he said and dropped a carrier bag on a table. 'Bacon butties all round, everyone, courtesy of me! But you can make your own tea. And mine, while you're at it.'

Harry made to rise from his chair when Jadyn appeared in front of him.

'Here you go, Boss,' he said, and handed Harry a paper bag spotted with grease.

Harry took the bag, pulled out the butty.

'Thanks,' he said, taking a mouthful. Swallowing, he asked Jadyn if he'd found anything out about the Rotary Club.

'Not really,' the constable said. 'They meet over in Leyburn, that much I do know, and I have the address, so I know where I'm going tomorrow.'

Harry wondered if it was fair of him to send Jadyn, but on the other hand, he really didn't fancy going himself.

'What do they get up to? Who's in charge?'

'Seems to be a mix of networking, social stuff and charity events,' Jadyn explained. 'They meet every couple of weeks, plus there's special events with speakers and meals out and whatnot. The charity stuff is everything from sponsored walks and runs to clay shoots, providing bursaries for school kids, that kind of thing. Can't remember who's in charge, but there's a committee, a president or a chairperson I think, the usual with anything like that.'

'Sounds fascinating,' said Harry and before he knew what he was saying he told Jadyn he'd join him the following evening.

'At least we can keep each other company,' he added, taking to his feet. 'And jab the other, if one of us falls asleep.'

Harry moved to the front of the room and his presence there was enough to have everyone's attention. Jadyn was already at the board, ready to add notes if needed.

'As we're all here,' he said, 'it makes sense to quickly run through where we are with everything. So, Jen...'

Harry gave them a quick update on how the constable was doing, having called her parents after they'd finished the search at the bridge. He'd seen her, yes, but then had to rush off, and hadn't managed to get any specifics on how she was.

'So, no broken bones or anything, then?' Matt said. 'That's amazing.'

'She'll be bruised and sore for a good while,' Harry said, 'and she's being kept in tonight, just for observation. After that, she can head home, and her parents will be collecting her and taking her to theirs, which makes sense. So, we won't have her back on the team for a few days.'

Harry then told them about the man who had turned up claiming to be one of the paramedics who had taken Jen to the hospital.

'Swift went through all the security camera footage, but we have nothing worth anything I'm afraid. Whoever he was or is, he kept his face hidden, underneath a bloody great big hat, would you believe. Jen's given Swift a description, but she's still a little groggy, so he says it doesn't amount to much. We'll have her do an EFIT tomorrow when she's a bit more with it. Like I said, she's fine in herself, but I think things are still a little muddled and hazy and after a hit like that it can take a while for everything to start working properly again.'

Harry had suffered from a serious concussion himself and knew how it could affect even the simplest of tasks.

'Not much use then,' Jim said.

'Not yet, no,' agreed Harry. 'But it does tell us something, doesn't it? The fact that he knew to keep his identity hidden shows that he knew what he was up to. Whoever he is, he's clearly the driver of the car that hit Jen. And we have the details from Matt and Liz's visit, too.'

Harry looked to Matt and Liz.

'There were two people in the car,' Liz said. 'They were seen arguing as they drove at speed towards Wensley.'

'The witness, a very talkative Mr Heath,' Matt added, 'noticed the missing wing mirror.'

'On that,' said Gordy, 'I've managed to get a make and model from a dealer I know over in Catterick. Just sent over some photos and it's definitely a BMW 3 Series, only a couple of years old.'

'Might be able to get a lead on that, then,' Matt said.

'Exactly,' Gordy agreed. 'I've some other things to be on with tomorrow over Richmond way, but I think we should put Jadyn on this.'

'Really? Why?' Jadyn asked. 'I mean, great!'

'I suggest that you get on with contacting all the BMW dealers in the area. If they were heading towards Leyburn, I suggest you just spread out from there, do a ring round, visit if you need to. See if anyone's come in for a mirror repair, that kind of thing. Harry, what do you think?'

Harry wasn't given a chance to answer.

'That works for me,' said Jadyn. 'And I'm in Leyburn tomorrow evening anyway, with Harry.'

'How was Bill's wife?' Harry asked, eyes on Gordy in an attempt at an apology for still not having managed to speak with her himself.

'As you'd expect,' she said, 'but I did learn some interesting details about her husband. I'll send you a detailed report on it this evening. And I need to get going soon, to drop something off with forensics.'

Harry jumped at this.

'Forensics? What are you dropping off? And how come I don't know about it?'

Gordy held up an evidence bag and Harry saw some sheets of paper inside.

'Are you going to give us a clue, or do we have to guess?' Harry asked.

'Turns out that the DinsDales and Mr Adams were buying Hawes Chapel.'

This raised a few gasps of disbelief from the room.

'Why on earth would they want to do that?' Matt asked. 'A chapel? What would a farmer want with a chapel?'

'And what does that have to do with what's in the evidence bag you're holding?' Harry asked, desperate for something to start making some sense.

'I remember something about the chapel being bought,' Liz said. 'Bit of local gossip, that kind of thing, but I've heard nowt about it for ages now or who was buying it.'

'Bill had this plan to turn it into a safe house,' Gordy said. 'Somewhere for people who needed help, who needed a temporary roof over their heads, that kind of thing.'

'In Hawes?' Jim said. 'You're having a laugh, aren't you?'

'Bill certainly wasn't,' Gordy said. 'Neither was Hannah. Only one who didn't know was Danny.'

'Why's that?' Liz asked. 'Why keep that a secret from their son?'

'Not sure they trust him entirely,' Gordy said. 'Not least because he's set to inherit the farm. And he's been away for years as well, so I think they're just wary.'

'Fair enough,' Matt said. 'I can't imagine him being too happy on finding out his dad's spending money on a chapel.'

'Which leads us all back to the contents of this bag,' Gordy said, again holding it up for everyone to see.

'How?' asked Jadyn.

'These are threats,' Gordy said. 'That's how. Proper ones, too, inasmuch as whoever did them has obviously watched too many crime shows on the telly, if you know what I mean.'

'No, I don't know what you mean,' Harry said, aware he

was sounding very, very impatient with it all. 'Get to the point.'

'Letters and words, all cut out from newspapers and magazines,' said Gordy. 'All warning Bill and Mr Adams off what they were planning to do with the chapel.'

'You're having a laugh!' Matt said.

'I'm not, no,' said Gordy. 'And neither was whoever put these together.'

'Notes though? Cut out from newspapers? No one does that, do they? No one serious, anyway.'

Harry could see from Gordy's face that the notes were very serious indeed.

'What do they say?' he asked.

He was also wondering why Mr Adams hadn't mentioned these notes to him that morning.

'The first couple aren't much,' Gordy said. 'Vague, too, as well. *Stop now before it's too late*, and *You're making a big mistake*, and a few others. Nothing too crazy.'

'They're not really threats, though, are they?' said Harry. 'They're warnings.'

'Polite, too,' Jadyn said. 'Where I grew up, if you wanted to threaten someone, you'd set their car on fire.'

At this, everyone, including Harry, turned to look at Jadyn.

'What?'

'Are you speaking from experience there, Constable?' Harry asked.

Jadyn's face almost fell on the floor.

'Me? No! Of course not! I've never set a car on fire! Why would I do that?'

Harry made a rumbling growl of a sound in his throat.

'I'm serious!' Jadyn said. 'I never did! I was just making a comparison, that's all. Wish I'd never said anything now!'

'A thought you should hold close, I reckon,' said Harry.

'The tone changes, though,' said Gordy. 'And the last one says, *This is your last chance: stop now, or suffer the consequences.* I don't know what the ones Mr Adams' has are like, but I suggest we get those tomorrow as well.'

'You think there's a connection,' Harry stated.

'I think,' said Gordy, 'that what happened yesterday was made to look like an accident, and that the victim had been receiving increasingly overt threats for a number of weeks prior to the event. It could be a coincidence, but I'm not a massive believer in that.'

'Which leads us back to the mystery of the disappearing son.'

Harry was beginning to get dizzy with the number of circles it felt like they were going around in.

'It also makes me rather concerned for the safety of Mr Adams. Matt?'

'Yes?' Matt's face dropped. 'I know what you're going to ask, don't I?' 'Yes,' Harry said. 'Once we're done, I need you to head over to Mr Adams', get those notes of his, and I suggest we keep an eye on him. Nothing too heavy, but I think we'll need a car sat outside, certainly for tonight at any rate. Tomorrow, we'll need his movements, that kind of thing.'

'No problem,' Matt said. 'I'll sort a rota out with the rest of the team.'

'A proper stake out!' Jadyn said. 'Awesome!'

Harry ignored the young constable's excitement.

'We do need to find Danny, though,' he said. 'Those threats and what we know so far don't mean that he's responsible for his father's death, in fact, nothing we've uncovered points at him, but someone is, that much is certain. And I don't like him being out there without us knowing where he is.'

'He can't have just disappeared though, can he?' Matt said. 'This is the Dales! People notice things!'

'Particularly when he was spotted this morning,' Harry agreed, looking at Jim.

'The trunk?' Jim said. 'I've put it in the evidence room, but the contents clearly belong to Danny. He was spotted at a barn just over a mile away from the field Bill was found in.'

'We think,' Harry said, 'that Danny, for whatever reason, has been camping out there for quite some time.'

'Why would he do that?' Liz said.

'The stuff in the trunk is a collection of camping equipment, a sleeping bag, stove, that kind of thing. So, it looks like he's been going over as and when it suits him, but for what reason we haven't the faintest idea.'

'Would Hannah know?' Liz asked.

'We can check that tomorrow,' Harry said. 'But what we do know is that Danny was there last night.'

'His mum described him as wayward,' Gordy said. 'When he was younger, anyway. Did a bit of community service apparently, for stealing fireworks.'

'Can't see how that links to this,' said Harry.

'There's that scrap of material I found on the fence by the road,' Jim added. 'Ripped off a checked shirt I think. Probably nowt, but it can go off to forensics with those notes, just to make sure.'

Matt leaned back in his chair, scratching his head.

'If you don't mind me saying so, Boss, all of this is very confusing.'

'We have two things to be going on with, so best to not get them tangled up,' Harry said. 'Like I said, what we really need now is to find Danny. So I want everyone on with this tomorrow. Knocking on doors, contacting friends, anything that can help us find him. He's missing for a reason, and the longer he stays missing, the more suspicious we're going to get.'

'What about Jen?' Liz asked.

'Well, with Jadyn looking into the wing mirror, that might come to something, so we'll have to go with that for now.'

The meeting over, Harry headed home to his flat. As he approached, searching in a jacket pocket for his keys, Smudge at his heels, the front door opened and Ben came strolling out.

'Harry!'

'Evening,' Harry said as his younger brother gave him a hug. He was getting more used to it now, but he still felt a bit awkward. 'Heading out?'

On seeing Ben, Smudge's tail turned into a flail, thwacking hard against Harry's legs. Ben ducked down to stroke the dog and she flipped over for a tummy rub.

'Fridge is empty,' Ben said. 'Thought I'd grab us something from the Spar.'

'You sure it's still open?' Harry said. 'That place has the weirdest opening times. I'm still not used to it.'

Ben checked his watch.

'I have fifteen minutes, so I'd best be quick!'

As Ben dashed off, Harry pushed his way into the flat. Smudge, now off her lead, raced ahead and Harry found her in the lounge with a sock hanging from her mouth.

'That's mine, you little bugger!' Harry said.

Smudge's response came in the form of her tail thumping hard on the floor.

Harry walked over to Smudge and grabbed the end of the sock. As the dog snarled playfully, tugging at the other end, Harry's phone buzzed. It was a one-word message from Dave Calvert: 'Pint?'

Harry thought back over his day. He was weary. Ben was sorting dinner. A pint once they'd eaten, he decided, would be a very good idea indeed.

CHAPTER TWENTY-FIVE

Having enjoyed just a couple more pints than the suggested one with Dave down at the Fountain Inn public bar, Harry was making his way back to his flat. Dave had heard about Bill because Hannah had called him, and that was the first Harry had known about Dave being friends with them.

It also turned out that Dave knew about Bill's plan for the chapel, because Bill had confided in a few friends, probably to help get local support for the whole thing. And it had worked, too, according to Dave. Which made Harry wonder even more as to who would dislike the whole idea so much as to not only send Bill threats, but to even go so far as to kill him.

Dave was as shocked as anyone would be at the loss of a friend, but his approach to grief hadn't been to then sit and focus on the sadness, the tragedy. Instead, it had been to tell as many stories as he could about how great a man old Bill Dinsdale was. It had been an easy evening, really, for Harry, who'd had to do little more than say thank you for the beers and then just listen, giving Dave a willing ear as he talked.

The walk back to the flat was only a few minutes from the bar and Harry rather fancied a bit of a stroll. The night was a clear one, the sky resting over Hawes shimmering with stars, and after all of Dave's stories, he needed a little bit of quiet time to himself.

There was also the little task of reading the report that Gordy had sent through while he'd been at the bar buying a round. He could do that at home for sure, or he could continue trying to enjoy the night at the same time. Harry also figured that if he waited until he was home to read what Gordy had sent him, he'd soon be asleep on the sofa, Smudge curled up on his lap. At least out here, reading the report on his phone, the chill of the night would keep him awake enough to read and alert enough to take it in. So, instead of turning towards the flat, Harry continued on past, taking a left over the road, passing the primary school, and then up the hill towards Gayle.

The roads were quiet, the air still, and as Harry started to read what Gordy had sent him, far off he caught the faint bleat of sheep and lambs. The silent vastness of Wether Fell was set above the now sleepy dwellings below, its black bulk seeming to almost loom out of the night sky like a tidal wave of darkness just waiting for the perfect moment to come crashing down. On the small screen in front of him, Gordy's report wasn't making what had happened this past couple of days any easier to get to the bottom of.

As she had said at the community centre, Bill had bought Hawes Chapel with the proceeds from the sale of a couple of barns and a little bit of land. He wasn't alone in this purchase either, Mr Richard Adams being the other partner. Gordy had touched on the reasoning behind the purchase, but the detail in her short report went further, showing that there was much more to it than a mere whim.

Harry read how Bill and his parents had arrived in the country during the war, escaping the hell sweeping through Europe for anyone who didn't fit in with the Nazi dream of a master race. They hid their Jewish background behind new identities and settled into the Dales life. And it was this which had, according to what Gordy had found out from Hannah, driven Bill to push forward with the chapel: the dream of being able to provide, in the place that had welcomed his own family so openly, a sanctuary for other people fleeing conflict.

They'd kept the whole thing from their son, Danny, because being the only heir, and thus the one in line to inherit the farm, they guessed that he might not entirely agree with what they were doing with what would, eventually, be his. Though Harry wondered why that would be, when the lad himself had been adopted by Hannah and Bill.

On past the creamery Harry walked, taking in what he was learning about Bill, trying to figure out if there was anything that pointed conclusively to Danny or to anyone else. But his mind was also trying to deal with what had happened to Jen and it was almost impossible to stick to any one thought without another barging it out of the way.

Having taken a left along the flagstone path that followed Gayle Beck, and which ran almost like a thin vein of life between Hawes and Gayle, Harry strode on, mulling everything over, rereading Gordy's report a few more times. The moon, bright enough to bring into sharp relief the way ahead, gave him enough light to walk without concern of tripping over a loose stone or grassy tuft. To his right, the water of the beck chattered and gossiped its way onwards, cutting then through Hawes, under bridges, and on through the fields beyond, joining up with the greater River Ure.

It was as Harry drew close to Hawes again that he started to take more serious notice of the footsteps behind him. He had noticed them on his way up the hill to Gayle, but thought nothing of them, because he assumed that he wasn't the only one walking home in the dark after a pint or two in a pub.

However, as he'd walked along the path from Gayle and back to Hawes, it had struck him as strange that the footsteps had followed. Again, Harry had guessed that he wasn't alone in wanting to enjoy the bright, clear night, because it really was quite beautiful and an opportunity not to be missed. But when the footsteps seemed to speed up or slow down, matching his own pace, he began to wonder just who was behind him and what they were up to.

Harry had been followed many times during the course of his career in the police, and even more often he'd followed others. Then there were the times, back in the Paras, where the following and being followed was considerably more deadly.

Senses alert now, Harry took a left, down between the church and the small, overgrown graveyard and, with the darkness here thicker, like ink almost, he dropped quickly in amongst the graves. Slipping behind a large stone, Harry watched and waited as a figure left the path as he had done and followed on down, hesitantly it seemed, because their pace was now slowing.

The figure stopped. Harry waited. Then the figure moved on. Harry gave them a couple of minutes, then edged out from behind the gravestone and back to the path. Aware now that the person he suspected of following him was either now long gone or hidden somewhere ahead in the shadows, Harry was presented with two options: turn back and take the other path, which led down to just in front of Cockett's, or to continue onwards. Harry decided to march on, figuring that whoever had been following him hadn't been desperate to get close, so being jumped probably wasn't too much of a worry.

Following the path down, Harry slipped past darkened windows of cottages, along a short, dark passageway, and then out into Hawes marketplace. He glanced left and right, saw no one close by other than a couple making their stumbling way home and someone out for a very late-night walk with a dog.

Hunching his shoulders against a breeze coming down the passageway behind him, Harry turned left and walked back through Hawes. He hadn't the faintest idea of who'd been behind him or where they'd disappeared to. Approaching his front door, he wondered if perhaps his imagination had simply got the better of him. It happened, particularly on dark nights and lonely footpaths.

Harry pushed into the flat to find a note on the floor from Ben. He crouched down to read it: *With Liz, see you tomorrow. Ben.* Then the clipping sound of Smudge's claws on the floor ahead caught his attention and he glanced up to see her sitting at the end of the short hall staring at him. Not his socks in her mouth this time; his boxer shorts.

'Miss me?' Harry said.

Smudge's tail thumped against the floor.

Smiling, Harry went to stand up when a sharp, rapid knock cracked against the door behind him.

Harry turned, stared. Behind him, Smudge kept on with

the tail wagging.

The knocks came again.

'Ben?' Harry said. 'That you?'

More knocks. Definitely not Ben, then, Harry thought.

'Please,' came a hissed voice. 'Please, I need to speak to you!'

Harry wasn't about to let just anyone walk into his flat.

'Who are you?'

'Please!' came the reply. 'Can you let me in?'

Another flurry of rapid knocks.

Harry looked around for something to protect himself with, walked through to the kitchen, and found a rolling pin in a drawer. It wasn't much, but if whoever it was came at him, he'd at least have something to hand. He took a practise swing at an open palm. Yes, he thought, that would do very nicely indeed.

'Stand back from the door!' Harry called out.

'But I need to come in! Please!'

'And I need you to stand back from the door!' Harry called back. 'Who are you? I need a name before we go any further. You clearly know who I am, otherwise you wouldn't be here. But I need the same from you. Or you can just stand out there and freeze for all I care!'

Harry waited, heard the shuffling of feet.

'It's about Bill,' said the voice beyond the door.

'That's still not your name, is it?'

'But I don't know who's listening! There could be anyone out here!'

'The only person listening is me,' said Harry. 'And my dog, and right now she's more interested in the underwear of mine that she's chewing, than whoever the hell you are. So, name now, or I'm off to bed!'

Silence.

'Right, it's bed for me, then!' Harry said. 'Nighty-night!'

'No, wait!'

Another pause.

'My name... I'm ... I'm Danny. Danny Dinsdale, Bill's son!'

'Prove it!'

'What?'

'I said prove it!'

'I can't!'

'You can bloody well try!' Harry replied.

'I'm his son! You have to believe me! Why would I lie? I've not even been to see Mum about what's happened because I need to speak to you first! Please!'

That was enough, Harry thought and he opened the door only to have a figure rush at him from out of the dark.

'Stop!' Harry bellowed, his voice loud enough to halt the figure in a beat. 'Stop! Now!'

'But I need to come in!'

'And this is my home and the only people who come into it are family and friends. And you're neither of those, are you?'

Standing in the dark, the man claiming to be Danny stared back at Harry, hugging himself against the chill of the night.

'I need to speak to you! It's urgent! Please!'

He was jumpy, twitchy, constantly looking around him as though he was afraid of being seen.

'If it's so urgent then I can't help but wonder why you've not come to speak to me before now,' Harry said. 'And moving on from that, why you think the middle of the night is entirely appropriate to do so!'

The man stared at Harry, silent.

'One more thing,' Harry said. 'And I know I'm only hazarding a guess here, but let's call it a very well-educated hunch, perhaps you can explain why you thought following me was entirely necessary?'

The man said nothing to confirm nor deny it had been him on the path, but Harry was confident that his hunch was correct. Instead, he just stared at Harry from behind tired, terrified eyes, shuffling from foot to foot.

Harry gave up waiting and instead ducked back inside the flat to grab his keys for the community office. Then, after quickly ruffling Smudge's fur, he exited the flat, pulled the door shut behind him, and took his first proper look at the man claiming to be Bill and Hannah's son.

His eyes were sunken deep, black holes, his face weary, and his hair was a mess. His clothes were crumpled, like he'd been sleeping rough, with scuffed, grubby jeans, and what Harry could only describe as a tired, faded lumberjack's shirt, with a sharp rip in the left sleeve. Harry thought back to what Jim had found in the field earlier in the day.

'I'm sorry,' Danny said. 'I didn't know what to do.'

'And this was what you came up with?' Harry asked. 'Really? Not a phone call to the police first? Or perhaps, and this is just a suggestion for future reference, contacting your mum?'

Danny said nothing, just shivered in the dark.

'Right, you walk in front of me,' Harry said. 'And yes, I am carrying a rolling pin, so don't get any funny ideas.'

'Where are we going?'

'Just walk,' Harry said and directed Danny back into town.

CHAPTER TWENTY-SIX

Inside the community centre, Harry flicked on the lights and sent the darkness racing back outside as he locked the door behind them. The chill of the building wasn't going anywhere anytime soon, but he was pretty sure he'd seen an old electric blow heater in the main office and after a quick scout around, found it. Harry then led Danny through to the room he had, earlier that day, sat in with Mr Adams, plugged in the heater, and switched it on full. The aroma of warm dust drifted into the room.

'Take a seat,' Harry said, sitting down himself, rubbing his eyes, and doing his best to not yawn.

The warmth from the heater was already having an effect, helped by Harry positioning it under the table.

Danny stayed on his feet, fidgeting, like he would, at any moment, just bolt for the door and disappear, nervously rubbing his left arm with his right hand.

'Look, whatever it is you need to talk to me about,' Harry said, 'if you think you're in danger, whatever it is that had you decide to knock at my door only just short of midnight on a Monday night, I need to know, right now.' Harry signalled to a seat opposite. 'My name is Detective Chief Inspector Grimm. Please, if you could sit down?'

With no movement still from Danny, Harry's patience, thin at the best of times, was now as fragile as a bee's wing, particularly after having read what Gordy had sent through to him earlier that evening.

'Either sit down or I'm sodding off!' Harry said, his voice gruff and grumpy and louder than even he had expected it to be. 'I'm tired. I'm more than a little bit grumpy. And I've a few more pints in me than I should have, which doesn't bode well for you to begin with, does it? So, what's it to be?'

At last, Danny dropped into the chair, half willingly, Harry thought, though it was clear that the main reason was that his legs seemed to be unable to hold him up any longer.

Danny's eyes flitted around still, constantly looking up at the door as though he expected someone to burst through it at any moment.

'That's good,' Harry said. 'Much better, I think, don't you? And now that you're settled, and hopefully enjoying the warmth from this little heater I managed to find, how's about I get you and me a drink? I'm not sure we have any biscuits, but I can have a look. What do you want? Tea? Coffee? Water? Might even be able to push to some squash if that takes your fancy.'

Danny shook his head.

'No, I'm fine, thank you.'

Harry, on the other hand, wasn't, and nipped out, returning a minute or so later with a jug of water and a couple of glass tumblers.

Harry filled both glasses. Leaning back, his chair complained just enough to have him ease off in case it collapsed. Then, with the recorder in the middle of the table on, and his official statement made, noting location, date, time, and his name and professional title, he asked Danny for his contact details.

'Name, address, date of birth, and telephone number, please. For the record.'

'I'm kind of between addresses,' Danny said. 'My post gets sent to the farm because that's where I stayed when I came back, but I'm in my mate's spare room at the moment. Have been for a good while now.'

'Just give both,' Harry said.

Danny gave up the information without any complaint, then asked, 'Does this have to be recorded?'

'You're not under arrest,' Harry said. 'You're free to leave whenever you want.' Harry noticed Danny was still rubbing his arm. 'You alright there?'

'What?'

'Your arm.'

Danny stopped rubbing, stared at his arm.

'Scratched it,' he said, then clasped his hands together. 'It's nothing.'

'Well, then,' Harry said, pleased to be making progress, 'why don't you start from the beginning? I'd say we have all night, but we don't, so if you could get a move on, I'm sure we'd both appreciate it.'

'You're sure I'm safe, right?' Danny asked, his eyes dancing from Harry to the door behind him. 'In here, I mean? No one can get me in this room, can they? I'm definitely safe?'

'Very much so,' Harry said, wondering just what it was that Danny was so scared of. 'So, like I said, in your own time...'

For a few moments, silence sat between Harry and Danny. The two men sat staring at each other, the only sound in the room the low, over-enthusiastic hum from the heater at their feet. To hurry Danny along, and to show that he was taking this seriously, Harry pulled out his notebook. Then, after a deep sigh, Danny spoke.

'I know I should've come in earlier,' he said. 'But... I was scared, you see.'

Harry noticed that Danny's accent wasn't as full of the Dales as he'd expected.

'Go on,' he said, encouraging Danny to offer an explanation rather than be led.

'I was with Dad, in the field,' Danny said, struggling to keep his voice steady. 'We argued, I left, but then I went back, to apologise, which was when I saw them. The men.'

At this, Harry perked up, whatever tiredness was in his bones evaporating.

'Who did you see, Danny? Where?'

'In the field, with Dad, that's where!' Danny said. 'I drove back and parked further up the lane because there was a car just pulled up outside the gate.'

'Do you remember the colour?' Harry asked.

'Black,' Danny said. 'It was a black BMW.'

'So, you parked up,' said Harry. 'Then what?'

'I walked back down to the field,' Danny explained. 'I walked over to where Dad was, behind the spinney. I saw Dad was talking to these two men. I didn't know about what, but I headed over anyway.'

'Did you recognise them?'

Danny shook his head.

'They had their backs to me,' he said. 'And they were on the other side of the field so I couldn't really see them.'

'Can you describe them?'

'One was tall, probably over six foot, the other a bit shorter than that. Dad couldn't see me either, I don't think, because they were blocking his view really. And...'

'And what?'

'They had something pulled over their heads,' Danny said, gesturing to his head and face with a wave of a hand. 'I didn't notice at first, but later, that's when I saw.'

'Saw what?' Harry asked. 'What happened?'

Danny lowered his head then, rubbed his eyes. Whatever he was here to say, Harry could see that doing so was taking a hell of a lot of effort.

'I started walking over towards them. Like I said, I'd had this big argument with Dad that morning, about the farm, about what he was doing with it, this mad idea of his to buy Hawes Chapel! I mean, that's insane, isn't it? A chapel? What was he thinking? It didn't make sense to me. But I wanted to clear the air, start again. He's my dad, you know? I mean, we have our differences, but I never wanted to fall out like that.'

Harry kept quiet on what he knew about Bill and the chapel. He didn't mention the threats.

'Did you speak to the men?' Harry asked. 'To your dad?'

At this point, Harry saw what little colour was left in Danny's face drain away completely.

'There was an argument,' Danny said. 'Dad was shouting, the two men were shouting. I've no idea what it was about, but it was proper loud. Then the smaller one approached Dad, but Dad kind of just walked up to him, challenging him I suppose, because Dad was never one for being pushed around, just wasn't in his nature. He reached out for the thing the other man was wearing on his head and that's when I saw what it was.'

'And what was it?'

'A balaclava,' said Danny.

'He was wearing a balaclava?' Harry asked. 'You sure about that?'

Danny nodded.

'They were both wearing them! I mean, what's that about? Why would two blokes in balaclavas be arguing with my dad in the middle of a hayfield? I think Dad probably thought the same. He was never one for putting up with nonsense, if you know what I mean. I reckon he just lost it and tried to yank the balaclava off. But as he did so, the other man, the taller one, he smashed Dad over the back of the head with what looked like a fence post. He'd pulled it out of the baler. What it was doing in there in the first place, I've no idea.'

Harry turned a page in his notebook, having run out of space.

'What did you do?'

'I froze!' said Danny. 'I just stood there in shock. What I was seeing, it just didn't make sense! I didn't know how to react. It was like I was just frozen to the spot, you know? The shock of it.'

Danny's voice broke, unable to say any more.

'Danny?' Harry said, his voice calm, quiet. 'What happened? What did you see?'

'They had the tractor going again,' Danny said. 'I think that was the tall bloke, but I'm not sure. And then they... well, they both just lifted Dad up and...'

Harry watched as Danny mimed lifting something heavy, throwing it through the air.

'They just threw him into it, into the baler! My dad! I saw him go in! And then the baler was making these awful sounds and...'

Danny choked.

'And you saw all this?' Harry asked.

'Of course, I bloody well saw it! You think I'd make this up? I was there! They did it right in front of me!'

'Still, though, it's taken you a while to come to the police, don't you think?' Harry said.

Danny stared at Harry, his fists clenched tight, knuckle-bones white through his skin.

'They saw me!' Danny said. 'They saw me, and I ran!'

CHAPTER TWENTY-SEVEN

'Can you imagine it?' Danny said, his voice a raging thing of spit and fear. 'Seeing that? It was awful! I can't describe it!'

'And I'm not going to ask you to, either,' Harry said.

He had seen enough terrible things in his lifetime, in the police and back in the Paras, to keep most people from sleeping ever again. He wasn't about to force someone to make it worse for themselves when they'd do that all on their own and often with little control over it.

'They shoved Dad into that baler, then they saw me and I ran! They were shouting and I could hear them chasing me down and I knew that after what they'd just done to Dad they would do worse to me, because I was a witness, wasn't I?'

Harry let Danny's words run free. There was no stopping him, the memory just spilling out, the panic

'I just needed to get out of there. I had to, I had to run and go and I wasn't thinking, but I could hear them behind me, shouting and running and swearing, and I could hear the baler and the tractor, and all I could think about was Dad inside it and what it was doing to him and them doing the same to me, and...'

The panic and fear in Danny's voice was an animal breaking free and running wild now.

'What else, Danny?'

'I ran to my car. All I wanted to do was to get out of there. Dad was dead! They'd killed him! I don't know who they were, but that's what they did, isn't it? They killed him! Shoved him into a baler and killed him! I saw them do it! I saw them!'

Harry was trying to picture what had happened and asked, 'What happened then? What did you do? I need to know where you've been since you saw all of this.'

'I just drove,' Danny said. 'I jumped in my car and just went for it, I mean I drove like an idiot, I know I did, but I wasn't thinking anything other than to just get away, to run. I saw two cars coming the other way, one was Mum, but I couldn't wave, couldn't stop.'

'So, where did you go?'

'They came after me so I just kept driving! They'd appear in my mirrors then they'd not be there and I'd think I was fine, but then they'd be there again. I've never been so terrified in my life! I had enough of a head start, but their car was faster. I just floored it, didn't really think about where I was, what I was doing, anything. I drove all over the place. Went through Thoralby, ended up down Bishopdale way, trying to lose them down smaller lanes. It didn't work. Nothing seemed to work. And I knew they were going to kill me.'

'They followed you?' Harry asked, thinking that Danny really wasn't sounding like the kind of person who would've sent his dad those threatening notes. Though there was always the chance that he was and that this was all an act. Though, if it was, Danny was really going for it, Harry thought.

'I hid the car a couple of times, tried to lose them, but then when I headed back out onto the road, they were still driving around, looking for me! I was sure they were going to get me. I just couldn't get away, no matter what I did! Every corner I'd see them behind me, every straight bit they'd be getting closer!'

'They didn't though,' Harry said. 'You got away.'

'No, they didn't,' said Danny. 'I'd been driving around, I don't know, an hour, maybe a bit longer? Cat and mouse, it was. I threw up in my car at one point, thinking about Dad, about those two men trying to get me. Drove like an idiot through West Burton, out onto the main road. I saw this open gate into a field, just past that layby on the right, down the hill out of Aysgarth. I think I just panicked then. I threw my car into it, dropped behind this hedge. I nearly lost control of it, skidded, don't really know how I made it to be honest. I saw them go past. Heard them, too, tyres squealing. And I just stayed there. No idea for how long. But it was dark by the time I moved. I heard sirens, but that only made me want to not move even more. I wanted to hide forever because I knew, if I came out, they'd find me.'

Harry gave himself a moment to join the dots, not that it was a difficult task. Whoever these two were who'd fed old Bill into a baler, he was now fairly sure that they were the same two who had hit Jen, just after Danny had hidden himself in the field it seemed. He could check the story out later, at least with regards to having a look at the field Danny mentioned, to confirm what he was being told.

'That takes you up to yesterday evening, then,' Harry said.

'It's a bit of a blur from then on,' Danny said. 'I didn't dare go to the farm. I figured if they knew who Dad was, they'd know me, where I lived. So, I went to the only other place I could think of.'

'The barn, right?' Harry said.

At this, Danny looked surprised.

'How did you know?'

'You were seen this morning,' Harry explained. 'One of my team followed it up, found your trunk in the barn. We have it here, actually. Why didn't you go home? Why didn't you go and see your mum?'

'What if those men had followed me?' Danny said. 'What if they were just waiting outside Mum's place for me to turn up? I couldn't put her in danger, too, could I?'

'Why the barn, then?' Harry asked. 'I'm just trying to work out why you went there in the first place, and where you've been ever since.'

'Because it's my barn, that's why!' Danny replied. 'Well, it was supposed to be, until I found out Dad had sold it to buy that bloody chapel!'

Harry really needed a coffee. The kind he used to make for himself back in the Paras when they were out doing 'proper soldiering' as his sergeant used to call it. This was a cover-all term for anything and everything that involved being out in all weather, usually the rain, lying in a scrape and eating cold ration packs. Some of those patrols and exercises had been hell, yet he found himself often looking back on those days with affection. A brew was always important, good for morale and all that, but coffee always helped with tiredness. He'd always take his own instant sachets, but instead of sugar, he carried tubes of condensed milk. Worked as a spread, too, Harry remembered, on top of ration pack biscuits.

'This barn, then,' Harry said.

'Used to go up there as a kid,' Danny explained. 'It was my den! I'd have some bales up there, a tarp or two, and I'd just play. When I was older, I'd camp out, take a few mates for beers, that kind of thing. Always dreamt of turning it into a house for myself.'

'So, you were angry when you found out, then,' Harry said. 'About your dad's plans.'

'Too right, I was angry! Who wouldn't be?'

'But the farm was your dad's to do with as he wanted,' said Harry. 'Did he know you wanted the barn?'

'Of course he did!' Danny said. 'I mean, it's not like we talked about it loads, but he knew, I'm sure of it. Doesn't matter anyway, because of those plans of his. He should've spoken to me about it, shouldn't he? Why keep it a secret? But it wasn't just him, it was Mum, too. They just don't trust me. But I only came back to help them, to look after them, that's all! And I missed the farm, the Dales. It's impossible not to.' At this, Danny's voice cracked with a cold laugh. 'This bloody place! I spent years trying to get away, thinking there was more to life out there, beyond the fells. And now look at me, back here, like I've never been away.'

Harry allowed Danny a moment and flicked through his notes.

'Can you think of anyone who would want to harm your father?'

'Harm him?' Danny said. 'Really? That's the best word you could come up with, harm? They didn't harm him, did they? They smashed in his skull in with a post and fed him into a baler!'

'The question still stands,' Harry said. 'I know this is hard, and I know I'm not being very tactful, but if you know anything at all that can help us find who did this to your dad, you need to tell me.'

'No, I know,' Danny said, deflating a little. 'But I really can't think of anyone who would want to do that to Dad! This is the Dales, isn't it? Up here, it's all sheep and endless cups of tea and *by 'eck* this and *nay, lad* that! It's not the kind of place where something like this happens! People don't go around shoving each other into farm machinery!'

'And you're sure you didn't recognise these two men?' Harry asked.

'They were wearing balaclavas! How could I?'

'You said your dad pulled off the one the shorter bloke was wearing.'

'Not completely,' Danny said. 'That was when the other one hit him. And then...'

Danny slumped forward, elbows on the table, head resting in his hands.

'I'm so tired,' he said.

'Where have you been today?' asked Harry.

'What?'

'Today? Where've you been? You were seen at the barn early this morning and you turned up to see me in the middle of the night. There's a few hours missing.'

'What does that matter?' Danny replied.

'Details,' Harry said. 'Details always matter.'

Danny was quiet, and he rubbed his eyes, yawning.

'Well?' Harry said.

'I headed back to my mate's place. I've known him since

we were kids at Hawes primary, you see? I didn't tell him what had happened, just disappeared upstairs. I needed to be on my own, try to clear my head, work out what to do next.'

'This friend have a name?'

'Nigel Thwaite,' Danny said. 'Lives just outside of Hawes. Odd little row of houses on the left in the middle of a field. Nice, though. Most of them are holiday cottages but he lives in one. Has done since his divorce.'

Harry took down the contact details and address.

'I'll speak with him tomorrow,' Harry said. 'Just to confirm this.'

'Oh, he'll confirm it,' said Danny. 'He's a good lad. Proper gentle giant!'

Harry cast his eyes back over his notes.

'Is there anything else you can think of to tell me?' he asked. 'Any other details at all, about the men, what happened, anything at all?'

Danny shook his head.

'No, that's it. There's nothing else.'

Harry saw now that the fear in the man in front of him had been replaced by utter exhaustion. Interview over, he asked if Danny wanted to clarify anything, which he did not, stated the time and that the interview was over, then he switched off the machine.

'You need to get some sleep,' Harry said, removing the cassette tape, sealing it in an envelope, and then signing it before asking Danny to do the same.

Danny gave a nod.

'My suggestion is that you head home, and by that I mean to the farm, to be with your mum.'

Danny shook his head.

'It's too dangerous. I can't.'

'I don't think so,' Harry said. 'Whatever this was or is, it was with your dad, not your mum, not you.'

'They saw me.'

'How far away were they?'

'In the field?' Danny asked. 'Couple of hundred metres I guess, maybe a bit more.'

'So, they didn't see you,' said Harry. 'What they saw was a blur, a distant figure, someone who turned and ran and drove off. That's all. Anyway, we'll have someone outside the house for a while, keep an eye on things.'

'They'd know my car, though. They chased me!'

'To scare you, I'm guessing,' Harry said. 'Or maybe they were panicking themselves.'

'You can't be sure of that.'

'Where's the car?'

'Hidden,' said Danny. 'Little bit of woodland on the farm.'

'Then I'll drive you,' Harry said. 'How's that sound?'

Danny hesitated.

'Your mum needs you,' said Harry, his voice as soft as he could make it. 'At times like this, family is everything. You're her son, aren't you? Start behaving like it.'

Danny gave a nod.

'You're right.'

'Not all the time,' Harry said, 'but right now? Yes. So, let's get you home, shall we?'

And with that, Harry turned off the electric heater and stood up.

Danny followed suit, pushing himself to his feet, then following Harry out of the room, out of the building, and back down through Hawes marketplace to where Harry had parked his Rav4.

On the way over to the farm, Danny slept, waking only when Harry pulled up in the yard.

'Thanks,' Danny said, unclipping himself and opening the door.

'Not a problem,' Harry said. 'I appreciate how hard it was for you to come forward, to tell me what happened.'

'Yeah, it was.'

'Do me a favour though,' Harry said as Danny climbed out. 'I'm not assuming there will be, but if there is a next time that you need to chat, make it closer to midday than midnight?'

Danny shut the door. Harry waited till he saw the front door open and Hannah, Danny's mum, welcome him in with a hug, then he turned around and headed home. On the way back, he parked up and called Jim.

'We've another house I need someone to keep an eye on,' he said.

Jim was there in thirty.

CHAPTER TWENTY-EIGHT

JADYN WASN'T HAVING THE BEST OF DAYS. IT WASN'T THE worst either, but it wasn't exactly thrilling him. Yes, he knew that police work wasn't all chasing down criminals and dodging bullets—actually, he'd never dodged a bullet in his life and would be very happy for it to stay that way—but sometimes, the tedium of the work was a little wearisome.

Everyone else seemed to be on with really important stuff, keeping an eye on both Mr Richard Adams, and Hannah and Danny. That was proper police work, wasn't it? But what he was doing, well, it just wasn't as sexy. Not that he was in the police for that at all, but sometimes, he had to admit, that was what he wanted.

With a list of every BMW dealer in the area, Jadyn had spent most of Tuesday on the phone, calling around garages and dealerships, and in a number of cases, heading over to speak to them in person. This hadn't been necessary with the organised garages, the ones able to tell him immediately what they had in, the repairs they'd carried out or were planning to.

There were a few though, where whoever he'd spoken to on reception just hadn't had the foggiest idea about anything that was actually going on in the very establishment in which they worked. And so, off Jadyn had headed, from garage to dealership to garage, trying to track down a needle in a haystack in the shape of a black BMW with a wing mirror missing. And so far he'd come up blank. Plenty of black BMWs for sure, but none with a missing mirror. Hadn't stopped a couple of the establishments from having a go at trying to sell one to him, either. And one of them had clearly read a script on selling cars from the 80s, including all the bits on being politically incorrect.

'It'd suit you, this one.'

'Would it? Why?'

'Well, a young lad like you, nice car like this, know what I'm saying?'

'Not really, no.'

'The birds, mate! Think of it! They'd love it!'

'Birds?'

'The women!'

'Would they? Why?'

'They just would! Can't get enough, can they? The birds bloody love a car like this! They'd be all over you, I promise! And that's my guarantee, that is. In fact, I'll even knock five-hundred off the price for you, that's how confident I am. So, what do you say? Deal?'

The man who'd attempted to sell him the car had been about the size and shape of a wrecking ball, with yellow teeth and breath thick enough to chew on. Jadyn had, much to the man's disappointment and surprise, turned down the offer.

'Won't get another like this, you know. It's a proper bargain.'

'I'll take the risk, thanks.'

Now, with the afternoon nearly gone, and an evening at some meeting or other of the Rotary Club, Jadyn had a couple of hours to kill before Harry arrived to join him. He could go home, crash for an hour, but Richmond was in the wrong direction now, so he figured it best to head over to Leyburn, as that's where he was heading anyway. He could grab something to eat, have a walk around, and there was never any harm in being visible to the public, was there? That was all part of the job.

Arriving in Leyburn, Jadyn parked up and did a quick three-sixty of the centre of town. It was a busy place, even with the day coming to an end, and Jadyn's first port of call was a bakery to grab something for dinner. He remembered Matt waxing lyrical about some kind of special pie, but he wasn't in the mood for that right now. Just a sandwich would do, a can of pop, some crisps. Hell, maybe even some cake.

Walking over to the bakers, Jadyn found out his choice was a little limited.

'End of the day, mate,' the man behind the counter said. 'So, you've a choice of... chicken salad, egg mayonnaise, or... No, that's it, that's your choice.'

That was no choice at all, Jadyn thought, because he'd always felt that there was something inherently wrong with egg mayonnaise. The texture just wasn't right, all lumpy and soft and gloopy. The taste was odd, sort of sweet but savoury, that tang of mayo and then the egg. But the worst of it was the smell, the godawful reek, the stink that would haunt you for the rest of the day, wafting around like some rotting ghost of what a sandwich should never be.

Back outside the shop, Jadyn was tempted to grab himself a seat, but after all the driving that day he needed a walk, so off he wandered, first up out of town and towards the secondary school, then back into town and through the marketplace. Ahead, he saw the tower of the church poking above some trees, grass around its flanks, and he took a wander then, up the path to the door then sat himself down on a bench to finish off his food.

With his lunch gone and now being digested by an adequately satisfied stomach, Jadyn stretched then leaned back, staring up at the sky, then around at the church. Having grown up in Bradford, he was used to seeing churches with mesh on the windows, in some cases plywood boards. Here though, the colours of the stained glass caught the sun as it slowly dipped lower and lower in the sky. The front door was open, with a sign inviting people in.

Okay, so there was some hint at being security-aware, with a couple of cameras visible, one at the front of the church, on the corner of the tower, another above the main door in the side of the building, but other than that, this was a building open to the public, and that, Jadyn thought, was really rather lovely, all in all.

Checking his watch, Jadyn saw that he had another hour and a half to kill before Harry arrived, assuming that the DCI would be on time, so he picked up the rubbish from his dinner and made to walk back up into town. Maybe he'd show his face in a couple of pubs, he thought, help build relationships with the owners and customers, that kind of thing? It was as he was walking away from the church that Jadyn stopped and turned around to look at the building again. An idea had struck him, probably a stupid one, no doubt, but then, maybe not.

Walking back to the church, Jadyn looked up at the

building, saw the camera on the tower then tried to track where it was pointing. Definitely the road, he thought. Remembering what Matt and Liz had said the day before, that the black BMW had been, at the very least, heading to Wensley, then there was a good chance it had gone through Leyburn. Gordy had tried to get help over from elsewhere, to go around checking on this kind of thing, but that had come to nothing. Something to do with 'resources needed elsewhere,' which Jadyn was fairly sure was code for 'too far away, not exciting enough.' And that meant that right now, if anyone was going to check up on what he'd noticed, then it was going to have to be him.

There was a slim chance that this camera had caught the car as it travelled through Leyburn, Jadyn thought. It was a long shot. For a start, he didn't even know if the cameras were on or, if they were, what they were set to record, if their range was only the church grounds or if they would pick up anything beyond that boundary. Only one way to find out, he thought. So, with just enough time left before Harry's arrival, Jadyn found himself at the church noticeboard and calling the number given after the vicar's name.

The vicarage, Jadyn discovered, was not a grand old building as he'd expected, but a nice modern detached family house on a new estate on the outskirts of the town. The vicar was at the door waiting for him when he arrived.

'Officer Okri, yes?' the man said. 'Good to meet you. Come on in. The study's just through here on the left.'

Jadyn followed the vicar into the house and through to the study, a room comprising a desk, a couple of sofas staring at each other over a low coffee table, and walls dedicated to books.

The vicar, a Mr John Williams, was in his late fifties, Jadyn guessed. He was a tall man with no hair but a beard as thick and white as cotton wool.

'So, security cameras, then,' Mr Williams said, sitting down at his desk.

'Yes,' Jadyn said. 'It's a long shot, but I was just wondering if you had anything from Sunday at all.'

'I'm sure we do,' Mr Williams said. 'It was a busy day. Had a Sunday wedding, which isn't all that common. Most people like to tie the knot on a Saturday, you see, so that they can then have Sunday to sleep it off, if you know what I mean!'

Jadyn smiled, quickly warming to the man.

'Was it a good wedding?' he asked, making conversation.

'Of course it was!' Mr Williams said with a smile. 'I performed it, didn't I? Best weddings around if you ask me. Try to make sure it's not too serious. Nothing worse than a wedding that feels like a funeral.'

'No, I'm sure,' said Jadyn.

Mr Williams clapped his hands, the sound as loud as a gunshot.

'Right then, you'll be wanting me to use my computer then, won't you? No easy task. I seem to forget everything about it as soon as I turn it off. And on that, why is it that I have to click 'Start' if I want to switch it off? Who on earth thought of that?'

Jadyn shrugged, not really sure what to say.

Mr Williams turned to his computer. After fiddling with the mouse, clicking the buttons loudly, then hammering his fingers down on his keyboard, he punched the air and shouted, 'Yes! I'm in!'

'Great!' said Jadyn almost punching the air himself.

'Best you come round and have a look yourself, I think,' Mr Williams said. 'You'll know what you're looking for better than I, that's for sure.'

Getting up, he then moved away from his desk and gestured to his seat.

'Make yourself comfortable. Just give me a call when you're done. Sure I can't interest you in a coffee?'

'No, I'm fine, thank you,' Jadyn said, and Mr Williams left him alone.

Opening a folder on the screen, Jadyn saw that he had a good number of files to get through. He checked his watch: still time, he thought. So, he clicked on the first and hoped for a miracle.

MAKING his way from the vicarage to where he was meeting Harry, Jadyn wondered what to do with what he'd found out. There'd been a good amount of luck involved in what he'd discovered, that was true, but that was no bad thing. During his time as a police officer, he'd realised that luck was important, but also that you made your own luck. If you looked for things in the right places, there was always a chance that you'd find what you were looking for. You had to go with a hunch, listen to your gut, and that's what he'd done. He could just as easily have dismissed the cameras at the church, but he hadn't, had he? Instead, he'd followed his instincts and found something interesting.

After a day spent unsuccessfully trying to track down the BMW they were looking for, to find the fleeting image of it on the files from the camera had been the longest of long-shots. And yet, he'd found something, hadn't he? Okay, so the image was grainy, but that was to be expected. However, there was something else: the car had stopped, outside the church, and the passenger had clambered out and for the briefest of moments, been on screen.

Jadyn had printed off some images, not just of the car, but the passenger. He'd zoomed in as best he could to get a better impression of who the person was, but to also check that it was the right vehicle. At first, he'd thought his excitement had been misplaced, but then he'd spotted it—the missing wing mirror on the passenger side. So, it was the car. And he had a face, albeit it a grainy, blurry one, to go with it.

Now, if he could track down the passenger, then the driver could be found, too, for sure. But there was something else, too, which had jogged his memory about something Jim had said that he'd found when he'd gone back to have another look around the field. He'd be speaking to him about that tomorrow for sure.

Parking up again in the centre of town, Jadyn checked his watch. He had half an hour left before he was meeting Harry. In his hands he had a lead, didn't he? Something he could follow right now if he wanted to. And he really, really wanted to. Wouldn't it be fantastic, if he was able to develop that lead into something more tangible, a name perhaps, an address? He was on his own, which meant traipsing around and knocking on doors wasn't an option, so he needed something that would allow someone on their own to have a bigger hit.

Pubs, he thought, that's what he needed. And with that half an hour, he reckoned he could get in at least two or three before seeing Harry. Maybe he'd even have a lead by then, which would be amazing! And if he didn't, well, he'd just do a few more pubs after and hope for the best. Then, tomorrow, he could tell the team as a whole what he'd found and he'd been doing.

Climbing out of his vehicle, Jadyn locked up and headed to the closest pub, unable to ignore the adrenaline surging through him at what he was about to do. He loved this job and couldn't imagine doing anything else.

CHAPTER TWENTY-NINE

HARRY ARRIVED AT THE BUILDING WHERE THE ROTARY Club was meeting to have his absolute lack of interest in what he was attending be smashed to pieces by the approaching excitement of Police Constable Okri. Jadyn had a bounce in his step and a smile on his face so wide, so broad, Harry wondered if it was actually in danger of cutting his head in half. He'd spent the day following things up and somehow it was now the evening. Where the hell had the day gone?

'Constable Okri,' Harry said. 'I know I'm going to regret asking this, but why do you look so bloody cheerful?'

'I've been to see the vicar!' said Jadyn, dropping down to say hello to Smudge.

The dog immediately flipped over, requesting a tummy rub. Harry wondered if Smudge would ever do anything else.

'Can't say that was the answer I was expecting,' Harry replied. 'And what did you go to see this vicar about, exactly?'

Jadyn went to say something then stopped himself.

'I'm not sure, yet. It's just a hunch, but something I wanted to follow up.'

'And is this a hunch you want to share with your chief inspector?'

'Tomorrow,' Jadyn said.

'You mean now, I'm sure,' Harry said.

Jadyn shook his head.

'No, there's not much to say, not yet, anyway. I just need a little more time to think it through, if that makes sense.'

Harry frowned. More secrets, he thought, and that made him nervous, but on the other hand, it was good to see that Jadyn was showing a nice bit of initiative. He was also pleased to hear that instead of acting first and dealing with the consequences later, the young constable was thinking things through. All good signs that he was developing into a great police officer.

'Fair enough,' Harry said 'but I'll expect something tomorrow, understand?' Jadyn gave a resolute nod. Harry glanced up at the building in front of them. 'Right, then, you ready for this, Constable?'

'No idea, Boss,' Jadyn said, 'because I don't actually know what this is.'

'Between you and me, neither do I,' said Harry. 'So, it looks like we're both in good company, doesn't it?'

Once inside the building, Harry and Jadyn were greeted by none other than Mr Richard Adams himself. Harry was fairly sure that he didn't like the man at all, but each time they met he did his best to give him another chance. Trouble was, there was just something about him that made it almost impossible. He couldn't quite put his finger on it and in the end, had just chalked it up to the fact that every time he met the man, he came across as a wealthy, controlling, and insufferably puffed-up egotistical git. And that was Harry being his most polite. Not exactly the type of person he would ever consciously choose to spend time with. One life and all that, Harry thought, and he'd always been very choosy as to who he decided to share it with, which, in the end, turned out to be very few people at all.

With what was going on in the Bill Dinsdale case, and whether he liked him or not just didn't matter, Adams was someone they were keeping an eye on. He'd received threats, Bill was dead, so being here with him was probably a good thing. He'd just have to put up with the man as best as he could.

'Ah, DCI Grimm,' Mr Adams said, approaching Harry with a wide, fake smile slapped across his face. It dropped as soon as he caught sight of Jadyn. 'And I see you've brought your dog and another guest...'

The man's eyes flickered awkwardly between Harry and Jadyn and then at Smudge. His smile looked for a moment like his face had short-circuited.

'Didn't think you'd mind,' Harry said. 'They're both well behaved, though I think Smudge here is better at sitting still.' He then added, 'And Jadyn here will be working as my key liaison with local businesses. Won't you, Constable Okri?'

Harry gave Jadyn the kind of stare that made it very, very clear that his response should be to just nod and say yes.

Jadyn looked up at Harry, eyes momentarily wide at what Harry had said. 'Yes, absolutely. That's what I am, key liaison! With local businesses. It's a very important role and I'm here to make sure that I do it importantly. I think it even comes with a badge.'

Well, Harry thought, at least the constable had picked up

on what he'd said, so that was something. Though he'd have to have a word with him about the badge thing.

'Really? Oh, well then, that makes perfect sense, of course!' Adams said, his smile firmly back in place. 'Best you both come on in.'

Harry, Jadyn, and Smudge followed as Adams led them through into a small hall laid out with rows of chairs. In front of the chairs, and sitting on a small, raised stage, was a table at which four further chairs were placed.

'About the notes,' Adams said. 'I know I should've mentioned them. I can only apologise.'

'These things happen,' Harry said.

'Your officers have been excellent,' Adams said. 'I feel very safe now, that's for sure. Though I doubt it's necessary.'

'Just a precaution,' Harry said.

Adams pointed to the front of the room.

'That's where the chairperson, Mr Turner, sits,' he said, 'with the rest of the council.'

A number of other people were in the room and others were following in behind. There was lots of handshaking and back-slapping and Harry wanted to leave immediately.

'So, what's tonight's meeting about, then?' Harry asked, having not the faintest idea what to expect.

'We were due to have a speaker, actually,' Adams said. 'Giving a talk on rewilding, I believe. But that's been cancelled in light of what happened at the weekend, with Bill, I mean.'

'Really?'

'It was quite a shock to the club because Bill was very well-liked by everyone,' Adams said. 'Hannah is coming along herself as well to help us discuss what to do next.'

'You mean the funeral and a wake or something?' Harry asked.

'That and the business with the chapel, of course.'

'Why, of course?'

'Because the Rotary is like a large family,' said Adams. 'And we look after each other and right now, Hannah and Danny need looking after, too, don't you think?'

Harry was still a little confused, but was given no further opportunity to ask questions as they were then interrupted.

'I see we have guests, Richard!'

A tall man with grey hair and expensive shoes was now standing with Adams. He reached out a hand to Harry. It was clad in just enough gold to let everyone know the pockets it dipped into were both deep and full.

'Henry Turner!' the man said, though his enthusiasm at delivering his name faltered when he saw Harry up close.

Harry shook the extended hand.

'DCI Grimm,' he said.

'Ah yes, I remember now,' Turner nodded. 'I'm sorry, I didn't mean to look so shocked then. But Richard here hadn't told me.'

'Told you about what?'

'Your, er...' Turner's voice stalled and he gestured at his own face with a weak wiggle of a finger.

'Oh, that's old news,' Harry said. 'Bit of an argument with an IED, back in the Paras. It didn't win exactly. More of a draw, I think.' He turned his attention then to Jadyn. 'And this is Police Constable Okri.'

'I see you also have a dog,' Turner said, glancing at Adams, an eyebrow raised momentarily.

Obviously not expecting three visitors either, Harry thought, though he really couldn't think why it would matter.

'I'm the key liaison officer for local businesses,' Jadyn said. 'I'll be working closely with people across the Dales to see how we can all work better together, businesses and the police.'

Well done, Jadyn, Harry thought, bloody well done indeed.

'Very interesting,' Turner said, 'and you know what? That gives me an idea; perhaps you would be able to tell us a little more about it this evening? I'm sure we'd all find it fascinating to know what it is you do.'

Harry made to step in, not entirely sure how serious Turner was being, but Jadyn was in there first.

'I'd be happy to!' he said.

'Excellent!' said Turner. 'Now, if you'll excuse me, I need a quick word with Nigel and then I'd better act like the chair and get things going, hadn't I? See you for a drink afterwards, yes?'

Looking over behind Jadyn, Harry watched Turner head off towards a tall man at the other side of the room who had a cigarette in his mouth. They then walked out together, through the main doors.

'I should go and wait for Hannah at the door,' Adams said. 'Take a seat, won't you?'

With Adams and Turner gone, Harry glared at Jadyn.

'Is there any particular reason you volunteered to speak?'

'I'm the key liaison officer,' Jadyn said. 'I should say something, shouldn't I?'

Harry rested a firm and heavy hand on the constable's shoulder and leaned in, his voice quiet.

'You do know I made that up on the spot, don't you?'

From the look in Jadyn's eyes, no, he didn't.

'There's no such thing as a key liaison,' Harry continued.

'Or at least there wasn't until you volunteered to talk about it!'

Harry couldn't help but laugh, though, and he managed to keep the sound quiet enough for no one around them to notice.

'I'll jot a few notes down,' he said, then led Jadyn to a seat, ready for the meeting.

CHAPTER THIRTY

HAVING SURVIVED A FULL TEN MINUTES OF TRYING TO explain a role that didn't exist, to a group of strangers who hadn't expected him to be there in the first place, Jadyn finally sat down. Harry had an urge to take the constable to the nearest pub and buy him a pint. He'd done well, fielded questions, and generally given the impression that he knew what he was talking about. Now, during the break, they were alone for a chat over tea and biscuits.

'You really do want a badge, don't you?' Harry asked.

'It's not important,' Jadyn said.

'You mentioned it five times.'

'Really?'

'I counted.'

Jadyn gave a shrug.

'I did alright though, didn't I?'

'You did indeed,' said Harry. 'Even the bit about creating a, what was it now...' He checked his notebook. 'Ah yes, here it is! An integrated system of cross-business and police communication!'

'Yeah, about that...'

Harry held up a finger; he hadn't finished.

'Which will,' he continued, 'utilise both analogue and digital modes to ensure a timely response to specific needs throughout the Dales. It sounds wonderful, Jadyn! Marvellous even! I can't help but be almost as excited about it as you are!'

'Really? Thanks, Boss!'

'Now all you have to do is help me with one small detail.'

'Of course, no bother at all!'

'What is it?' Harry didn't give Jadyn a chance to look downhearted, giving him a gentle pat on the back. 'Anyway, what do you think so far?'

'Not really my thing, if I'm honest,' Jadyn said.

'No, I'm with you on that,' said Harry. 'Don't think Smudge here is too impressed either.'

At his feet, Smudge was stretched out and fast asleep, occasionally kicking her legs as she chased something in her dreams.

'How are you finding this so far, then, gentlemen?'

The voice belonged to Adams who, Harry noticed, had an uncanny ability to appear seemingly out of nowhere, much like the shopkeeper in Mr Benn, a children's television series he had the faintest memories of. He'd watched it not so much himself, as later with Ben, who had loved it, even though, at the time, it had already been superseded by plenty of other luridly coloured nonsense on the television.

'Very interesting,' Harry said, unable to come up with anything better.

'"Yes, well, like I said, the original speaker was cancelled. However, it was decided at the last minute that a little distraction would be sensible after all. I wasn't expecting someone to be able to fill in, but thanks to your excellent constable here, and of course Jerry over there, for his last-minute talk on beekeeping." He waved to a man on the other side of the room who was wearing a beekeeper's hat over a face that wore, with clear pride, a moustache so bushy and long he looked from afar like a walrus. 'How he persuaded Henry to say a few words, I don't know! And do you know, this is the first time I've heard anything about our chairman's own interest in, now what was it, apiculture? Yes, that was it. The meeting has been rather more interesting than expected that's for sure!'

'It has?' Harry said. Then realising that had come across like a question rather than agreement, asked, 'And what's next?'

'We're just going to have a chat about Bill,' Adams said. 'Share a few stories, that kind of thing. See if we can help Hannah in any way.'

Harry saw over Adams' shoulder that Hannah was talking to a few others members from the club.

'How is she?'

'So-so,' Adams said. 'How would anyone be under such circumstances? Obviously, the thing with the chapel is a bit of a worry for her now, too, but I'm sure we can sort something out there as well.'

When the break was over, Harry sat back down with Jadyn and saw that Hannah was now sitting in the front row of chairs. Turner called everyone together and once everyone was sitting, invited Hannah to the stage. Sitting down behind the table and beside Turner, her hands clasped tightly together on the table in front of her, Hannah spoke with a quiet, soft voice cracked through with thin lines of pain.

'I'm not going to speak for long, if that's alright with you all,' she said. 'Were Bill here, you'd be better off, because if ever there was a man who could talk, it was him!'

A ripple of laughter ran through the listeners.

'I've had some lovely messages from you all, and I thank you all for your support. Some of you have even been so kind as to pop round with food and I didn't really think I needed it, but I did. I've not the energy, really, to cook for myself quite yet. So, yes, thank you for all of it.'

There were some calls of 'Not a problem' and 'Anything you need, just ask'.

'I'm not sure when the funeral is, due to various factors, as you are all aware, but I'll let you know as soon as I can. The only other thing, really, is what to do about Bill's plan for Hawes Chapel.'

Turner rested a hand on Hannah's arm.

'Before we go into that,' he said, 'I thought it might be good if we all spent a few moments remembering Bill. We all have stories to share, I'm sure; he was well-loved. What do you think, Hannah? Would that be appropriate?'

Hannah smiled.

'Yes, actually, that would be lovely.'

For the next twenty minutes or so, the members of the club all shared their own memories of Bill. Harry had his eye on Hannah most of the time and could see how the tales being told affected her. There was sadness there, but he saw warmth and love coming through as the memories danced around them, often chased by laughter and applause. Bill, it seemed, had been a character, well-loved and respected. Okay, Harry thought, it was often the case that most people were sainted after death, the bad stuff, their mistakes long forgotten, but from what he could tell, Bill was the real deal.

This had been a man who had lived well, worked hard,

and grown to become a well-loved member of the wider Dales family. And considering his beginnings, the way his family had arrived all those years ago, that was no small achievement. The trouble was, the stories only served to confuse Harry even more. If Bill had been so well-liked, then how had he ended up fed into a baler by two blokes in balaclavas? Why would anyone have any issue with what he was planning to do with the chapel?

As the stories came to an end, Harry watched as Hannah leaned forwards again, calming herself with some slow, deep breaths. She thanked everyone for the stories, the memories, then moved on.

'As some of you know, Bill had his plan for Hawes Chapel,' she said. 'I share that information this evening because I know that Bill, and those working with him on it, had kept it all quiet. That was Bill's prerogative, as it was his idea. Now though, with Bill gone, and on the kind advice of Richard, here, I thought it best to get his plan a little more out in the open and to also state my own intentions.'

Harry noticed a shuffling of chairs at this point, though from where he couldn't quite discern.

'A good number of you have sent your thoughts through, and that was most appreciated. Your concern for Daniel and me, I understand, and I want it to be known that I have thought long about this, about whether to go ahead with it or not. Bill's gone after all, so there's a lot to be thinking about.'

More chair shuffling, a few throats being cleared.

'Now, I fully understand why some would like to see this project of Bill's be put to one side. But the Dales welcomed Bill and his parents all those years ago and it was his dream to do the same for others. The Dales, the people, we pride ourselves on the welcome we give, so I wish to state here and now that my aim, and Daniel's, is to fulfil Bill's wishes.'

At this, Harry heard a few sharp breaths, just enough to let him know that not everyone in the room approved. And that was interesting.

Hannah was still speaking.

'Daniel and I, we loved Bill, everything about him, and we think that this, what he wanted to do, well, it's the most fitting memorial to the man, that we can think of. However, I think it worth stating that it was the idea that was important, more so than the building. So, for now, although Bill's dream is not dead, we will hold off on going ahead with Hawes Chapel.'

A rumble then of muted voices and whispers, but they were soon drowned out by Richard Adams who rose to his feet just a couple of rows in front of Harry and Jadyn and turned to address the members.

'I think I speak for us all, indeed I hope that I do, when I say, Hannah, that you have the full support of the club.'

More faint murmuring, but Adams ignored it.

'I backed Bill with this when he came to me with the idea right at the beginning. And I supported it because, speaking from experience, I know the welcome the Dales gives those from elsewhere. And I thank Hannah, now, for what she has said.'

Applause then, but Adams held up a hand to still it.

'As Hannah has said, the dream is what is important, not the building. So, we will, I'm sure, all support her in that. I have also said to Hannah and Danny that, for now, I will look into the building and what else can be done with it. At a time such as this, they do not want to be concerned with all that could entail.'

Adams turned to Hannah.

'To Bill!' he said and started to clap. Others around the room soon joined in.

When the meeting finally drew to a close, Harry found himself standing outside with Jadyn thinking through what they'd both just experienced. He'd learned nothing new, really, thanks to Gordy's report, and he was as confused as ever about Richard Adams, a man he didn't like, yet who clearly had some goodness in him, demonstrated by his support for Hannah and Bill's wishes.

Well, at least there was Jadyn's new role, he thought. It would give the police constable something to really get his teeth into, and it might even be something rather worthwhile. Harry knew from experience that he probably wasn't the best person around for developing good working relationships. Jadyn, on the other hand, was blessed with the innate ability to be liked.

'I'd best get off,' said Jadyn.

'Same here,' said Harry. 'Nothing like arriving home just in time to go to bed.'

'See you tomorrow, then.'

'That you will,' said Harry. 'And Jadyn?'

Jadyn turned to look up at Harry.

'Well done this evening. You really did a great job up there. I mean, you put yourself there in the first place, but regardless, I'm impressed.'

'Thanks!' Jadyn said, then he strode off into what was left of the night, that huge grin once again on his wide-eyed and ever-keen face.

Harry, with a tired Smudge at heel, walked over to his own vehicle and climbed in. Checking his watch, he saw that the time had just knocked past ten. He pulled his phone from a pocket, thought twice about using it, then hit the number he'd pulled up anyway and waited for his call to be answered.

A while later, Harry pulled up outside Grace's house and knocked on the door.

'Thought you might want some company,' Harry said when Grace opened the door.

Grace dropped to the ground and gave Smudge a scratch under the chin.

'How can I say no to a face like this?'

'What about this one up here?' Harry asked.

Grace stood up.

'What about it?' she said, leaning in with a kiss, then hurrying Harry and Smudge inside, out of the cold.

CHAPTER THIRTY-ONE

WALKING INTO LEYBURN, JADYN WAS TRYING NOT TO feel too pleased with himself. Trouble was, that was impossible. He was absolutely convinced that he had uncovered something potentially hugely important with the church's security camera, and that in itself was rather exciting. Then there was his new role as key liaison officer. Today had, in the end, turned out to be brilliant!

He'd call home about it tomorrow. His parents would be seriously impressed, he was sure. They'd worried when he'd decided to join the police straight out of university, which was understandable. He'd looked into other jobs, of course he had, but the idea of spending his life in an office, being a trainee manager, then a manager, then a department manager or whatever other kind of manager there was, well, that just wasn't him. He'd wanted more, and for whatever reason, the police had ticked all the boxes.

'And you're sure about this? The police? It's what you really want?' his dad had said.

'It is.'

'Why?'

'Because it's interesting, the job's varied, and I can do some good, can't I?'

Jadyn remembered his dad shaking his head at this.

'You can do good by doing something else,' he'd said. 'The police, though? You know what it's like, don't you?'

'It's not like it used to be, Dad,' Jadyn had said. 'This isn't the seventies or the eighties now. Yes, racism is still a thing, of course it is, but things really have changed.'

'You believe that?'

'I do.'

'Then you're a fool! Albeit a fool with a good heart and mind. I just don't want to see that part of you broken, that's all.'

'It won't be.'

Jadyn understood their concerns, still did. But they'd grown to accept his chosen career, supported him in it. No, he wasn't a bank manager like his older brother, and he was certainly never going to be into whatever it was his sister did —something to do with marketing, he remembered, though marketing what he hadn't the faintest idea—but he had a job, with prospects, a pension, and that was something for sure. And he was proud of it, too.

Realising the evening was getting on, Jadyn considered just heading home. But he was still buzzing and he just couldn't resist the opportunity of turning up in the office tomorrow with more than just a few black and white printouts. If he could support those with a name, now that would be something else, wouldn't it? So, rather than head back to his vehicle, he pulled out his phone, found another pub, and headed there instead.

Walking into the pub, Jadyn found the place to be warm

and busy, the bar in front of him well-stocked with customers buying drinks to take back to their tables. Above the general murmur of conversation and laughter, the electronic jingle of a games machine did its best to attract new punters happy to empty their pockets into its greedy slots.

He could smell food in the air, too, though no one was eating unless it was the usual collection of bar snacks. He saw a dartboard in one corner, a serious game going on judging by the faces of those involved and spectating, and the walls of the pub itself were decorated with everything from horse brasses and fading copies of oil paintings, to random displays of matchboxes, postcards, and old coins glued to the wall.

Jadyn approached the bar, finding a gap and squeezing in.

Behind the bar were three staff. The first and oldest was a woman who, judging by the way she cast her eyes around the place, like a lighthouse on full beam in a storm, was the proprietor. The other two, a boy and a girl clearly the younger side of twenty, and doing their utmost to look and act older, both had long hair, piercings and T-shirts of bands Jadyn had heard of but never listen to.

'Hi,' Jadyn said, catching the eye of the girl.

She approached with a smile.

'What can I get you?'

'Oh, nothing actually,' Jadyn said. 'I don't drink.'

'Of course, you're on duty,' the girl said. 'Unless you're a stripper?'

'I'm definitely not a stripper.'

'If you say so.'

'I do, because it's the truth,' Jadyn said. 'Anyway, it's not because I'm on duty, it's just that I'm not drinking. At the moment, I mean. Bit of a health thing.'

Jadyn knew he was rambling and quickly shushed. The statement had clearly confused the girl, her smile dropping just a little.

'We've other drinks,' she said. 'Non-alcoholic beer, too, and it's not that bad actually.'

'Not-that-bad never really struck me as a great way to promote something,' said Jadyn.

'So, why are you here, then?' she asked. 'In a pub?'

'I'm looking for someone,' Jadyn said. 'Just wondering if they'd been in here at all.'

Jadyn wasn't sure he was approaching this in the best way, but he'd managed to strike up a conversation so was just going to roll with it for now.

'And who's that, then?' the girl asked.

Jadyn pulled the printed sheets out from his pocket, unfolded them, and showed the girl the one on top. She leaned in, squinting.

'Friend of yours, is he?'

'Just looking to have a chat with him, that's all,' Jadyn said. 'Do you recognise him?'

The girl was still staring.

'Can't say that I do, no,' she said. 'But that's not the best photo, is it?'

A shadow crept over the bar and Jadyn looked left to find himself being stared at by the older woman.

'Can I help, Officer?'

Jadyn gave the woman his best winning smile and told her why he was there. The woman looked at the photo, but didn't smile back.

'Not a good likeness, whoever he is,' she said.

'You don't recognise him, then?'

The woman shook her head.

'I don't, no. But we get a lot of people in here, locals and tourists alike. That's a lot of faces to be remembering, I think you'll agree.'

'Would you mind if I left you with this, then?' Jadyn said. 'And my contact details? Then, if you do see him, perhaps you could give me a call?'

'He's in trouble, then, is he?'

'We just want to speak to him,' Jadyn said.

A sharp gust of wind swept in from behind Jadyn and he turned to see the door closing.

'I'll keep that, then,' the woman said. 'Can't promise anything, though.'

'I really appreciate it,' Jadyn said. 'Thank you. Would you mind if I had a walk around the place a bit, see if anyone else has seen him?'

At this, the woman frowned.

'I've helped as much as I can,' she said. 'It's hard enough as it is to make money running a place like this, and between you and me, I'm not sure having a police officer running around asking questions is going to help much, do you?'

'I'll be discreet,' Jadyn said.

The woman pulled out her phone, pointed it at Jadyn, then flipped it round.

'What do you see?'

Jadyn looked at the screen to see a photograph of himself staring back.

'Me,' he said.

'Exactly,' the woman said. 'Dressed head-to-toe like Mr Police. Only thing you're missing is a flashing blue light stuck on top of your head! Nice though it is, it's hardly discreet, now, is it?'

She had a point, Jadyn realised.

'Well, thanks for your help,' Jadyn said. 'I'll maybe call back in later in the week?'

'You do that,' the woman said. 'We'll be here. Not like we've anywhere else to be going to, is it?'

Conversation over, Jadyn made his way back outside. Checking his watch, he saw that he had just enough time to get to one more pub. Hunching his shoulders against the cold wind now twirling its way through the town, he headed off into the dark.

About five minutes on, and with the next pub just around the next corner, Jadyn was about to cross the road when a van pulled up directly in front of him. The door opened and two figures, clothed in the night's darkness, jumped out and grabbed him, knocking the printouts from his hand, wind snatching at them and scooping them up into the darkness.

'Hello, mate!' said one of the figures. 'How do you fancy coming on a little trip, then?'

Confused by what was happening, but alert enough to not go down without a fight, Jadyn fought back.

'Stop!' he yelled out, thrashing around with his arms, kicking out with his legs. 'Stop! I'm a police officer! Stop!'

He hoped at least that his shouting would alert someone. It didn't.

Hands tried to grab him, but he twisted and turned as the arms around him struggled to hold him still.

A fist crashed into the side of his head. Jadyn saw stars. Another fist came in at the other side of his face and his head snapped back with the impact.

'That should shut you up!' a voice spat.

Jadyn struggled, but an arm was around his neck as hands tried to pin his arms behind him. He thrashed again, the pain in his head a thick throb making his actions sluggish, then an arm was free, a hand, and he reached out, found flesh, and dug his fingers in deep, nails cutting into flesh.

'You little bastard!'

The punch that followed was harder and more violent than the previous two combined. It came full-on at Jadyn's face, crashing into his nose, splitting it in a spray of blood and snot. Then he was in the van, dazed and bleeding and in pain, face down, two heavy bodies leaning on him, pressing him down into the floor.

The door slammed shut.

'Bloody hell, look at his face!'

'Search him.'

Hands shuffled through his pockets as Jadyn felt the van jolt forwards.

'Anything?'

'Just this lot. Here you go.'

A gust of wind blasted into the van from somewhere up front, a window opening, Jadyn guessed. He'd noticed three voices so far, one up front, two directly above him.

'No one will find you now, pal, that's for sure,' came from fourth voice, the words shouted out and lit with cruel intent.

The wind died, the window now shut, and Jadyn knew that the contents of his pockets were now scattered behind them somewhere in the dark.

Jadyn could hardly breathe and the realisation of where he was, or wasn't, was hitting home hard enough to make him gasp. At first, the shock of it all had taken him by surprise. It hadn't seemed real and had played out almost like a scene from a film, a dream maybe, but this was real, too real in fact, and the panic in his gut was burning hot enough to set his veins on fire.

'Who are you?' Jadyn gasped, his voice a crackled rasp. 'What do you want? You have to let me go!'

A hand grabbed his hair, yanked his head back then slammed it into the floor of the van.

'We want you to shut up, mate, that's what.'

Jadyn tried to move, to pull his hands free, but all that resulted in was laughter from whoever was sitting on top of him.

'Ha, the little bastard wants to get free I think!'

'Good luck with that, seeing as he's got your fat arse on him!'

'Wriggles like a rabbit in a snare!'

'That gives me an idea...'

Jadyn heard the rattling of metal, like a clasp being opened.

'Here we are! Now, let's see if it fits...'

Once again, Jadyn's head was slammed against the floor of the van. Dazed and in pain, he barely registered something being slipped over his head and then down around his neck. Until it was too late.

'Fits perfectly!'

Thin wire cinched around Jadyn's neck with such a violent snap that the pain of whatever was now cutting into his skin overrode the realisation that he was being choked.

Jadyn tried to breathe, but the thing around his neck was tight and being pulled back even tighter.

'Bit tight, is it?'

The wire went loose, Jadyn gasped, sucked in air.

'Let's try that again, shall we?'

The wire was tight again, tighter than before, and Jadyn's ears were filled with the sound of his own heartbeat, and behind that laughter, cold and mean.

Again the wire slackened.

'Don't want this over too soon, now, do we?'

A hand tapped Jadyn gently on the cheek.

'You can't do this,' Jadyn gasped. 'I'm.. I'm a police officer!'

Hot breath sloughed against his skin, thick and foul with the stale reek of tobacco.

'We don't give a fuck what you are, mate. Where you're from, though? Well now, that's a different matter altogether, isn't it?'

Jadyn was confused. Adrenaline was racing through him, but he could neither fight nor take flight. He was trapped.

'I'm... I'm from Bradford!' he said.

A laugh came then, gruff and terrifying.

'You hear that? He's from Bradford!'

More laughter, though the sound of it was twisting like rope, like the wire still around his neck.

'Nice place, Bradford. Well, it would be if there weren't so many of you lot there, if you know what I mean.'

No, Jadyn didn't know what he meant. All he knew was that he was in the back of a van, half-strangled, and absolutely bloody terrified. Breathing was painful and almost impossible, his body ached, his head was bruised, probably bleeding. He tried to think, to work out what he could do to escape, but the more he struggled, the more the weight of those on top of him seemed to increase.

The van slowed and Jadyn felt it turn sharply left, his body wanting to tip with it, but barely shifting. Then the smoothness of the journey was replaced by a slow, painful jolting as whatever road surface they had been driving on was replaced with bumps and thumps.

'Nearly there, mate. Bet you're excited, aren't you?'

The van stopped.

'Right then, let's have some fun...'

CHAPTER THIRTY-TWO

HARRY WAS SITTING ON THE SOFA IN GRACE'S LOUNGE. The house was a cosy place, hunched down in a small row of cottages, and the cast iron log burner at his feet was nice and toasty, the orange flames licking at the glass set in the door. Curtains drawn against the night, Smudge curled up at his feet, and Grace's own dog, Jess, asleep by the fire, clearly enjoying some time away from the rabble that was her litter of pups, Harry found that the worries of the week were eased a little. The wine in his glass also helped and maybe he'd have a sneaky whisky before bed; it had been a happy discovery to find that Grace had a good little collection of malts in a cupboard beneath the stairs, and Harry had taken full advantage of it as soon as it had been offered.

'Well, just look at the state of you three!'

Harry turned at the voice to see Grace leaning in through the door.

'We're comfy,' Harry said.

'And nearly comatose. Hungry?'

'It's gone eleven.'

'Not sure what that has to do with anything.'

'Good point,' said Harry.

'I'll bring something through, then.'

The only sound in the room was that of the dogs breathing and the wind rustling its way through the trees outside. The television was off, there was no radio playing. Instead, it was just the blissful lullaby of a quiet evening and Harry was happily adrift in it.

'Here we go.'

Grace entered the room and placed a tray down on the small coffee table in front of the fire.

Harry leaned forward, sipped his wine.

'Cheese, biscuits, cake, and the rest of that bottle you're enjoying,' Grace said, then reached out and topped up his glass, her own already full.

'I hated cheese, you know,' Harry said. 'Before I came here.'

Grace cut a small slice of cake for herself and sat down beside Harry.

'How's Jen doing, then?'

'Brilliantly,' Harry said, though the worry of what had happened was still with him, the thought that those who had put her there in the first place were still at large. 'I know she's about the size of a pixie, but she's tough, that's for sure.'

'You don't look too happy though,' Grace said.

Harry reached for some cake, added some of the cheese, took a bite. It really had grown on him.

'Lot on my mind,' he said. 'One of those weeks where everything seems to happen at once and none of it's good.' He caught a look in Grace's eye. 'Except this, of course. I mean, this is brilliant.'

Grace rubbed his leg gently with her hand.

'Well, that's good to hear,' she said. 'It's okay to relax, you know?'

THE HOOD over Jadyn's head stank to high heaven, the tang of animal urine and God knew what else stinging his eyes. It was in his throat with every breath and it was all he could do to not throw up.

'Right then, out you get!'

The gruff voice didn't wait for Jadyn to respond and he was kicked out of the van, tumbling for a moment through the coldest air, only to land on his back in a puddle.

Laughter, cold and mean, stabbed at him.

'On your feet, then! Come on!'

A kick in the ribs, not hard, but still a shock.

Jadyn brought his knees up, rolled over, but it was hard to stand with his hands tied behind his back.

'What do you want? Who are you?'

There were hands on him then, pulling him to his feet.

'I... I can't breathe. The thing on my head, it's...'

Jadyn coughed.

'Stinks a bit, does it? Probably because it usually has ferrets in it, and they don't half reek!'

Jadyn was pushed forward, forced to walk, though it was more of a barely controlled stumble.

'Just a bit further and then we can get on,' a voice said in his ear.

A jab in his back forced him to keep moving.

'You can't do this!' Jadyn said, trying to sound brave, to not give them, whoever they were, the satisfaction of breaking him. 'I'm a police officer and you need to let me go! You're only making this worse for yourselves!'

More laughter, only the sound of it had changed. Now it came back with an echo. So, we were inside, Jadyn thought. But where? And why?

Something hard hammered into Jadyn's stomach and he doubled over, vomit in his mouth. Then something thicker than the wire that had been around his neck in the van was dropped over his head and pulled tight around his neck.

Jadyn knew what was coming next.

'I'M NOT ALL that good at relaxing,' Harry said. 'Not really in my nature, if I'm honest.'

'Then you need to learn how to,' Grace said. 'It's easy, I promise.'

Harry wasn't convinced, but he was happy to give it a go.

'How's your week going so far?' he asked.

'Oh, just the usual. Things get busy now with shooting season a few months off, so I'm checking pens, talking with farmers about birds, keeping an eye out for poachers.'

'Poachers?'

Grace nodded.

'We get a few. Not much of a problem, though, to be honest.'

'You do know that poaching is illegal,' said Harry. 'And that I'm a police officer.'

Grace gave a shrug.

'I do, but like I said, it's not much of a problem.'

'It's criminal.'

'Well, the last poacher I caught—that was last year, by the way—he was eighty-three years old.'

'Doesn't excuse it.'

'And having him arrested wouldn't have solved it either,' Grace said, and Harry heard an edge to her voice. 'The only thing we have to watch out for is hare coursing, and gangs and their dogs coming in from elsewhere. There's big money in it. Thankfully, they've not tried to move into the Dales yet. But it's only a matter of time.'

Harry took a hefty glug of his wine.

JADYN COULDN'T BREATHE, the rope lifting him up onto his toes, the sack over his head, the stench of it, only serving to make whatever breath he did manage to suck in to be the foulest possible.

'Ooh, that looks painful,' a voice said.

More laughter.

The rope fell slack. Jadyn dropped to the ground, the pain in his knees nothing compared with the panic and terror now filling every corner of his mind. He sucked in air, ignored the taste of it, sucked in more.

'Please... I...'

The rope was tight again and he was lifted, back up and up and up, and he did his best to keep his toes on the ground, to stop himself from being choked, but it was so hard, and the pain was crushing him.

'Why?' Jadyn managed, his voice a cracked thing, broken, ruined.

'You really want to know?'

The voice was closer than Jadyn had expected. The breath reeked of mint and stale tobacco.

'You're a message,' the voice said. 'That's what you are. And the thing about messages is, they need to be easily understood, don't they? Clear, if you know what I mean. No point beating around the bush, is there?'

Jadyn couldn't answer, didn't know how to.

'Best we make it very clear then, don't you think, what this message is?'

The next thing Jadyn felt were hands grabbing at his shirt, ripping the buttons. Then came a searing pain as something sharp cut into his skin.

And he screamed.

'HOW'S ARTHUR?'

'Out with Phil this evening,' Grace said. 'By which I mean they're down at the Bolton Arms, sinking a few and putting the world to rights.'

'You mean Phil with the pies?'

'The very same,' Grace said.

Harry had met Phil back when he'd been investigating some illegal dogfighting. He made the worst pies Harry had ever tasted. He was also the very proud owner of an enormous Shire horse called, of all things, Harry.

'Now, how's that relaxing going for you?' Grace asked, sitting down next to Harry.

Harry stretched out.

'You tell me.'

'Don't try so hard,' Grace said and leaned forward for a nibble of some cheese.

Harry took another sip of his wine. If this was relaxing, he thought, then it was definitely something he could get used to.

———————

JADYN'S WORLD WAS PAIN. His every thought, his every movement, the worst kind of pain, a thing of blades and teeth and flame.

His chest was wet like someone had thrown water on him, except that the water was warm and slipped slowly down his body, crawling almost, soaking into his trousers.

'Yeah, I think that's clear enough,' a voice said, further away now, as though the speaker was standing back to take a better look at their handiwork.

'Please...' Jadyn said, but the word was little more than a bubbled breath as he gasped, the pain from the marks the blade had cut into his chest mingling with the agony in his legs and feet as he tried to keep himself upright. But he couldn't last much longer, the hideous darkness of unconsciousness only moments away, he was sure. He would not wake from it, he knew that.

'Please...'

Jadyn felt once again that hot, stale breath against his cheek.

'Not long now,' a voice said. 'No hard feelings, right? This isn't personal. Well, it is, but no harm in trying to make you feel better, is there?'

The rope around Jadyn's neck yanked hard, heaving him off the floor. But that didn't stop him from trying to reach it, willing his legs to stretch far enough, to stop him choking. But he was swinging free now, the floor was gone, and so was the air he'd been breathing, his throat clamped tight now, lungs bursting, the pressure building and building and...

'The fuck is that?'

'The fuck is what?'

'Lights! Over there! At the gate!'

... Jadyn was lost to the pain, fading now, his mind flicking through memories and visions and faces and...

'I thought you said this place was safe?'

'It was! It's supposed to be!'

'Then who the hell is that?'

... only seconds to go now, not long at all, the darkness opening to welcome him in, embrace him, a deep pool he was falling into, a breathless dive into oblivion...

'Leave him!'

'What?'

'I said leave him! He's nearly dead anyway!'

'But he's not, is he?'

'Who gives a shit?'

'I do! Because if he IDs us...'

'And how's he going to do that, then?'

'I don't know, but—'

'Exactly!'

... Sleep, he just wanted to sleep now, that was all, to sleep and to sleep and to not wake up...

'Now, move it!'

'But what if he—'

'Look at him! If he wakes up at all, he'll be a cabbage won't he? And that's a result in my book. Now, get in!'

... because waking up was pain and torment and agony and he was beyond that now, so far beyond it. Beyond life and love and breath and...

... Jadyn fell, felt his body crash down, every part of it

crumpling in on itself. Then a sharp metallic taste burst in his throat, in his lungs. He opened his eyes. A kindly face stared back, old and weather-worn, eyes burning with horror and rage.

'I've got you, lad, I've got you...'

'YOU'RE FALLING ASLEEP.'

'I'm just resting my eyes.'

'That's the same thing.'

Harry opened his eyes to see Grace staring down at him.

'Get yourself upstairs,' she said. 'I'll sort this lot out, and the dogs, and I'll be up in five.'

Harry pushed himself out of the sofa, yawned, noticed a buzzing in his pocket. He pulled out his phone, held it to his ear.

'Grimm,' he said.

Two minutes later, he was racing through the dark.

CHAPTER THIRTY-THREE

Harry had no recollection of the journey, no memory of leaving Grace's or of arriving at the hospital. That time was a void, but it was nothing compared with the deep emptiness he now felt inside as he stared at the figure lying in the bed before him.

'Harry...'

Harry didn't respond, couldn't, didn't know how.

'Swift, he's on his way. He'll be here as soon as he can. I've called through to forensics as well and where Jadyn was found, it's all cordoned off. Liz is there now. Arrived pretty bloody quickly too, so I'll be having a word with her about the speed she rides that motorbike, that's for sure.'

Harry heard what Gordy was saying but still no words came.

A hand rested on his shoulder.

'This isn't your fault. It's no one's fault.'

At last, Harry looked up at DI Haig from where he was sitting. She was standing at his side, face stern, eyes hard, yet her voice was warm.

'What the hell is going on?' Harry said. 'What? I've had two officers in this hospital in the last three days! Two!'

'We'll find out,' Gordy said.

'He was with me this evening, at the Rotary Club thing. Turned up with that grin on his face. I knew something was up, but I didn't press. I didn't ask. I could see he was enjoying using his initiative and I didn't want to take that away from him.'

'And that was the right thing to do. You had no idea any of this was going to happen, did you? And that's a rhetorical question, by the way. None of us have any idea if whatever he was on with actually led to this! Not yet, so don't you go jumping the gun.'

'Don't we?' Harry said.

Gordy said nothing.

Harry turned back to Jadyn.

'You should've seen him at the meeting. He just got up there, full of confidence, and started talking! Spoke to them, a whole room of strangers! Just did it, proper professional he was. Impressive stuff.'

'He's a good officer,' Gordy said.

'He's a bloody idiot is what he is!' Harry snapped back. 'If he'd just told me what he was up to, then this wouldn't have happened, would it?'

'Again, you don't know that. We don't know what happened. No one does.'

'He must've put up a hell of a fight,' Harry said. 'His fists are all bruised, and they've managed to scrape his nails out for forensics to look at.'

'He scratched them?'

'By accident or not, there's hopefully something there for us. What about the bloke who found him?'

'We've taken a statement,' Gordy said. 'He's coming over to the office tomorrow.'

'Farmer, right?'

'Out doing some lamping,' Gordy said. 'Bit of a rat problem apparently, up at some old barns of his. The place looks derelict. Probably why they used it, whoever it was that took Jadyn there, I mean.'

'Go through it again,' Harry said. 'What he said, the farmer.'

Gordy pulled out her notebook.

'It's luck that he was there at all,' she said. 'Apparently, he's not been up there in a few months, but was clearing out the rats, getting ready to fill the place with hay.'

'Go on.'

'He thinks he was there at around eleven-thirty. Arrived to find that the gate was open. Saw lights.'

'Did he see how many there were?'

'He saw a van, that's all,' Gordy said. 'White, but that's all he could tell us. He was too busy with Jadyn, cutting him down...'

'Not too busy to stop him from taking a few potshots though,' Harry said, shaking his head. 'What is this, the Wild bloody West?'

Gordy was quiet, letting Harry rant for a moment.

'We have an attempted hanging, people shooting at each other! What the sodding hell is going on?'

Gordy said, 'We're lucky it was dark and that he didn't hit anything. His rifle, it's only a .22 calibre rimfire, but still, that's enough to do more than just make a scratch.'

'They strung him up, Gordy!' Harry said. 'They tortured Jadyn and then they tried to hang him in a barn! If you ask me, we're bloody unlucky that he didn't hit anything!'

Gordy said nothing. Probably for the best, Harry thought because he was very aware of what he was saying.

'Do we know what he was on with?' asked the DI.

'He said he'd been to see the vicar,' Harry said. 'That's all I know.'

'The vicar in Leyburn? What about? He was supposed to be looking for that missing BMW!'

'I haven't the faintest,' Harry said. 'I tried calling on my way over. No answer. I'll be popping in on my way back.'

'It's gone midnight, you know that, don't you?'

'I do,' Harry said.

'And most people are in bed.'

'I also know that Jadyn's lying here in front of us, rope burns around his neck, words carved into his chest!' Harry said, his voice shaking with anger. 'He's lucky to be alive at all! So, if it's all the same with you, I'll bloody well be waking up anyone I want to, you hear?'

'No, that's not what I mean,' Gordy said, seemingly oblivious to Harry's hot temper. 'Anna's a vicar as well, remember? Other end of the dale, but they work together, share services, that kind of thing.'

'And?'

'And,' Gordy said, 'if he's anything like Anna, then he always answers his phone. Between you and me, it gets a little annoying. It's like being out with one of us! It's always there, at dinner time, when we're watching television, going for a walk. It's like she's glued to the bloody thing!'

'So why didn't he answer, then?'

'Because he'll have been called away to something, most likely,' said Gordy. 'Maybe someone's ill or maybe just needing a shoulder to cry on. Last week, Anna was out all night with a family whose son had been rushed to hospital.

She was with them the whole time, just for support, that's all.'

'I get it, he didn't answer because he's not in,' Harry said.

'Actually, that gives me an idea,' Gordy said. 'I'll be back in five.'

Harry wasn't given a chance to say anything as Gordy turned on her heel and was gone.

Alone now with Jadyn, Harry forced his mind to clear. Whatever was going on, he had to get to the bottom of it and soon. It was all connected, he was sure of it, though why and by what, he hadn't the faintest idea, not yet, anyway.

Harry leaned back in his chair, Jadyn's deathly still body in front of him, wired up like Jen's had been. His neck was bruised from the rope, his wrists burned from the wire—a rabbit snare apparently—that had been twisted around them behind his back. He had fractured ribs, cuts and bruises across his body, scrapes and bruises to his head, his face.

It was the wounds on his chest, though, cut horribly deep by a sharp blade, words had been carved, which Harry just couldn't bring himself to say aloud. And he wouldn't either, because to his mind that would give the person who'd carved them into Jadyn's skin a degree of recognition that they just didn't deserve. The sentiment though... Harry would forever carry the knowledge with him that someone had done what they'd done to Jadyn because of the colour of his skin. It was fuel for him to burn, a furnace of rage.

Harry took a moment to calm down as best he could. Hot blood and the urge to find the person responsible and spill theirs, well, it just wasn't that conducive to thinking straight. When he eventually felt his heart rate drop a little, Harry felt as though he was staring at the scattered pieces of a jigsaw. Everything was there to make the final picture, he was sure of it, he just didn't know what piece went where. Start with the edges, Harry thought, that's how it usually worked, right? But how could what had been done to Jadyn have anything to do with Bill Dinsdale's death on Sunday?

Harry stood up, rubbed his eyes with finger and thumb, pushing stars into his brain. Sunday seemed so long ago, but he went there in his mind, retracing his steps as best he could, trying to put things in order of how they'd played out. And to help him he took out his notebook, his phone, too, which had photos of the crime scene and various bits of evidence.

So, Harry thought, this is how it had happened... Bill had headed out to the field. While there, Richard Adams had called Hannah about some threatening notes he and Bill had both received with regards to their joint project for the chapel. These notes were with forensics and as yet nothing had come back from Sowerby; Harry made a note to chase that up in the morning. It was morning now, yes, but even he wasn't mean enough to call Sowerby when she was already heading over to a crime scene in the middle of the night.

Next on the timeline, was Danny visiting his mum between the phone call and her heading over to speak with Adams. Once Danny had left, Hannah had then headed over to see Adams to discuss the threats. In the meantime, Danny had then headed out to speak with his dad. According to Danny, they'd argued about Bill's plans for the farm and the chapel and Danny had left, returning later to smooth things over only to witness two men kill his father.

Harry thought about that for a second or two, Danny arriving to speak to his dad, then witnessing what he had. Sometimes, he really wondered about humanity. Would the human race ever realise that the only way things were ever going to get any better was if everyone stopped being shitty to each other? He doubted it.

The two as-yet-unidentified men then chased Danny out of the field and followed him in their car. While this was going on, Hannah and Adams arrived to speak with Bill, found him in the baler, and called emergency services. The team arrived and Jen was called to a traffic incident just out of Aysgarth. While attending this, she was then hit by the car driven by the two men trying to get Danny, the two men who had killed his father, thus supporting what he had shared with Harry.

All of this was giving Harry another headache. He wanted to be back with Grace, finishing off that glass of wine he'd left half-full on the table.

Back to Danny... So, having hidden off the road, not far from the accident, Danny—terrified for his own safety, which was fair enough, all things considered, Harry thought—had scurried away to an old barn on the farm. A witness also saw the car that hit Jen, which supported Danny's report of the car he'd seen.

As to other evidence, Harry looked through the photos on his phone sent through by the crime scene photographer. From the crime scene, the only evidence seemed to be some blood on the baler, which didn't match that of the victim, and a scrap of checked cloth found at the fence from which a post was removed and used to batter Bill. Splinters of this post were found in the baler and scattered around it. There was the wing mirror as well, but they'd not found the car and until they did, it wasn't much use either.

Harry wanted to scream; so much had happened and in such a short span of time, and they had so little to go on. He was missing something he was sure of it, but what? So, Harry thought, what about motive, then? Maybe if he figured that out, he'd get somewhere.

In front of him, Harry noticed how Jadyn's breath sounded laboured and he reached out for a moment to hold the young man's wrist, giving it a squeeze. Silently, Harry made a promise to Jadyn, then was back to his thoughts.

Up to last night, and as far as Harry or anyone else on the team were concerned, the only motive for Bill's death seemed to be someone not approving of his plan to convert a chapel in Hawes into some sort of shelter or home for those who needed it. It was a little odd as ideas went, but there was merit to it, Harry thought. Though why anyone would hate it so much to do what they did to Bill, he just couldn't get his head around. But then he'd known people to do worse to each other over a lot less, that was for sure. Now though, with the attack on Jadyn, things had changed more than a little and he wasn't so sure it was all that simple.

At first glance, it was easy to think that the events weren't connected, but Harry was absolutely certain that Jadyn had been up to something that evening. He'd turned up with that grin on his face for a start, hadn't he? And he'd been a little coy about what he'd been up to. Harry's gut told him that whatever it was, that was the reason the lad had ended up strung up in a barn, words carved in his chest. Words that were still vivid and raw in Harry's mind and sent a hot charge of rage through his body.

'Harry?'

Looking over to the door, Harry saw Gordy and beside her was Swift.

'We need to stop meeting like this,' Swift said.

'I couldn't agree more,' Harry replied. 'Thanks for coming.'

Swift walked over, Gordy behind him.

'This isn't something that requires thanks,' Swift said. 'We've had two officers down in just a few days. We're all needed on this. I need to know exactly where we are and what we have.'

'I've just been running through it all myself,' Harry said.

'And?'

Harry shook his head.

'None of it makes sense. How the hell can a death in a baler be linked to this?'

'You think it is, then?'

'I do,' Harry said.

'And Detective Constable Blades?'

'That's linked, too, but only by the fact that she was in the wrong place at the wrong time. This, though? It's different. I'm convinced of it.'

'Why?'

Harry explained about Jadyn turning up for the Rotary Club meeting.

'So, you think he was looking into something to do with what happened on Sunday?'

'I do,' Harry said. 'And whatever it was, it ended up with him beaten, tortured, and lying here in front of us.'

Swift moved closer to Jadyn. He said nothing. He didn't need to.

'DI Haig mentioned something about letters or words cut into him?'

'Carved is a better description,' Harry said. 'Doctors think it was a short-bladed thing, like a Stanley knife, a box cutter.'

'You have a photo, yes?'

Harry gave a nod, found the photograph, turned the screen to Swift.

'Jesus...'

'You can see it quite clearly,' Harry said. 'The first two words are "go home". And the third one—'

'—is just as clear,' Swift said. 'So, this is racism, then?'

'Oh, I think this is off the scale,' said Harry. 'This is someone emboldened by something, though what, I haven't a clue because the only other thing is what happened on Sunday.'

'I see the problem,' said Swift. 'The grisly death, murder or otherwise of an old farmer seems very, very removed from what we have in front of us here.'

Gordy stepped forward.

'Harry?'

'What?'

'You needed to speak to the vicar, yes? The Reverend Bristow?'

'I'll do it tomorrow, as soon as I can.'

'No, that's not what I meant,' Gordy said and showed Harry a message on her phone. 'I checked to see if he was here, and for once, luck was on our side. He's just sent a message to say he can spare you a few minutes, if you have them?'

'Where?'

'Coffee machine, down in reception.'

Harry was already on his way.

CHAPTER THIRTY-FOUR

STRIDING ALONG THE CORRIDOR, DOWN TO RECEPTION, Harry pulled out his phone. He'd leave Sowerby a message asking about the notes sent to Bill and Adams, just in case everything that was going on forced it from his mind later and he forgot to call.

'It's DCI Grimm,' Harry said, as the phone went to the mailbox. 'Just wondering if we have anything on those—'

'Harry?'

Sowerby's voice took Harry by surprise.

'Yes, sorry,' he said. 'I was just leaving a message. Didn't expect you to answer. You're busy.'

'I am,' Sowerby said. 'Not that it mattered, really. I was awake anyway. Being called out to this, it was a good excuse to get out and do something instead of just lying there staring into the dark.'

'Why's that, then? The staring into the dark, I mean.'

'Insomnia,' Sowerby replied. 'I've suffered from it since university.'

'That's not good.'

'No, it isn't,' Sowerby said.

'What kicked that off? Exam pressure?'

Harry had never been to university, not exactly the academic type, but he knew plenty about it.

Sowerby was quiet, like she was thinking about telling Harry something important or personal or both, then she said, 'Something I had to deal with, that's all. And it just comes back to haunt me now and again, usually when I'm at my busiest!'

'Not what you need,' Harry said, as in the back of his weary mind, a memory tried to bubble up to the surface, something Sowerby's mum, the district surgeon, had mentioned ages ago now. But what it was, he just couldn't put his finger on. 'Look, it's nothing really, I'll call you back in the morning, after you've spent the next few hours not sleeping courtesy of work.'

'Well, you're on the phone, so you may as well get on with it,' Sowerby said. 'We have everything in hand here.'

'You've been told what happened?'

'I have,' Sowerby said. 'How is he?'

'I'm at the hospital now,' Harry said. 'They... they tortured him, strung him up.'

Sowerby was quiet for a moment.

'We'll get as much as we possibly can,' she said eventually. 'So, why the call?'

'I was just wondering if we had anything on those threats,' Harry said. 'Feels like I'm clutching at straws here, but there's so much going on and I'm having trouble connecting it all.'

'Not much to tell you, I'm afraid. We're seeing if we can identify the magazines some of the words and letters were cut from, but that'll take a while. All we have to go on is what's on the reverse of those pieces, so snippets of text, that kind of thing.'

'Some were hand-written though,' Harry said.

'And unless we have other writing to compare them with, to see if we get a match, then we can't do much with them.'

Harry shook his head.

'Well, thanks anyway,' he said. 'Best leave you to what you're on with.'

'Actually, I do have something to share with you, too,' Sowerby said. 'Came in late last night and I was going to call you early in the morning anyway. Now's as good a time as any, isn't it? And I suppose it is technically early morning.'

'Go on,' said Harry.

'The blood we found on the baler, remember?'

'It wasn't from the victim, yes, I remember,' Harry said.

'Well, the team was checking things through again courtesy of me being thorough and a slave-driving nightmare to work for, I'm sure.'

Harry wanted to laugh at that but was just too damned tired to even try.

'And?'

'And as I'm sure you know we don't take samples from literally every spot of blood that we find. If there's spatter caused by a firearm at a crime scene, for example, that could result in thousands of the tiniest spots. An impossible task.'

'I'm not sure what you're getting at,' Harry said.

'The team were checking the baler over again and found some threads of material and further blood. This time, though, there's a match.'

'That's hardly a surprise,' Harry said. 'You saw what happened to the deceased.'

'That's not what I mean,' Sowerby said. 'A DNA match came up on the system.'

Harry's breath stopped in his throat.

'Explain.'

'The DNA is Daniel Dinsdale's, the deceased's son. It relates to an offence back in the early nineties.'

'Stealing fireworks,' Harry said, remembering what Gordy had said earlier in the week.

'Yes, that's it,' Sowerby said. 'And those threads of material, they match the piece that one of your team sent through earlier in the week.'

Harry's mind was spinning now.

'Harry?'

'Yes?'

'I have to go.'

'Of course, thanks.'

'And I hope he's alright, the officer who, well, you know...'

'He'll pull through,' Harry said, then hung up.

Harry walked on, stuffing his phone back in his pocket, and pushing through doors into the reception area. He spotted the coffee machine. At a table close by he saw a man very clearly waiting for someone. The man saw Harry and he raised a hand in a small wave. So that was the Reverend Bristow then, Harry thought, returning the wave and walking over.

'Hello,' the man said. 'Reverend Bristow, but please, call me Chris. It's not my name, but I've always preferred it to Alexander.'

'What?'

'Sorry, my little joke!' the vicar said. 'Blame it on tiredness.'

'It's Alexander, then, yes?'

'No, Chris.'

'But you said...'

'Reverend Christopher Bristow.' He held out a hand for Harry to shake. 'I don't have long, but the other officer, the one with that fantastic Scottish accent, she said you'd like to speak with me?'

'Yes, she did,' Harry said, but his mind was on something else now and he wasn't exactly listening.

The vicar looked at his watch.

'I need to be back in another ward in ten minutes. I hope that's long enough. Coffee? Well, I say coffee, but it's basically just brown water pretending to be coffee. I wouldn't recommend it.'

Harry sat down.

'So, how can I help?' the vicar asked. 'I must say, that young police officer who came round this evening, he was a credit to you, that's for sure. So polite!'

'Mmm,' said Harry.

'He wanted to have a look at the files from the cameras we have on the church, you see? I had those installed a few years ago. Really didn't want to, but we'd had a few problems with vandalism, so we didn't have much choice. And insurance insisted on it.'

Harry looked across at the vicar.

'Can I call you in the morning?'

'I thought you wanted to talk now?'

'I did, but something important has come up. Can I take a number?'

The vicar searched in a pocket and pulled out a small, silver case. He opened it and pulled out a small card.

'This was a present from my wife when I was ordained!

It's not very me, if you know what I mean, but it's actually been very useful.'

Harry stuffed the card into a pocket.

'I'm really sorry about this,' he said, standing up and moving away from the table. 'We'll speak later.'

'I'm writing my sermon today,' the man said, 'so I'll definitely be at home. Unless I'm called away for something, but just leave a message and I'll get back to you as soon as I can. Feel free to pop in as well if you need to. Visitors are always welcome! And I make sure that I always have coffee and biscuits to hand; a key part of the job, I think, don't you?'

Harry was already moving towards the main entrance, the vicar's voice fading away behind him.

CHAPTER THIRTY-FIVE

'Jim?'

Harry was on his phone again as he hurried across through the dark to his vehicle.

'How's Jadyn?' Jim asked. 'Is he okay?'

Harry heard the concern in the PCSO's voice, an electric current causing his words to falter a little.

'He's okay, Jim,' Harry said. 'He's had a rough time of it, but he's going to be okay. He's a tough lad, is Jadyn.' Harry knew he was lying, but what else could he say? There was no point filling Jim's head with worry right now because he'd be worried enough as it was, as they all were. Best to keep him focused. 'Where are you?'

'I'm out at the Dinsdale's. Liz was due to swap with me, but she was called over to what happened with Jadyn. I can't believe it, Boss. I just can't...'

'No one can,' Harry said, 'but we'll deal with it because it's what we do. And we'll find those responsible.'

'Too bloody right we will!'

'Who's in the house?' Harry asked, deciding to say

nothing about the spark of lightning-like anger he heard in Jim's voice. They were all angry and right now that was a good thing because it might give them an edge, help them spot something they might usually miss.

'Mrs Dinsdale and Danny,' Jim said. 'Been in all evening, actually. I've been in there with them. Had a bite to eat, which was nice. Someone had dropped off this fantastic chicken and leek pie—'

'Jim!'

'Sorry,' Jim said.

'And you're sure they're still there?'

'Absolutely. I'm out in my vehicle now. Bit bloody cold it is, too, but I have the engine and the heater on and Fly's here with me; a nice bit of company. And a book. I'm not much of a reader, but thought I'd give it a go.'

'I need you to stay where you are,' Harry said. 'I'm on my way.'

'What? Why?'

'If you see either Danny or his mum between now and my arrival, don't mention that I'm heading over, but make sure they don't leave. Understood?'

'Of course,' Jim said. 'But something's up, isn't it?'

'I'll tell you when I get there,' Harry said and hung up.

Call done, and with a message sent to DI Haig to let her and Swift know where he was going, Harry left the hospital and was on his way.

During the day, the journey would take an hour, but at night, with empty roads laid out in front of him, he'd be shaving a few minutes off that, for sure. Harry switched the radio on, but the sound of it just annoyed him, becoming white noise infecting his mind, a swarm of wasps attacking his thoughts, so he killed it five minutes later. His mind needed silence and the almost hypnotic view of the road ahead.

Wide awake now, Harry focused, his headlights cutting a tunnel through the night's darkness, the white lines on the road ahead racing past in a blur. The sky was a starless thing, bereft of even the faintest stary twinkle, and to Harry, it seemed as though the darkness collapsed behind him as he went.

Slowing down for Leyburn, Harry slipped through the silent town, the marketplace populated only by litter dancing the night away and the flash of fur from a cat on the prowl. Further on, he cut through West Witton, for once not having to pull in behind any one of numerous parked cars to allow someone through. A few minutes later, he was flying down Temple Bank and across the bridge where Jen had been hit. He blocked that from his mind, no time to think on that now, not with what lay ahead.

Out of Aysgarth, Harry dropped back down the other side of the hill to the valley bottom. The moon broke through the clouds, its pale light falling on a small hill atop which huddled the spindly trunks of thin trees warped into twisted skeletons by wind and storm. With just minutes to go before his arrival, Harry was still trying to deal with what he'd learned from Sowerby.

They'd found more blood on the baler, blood that brought into question a hell of a lot of what Harry had been told. A part of him was more than a little irritated that the SOC team had missed it the first time around, but police work wasn't an exact science. Mistakes were made, things were missed, it happened, and dwelling on it wouldn't help anyone. That it had been reported as soon as it had been found, well that was enough for now. And there was the small matter of the threads matching the scrap of cloth Jim had found. None of it made sense, in fact, everything he'd been told seemed to both fit together and fall apart all at the same time. But Harry would be getting some answers tonight, that was for sure, even if he had to drag someone out of their bed with his bare hands.

The farm loomed out of the darkness ahead, a collection of buildings just off the road and surrounded by meadows clothed in the night. He pulled in a little too harshly, sending grit and gravel spraying into the air, hammering the brakes hard to bring the vehicle to a skidding stop. Engine off, he climbed out, spotting Jim just ahead do the same.

'Bloody hell, Harry!' Jim said, approaching him. 'In a rush, then? You nearly clobbered the gate post!'

Harry hadn't noticed and neither did he care.

'They're still in, then?'

'And awake now, I should think, after that grand entrance,' Jim said.

'Come on, then,' Harry said, walking past Jim and on towards the house. 'Best we get on with it, don't you think?'

'On with what?'

Harry raised his fist and hammered it hard against the worn wooden door.

'Ah,' Jim said, 'on with that, then.'

'That we are,' Harry said, and hammered his fist against the door once again. 'You're sure they're in, aren't you? They've not buggered off and you just didn't notice because you were too busy reading?'

Harry saw Jim's lips go thin, his jaw clench.

'They're in,' he said.

'Well, they're not exactly rushing down to answer now, are they?'

'It's the middle of the night!'

'I don't care if it's the middle of the last bloody night on Earth and they've invited friends round to spend their remaining hours getting to know each other biblically! They need to answer this sodding door!'

Harry was at the door again, this time adding a shout of, 'Police! Now answer the bloody door!'

A scuffling from inside the house caused Harry enough of a pause to stop him from kicking in the door.

The door opened, sending out a weak milky light from a less than enthusiastic bulb hanging in the hall behind.

'About bloody time!'

'What?'

Harry saw now that standing in front of him was Hannah, wrapped in a dressing gown, her bare toes curling against the cold of the flagstone floor.

'DCI Grimm,' he said.

'I know who you are!' said Hannah, her voice breaking with weary anger. 'What I don't know is what on earth you're doing at my door at this hour of the night! What are you doing here? What's going on that couldn't wait?'

'Can I come in?'

'No, you cannot!'

'We're the police,' Harry said. 'We only ask because we like to be polite. And I'm very far beyond being polite.'

'What's this about?' Hannah asked. 'You can't just turn up and demand things! You can't! I... I want a warrant! Yes, that's what I want. Do you have one?'

Jim spoke then, his voice considerably calmer than Harry's.

'Hannah, we don't need a warrant. We're here to ask

some questions, not here to search your house.' He glanced at Harry. 'Aren't we?'

'Mrs Dinsdale, Hannah, we need to speak with Danny,' Harry said. 'I've been told he's in.'

'Daniel? He's upstairs asleep,' Hannah said, backing into the house, her hands reaching for the door, edging it back towards Harry and Jim. 'Can't you come back tomorrow?'

'I'm afraid we can't, no,' Harry said, and he slid a foot forward just over the threshold.

'Well, you'll have to,' Hannah said, reaching out to close the door. 'We've had enough going on as it is and we're exhausted. Please, you need to go. Come back in the morning.'

'It is the morning,' Harry said, his foot preventing Hannah from pushing the door any further home. 'And we need to speak with Danny. Now.'

The quiet of the night stood between Harry and Hannah for a moment. Forcing himself to calm down, he said, 'Hannah, this is really important. Waking you at this hour is not something I wanted to do. Trust me, I would be as confused and angry as you, were this to happen to me. But it doesn't take away the fact that we're not going anywhere until we speak with Danny.'

Harry saw the fight leave Hannah like air from a balloon, her shoulders slumping forward, her chin dropping a little. She stepped back.

'Best you come in, then,' she said. 'And I'll go get him for you.'

'Thank you,' Harry said, and with Jim in tow, he stepped into the house.

CHAPTER THIRTY-SIX

When Danny walked into the room, Harry had to admit he was surprised. He had no real reason to suspect that the man would do a runner, but the police turning up at your door in the early hours could easily have that effect on someone.

'Mum said you wanted to talk to me?'

'Apologies about the hour,' Harry said.

'No, it's fine, really,' Danny said, his words barely making their way out through a yawn. 'I'll put the kettle on.'

'No need,' Hannah said. 'I'm already on with that. It's not like I'm going to be heading back to bed anytime soon, now, is it?'

Hannah made to leave the room and as she did so, Harry had a thought. He excused himself for a moment, followed Hannah out, spoke to her briefly, then came back in.

'Just thought I'd let her know that this is a bit of a private chat, that's all,' Harry said.

'What about the tea?' Danny asked.

'PCSO Metcalf here will see to that, won't you?'

Jim gave a nod and headed out of the room.

Harry took a seat.

'Nice and cosy,' he said, looking around the room. As lounges went, it was nothing fancy, and perhaps that was what Harry liked the most. There was no fuss, no nonsense, no shelves littered with things made of glass and pottery that looked like they'd been left behind by someone with too much creativity and not enough self-control. It was lived in, its singular purpose to make sure everyone in it was comfortable.

'It's better when the fire's on,' Danny said. 'Not been decorated since I was a kid, would you believe? I swear that wallpaper was up there when they brought me home.'

'You remember it, then?' Harry asked.

Danny stared at Harry, his eyes wide.

'Mum told you, did she?'

'One of my officers, yes,' Harry said.

'Well, it's no secret, is it? And no, I don't remember, really. I was only five when they adopted me. There are flashes of memory, but I don't know if they're actually real or not.'

'How do you mean?'

'Mum and Dad told me plenty about those days, plus there's a fair few photos around and about in albums and such like. It's easy to cobble all of that together in your head and turn it into a reality, isn't it?'

'I hadn't really thought about it like that,' Harry said. 'But yes, you're right, the mind is a curious thing, for sure.'

Jim entered the room carrying a tray laden with a teapot, milk jug, mugs, and a chipped dinner plate loaded with biscuits. Homemade, too, by the looks of things, Harry noted, waiting for the PCSO to rest the tray on a coffee table close by.

'I'll let you know when I need you,' Harry said to Jim, and then he was alone again with Danny.

Harry poured two mugs of tea, handed one over.

'I'm assuming there's a reason you're here,' Danny said, taking the tea. 'This isn't just a social call, is it?'

'No, it isn't,' said Harry, and placed his phone on the table.

'You're recording this?'

'I am,' Harry said. 'For your own good as well as mine, I assure you.'

Harry stated his name and rank, the location, date and time.

'Danny?'

Danny repeated the information he'd given Harry in the office. Then he looked over at Harry and said, 'You've found them, is that it? The two men who... who killed Dad?'

Harry leaned back, tried to get comfortable, look relaxed.

'I've been looking over a few things,' he said. 'The sequence of events, evidence, that kind of thing, and I wondered if we could go through it again?'

'That can't be why you're here, though, surely,' Danny said. 'Not at this hour.'

Harry ignored him and flipped open his notebook in his left hand.

'You said you saw two men, correct?'

'What?'

'At the field. You saw two men.'

'Yes,' Danny replied. 'They hit Dad on the back of the head with a post then lifted him into the baler. Why are you asking me this? I've already told you what I saw. It's not something I want to go over again. I can't.'

Harry ignored Danny's protests.

'You didn't recognise them or see them enough to give us a description.'

'How could I? They were wearing balaclavas!'

'It could be argued,' Harry said, 'that that's more than a little convenient.'

'For them, yes.'

'For you.'

Danny's face was drawn immediately into a look of shock.

'What? How? For me? What are you on about?'

'So, you arrived at the field where your dad was and you saw these men, correct?' Harry said.

'Yes, I mean no, I mean—'

Harry checked his notes.

'I have it here. You told me that you walked over to where your dad was, behind the spinney. You saw him talking to two men.'

'That's what I mean,' Danny said. 'I walked into the field but I only saw them once I was past the Spinney. I couldn't see them from the road because of the trees.'

'Well, that's a little clearer,' said Harry. 'And after that, after you'd seen the men and they'd seen you, they chased you out of the field. Then what?'

'I've told you this already!'

'Answer the question, please.'

'They kept chasing me, that's what!' said Danny, his voice growing louder and more irate with every word. 'They would've killed me if they'd caught me!'

'Why would they do that?'

'Because I saw them, that's why! Why else?'

'But you said they were wearing balaclavas,' Harry said. 'And I'm speaking from experience here, by the way, ex-Para you see, but one of the key characteristics of a balaclava is that it's worn over the face, isn't it?'

'What are you getting at?'

'What I'm getting at is if they were wearing balaclavas,' Harry said, 'then it was because they didn't want to be recognised. By anyone. And there's no way you'd have seen their faces. Unless I'm missing something, obviously.'

'Missing something? Like what?'

'Like the fact that maybe they weren't wearing balaclavas at all, Danny.'

'But they were!'

'And yet, you still ran from them?'

'I panicked, that's all! They'd just killed Dad! What the hell would you have done, just stood there and wait for them to come over for a little chat and then ask for an apology?'

'Maybe you recognised them,' Harry said. 'And you've just not told us.'

'But I didn't!'

'How's your arm by the way?' Harry asked.

'What?'

'Your arm. You were rubbing it when you came into the office in Hawes. After you'd followed me in the dark, remember?'

Danny's confusion was growing and Harry was pushing it on purpose, trying to get the answers that he still wasn't sure about himself. But sometimes, the only way to find them was to dig deep, follow the thinnest of veins, and keep digging.

'There's nothing wrong with my arm.'

'It was your left one I think,' Harry said. 'Can I have a look?'

'At my arm? Why would you want to do that?'

'Just concern, that's all,' Harry said.

'But there's nothing wrong with it!'

'Then you won't mind showing me, will you?'

Danny stared at Harry, disbelief and worry chiselled into his face. He rolled up his sleeve. Harry saw the scratch. It was long, had drawn blood but was now scabbed over.

'Looks sore,' said Harry. 'When did it happen?'

'What, this? I don't know, do I! It's just a scratch!'

'I do, though,' Harry said. 'Sunday, as it happens.'

Danny pulled his sleeve back down over the scratch.

'Jim!' Harry shouted, catching Danny by surprise, the sound of his gruff bark causing the man to flinch.

Jim popped his head around the door.

'You find it?'

'Yes. Now?'

'If you wouldn't mind.'

Jim's head disappeared and a moment later he walked into the room carrying something.

'Here you go.'

Harry took what Jim had in his hands, leaned forward to rest his mug on the table, then stood up and opened what he was holding: a faded, checked shirt, the one Danny had been wearing that evening when he'd turned up at the flat.

'That's mine!' Danny said.

Harry was checking the shirt over, looking for something.

'I don't understand,' Danny said. 'Why have you got my shirt?'

'Ah, here we go,' Harry said, then leaned over towards

Danny, holding the shirt out for him to get a closer look. 'See that there?'

Danny stared.

'There's a rip,' he said. 'What about it?'

'More than that,' said Harry. 'There's a little section of the material missing, isn't there? And here...' Harry held out the left sleeve. 'My guess is that this snag in the material here will match where that scratch is on your arm.'

'I don't know what it is you're trying to do,' Danny said, 'but whatever it is, you need to stop.'

'You see, Danny,' Harry said, 'we found a piece of material on the fence outside the field. That's important, you see, because the post used to batter your dad in the skull was pulled from that very same fence. And I'm willing to put money on that scrap of material matching this shirt.'

'No! I didn't do it! That's what you think, isn't it? That I did ... that ... to my dad? I didn't! I couldn't! Those two men did it!'

'We also found blood, and we've a DNA match,' Harry said, then stared hard at Danny. 'It's yours.'

'What?'

'Fireworks, Danny,' Harry said. 'Mean anything to you?'

'What? Why would they? What are you on about?'

'You were a bit of a naughty boy back when you were a teenager, weren't you? Thought you'd help yourself to something that wasn't yours.'

Realisation wrote itself across Danny's face.

'But that was decades ago.'

'That's as may be,' Harry said, 'but in a rather wonderful example of the police being thorough, your details were kept on file. Fingerprints, photographs, DNA.'

A flash of clarity lit up in Danny's eyes.

'I caught myself on the baler! That's where that's from! It was when I was talking to Dad! And I must've caught myself on the fence by the car.'

'You're the only witness we have who puts two men in balaclavas in that field,' Harry said. 'And right now, Danny, I'm thinking that there were no men there at all. Right now, I'm beginning to wonder if, after that argument you had with your dad, you went back to have it out with him, and things went, well, a little too far, shall we say?'

Danny was just staring at Harry now, bracing himself in his chair against the accusations coming at him.

'And by a little too far, I mean that you just couldn't take it anymore, could you? You found out about his plans and you lost it. It happens, you know, more often than you'd believe. People with no history of violence being pushed too far. A fist thrown. A knife slashed. An old man thumped on the head then thrown in a baler.'

'It wasn't me...'

'When you left, you realised what you'd done, so you had to come up with a story. A good one, nice and watertight. So, you were driving around, desperately trying to think of something, panic sending you half-mad, I should think. You saw two blokes racing along in a black BMW and right there you came up with the story of the balaclavas. I mean, I'm impressed if I'm honest. Shows real creativity, that. Real airport fiction, if you know what I mean. Thriller stuff.'

'I don't have to listen to this!'

'And I've been thinking about those notes as well, the ones that your dad and Mr Adams received,' Harry said. 'Maybe you found out about your dad's plans a while ago and you weren't too happy. So, you decided to try and scare your dad off. Didn't work though, did it?'

Danny was on his feet, but Harry was already between him and the door.

'You're insane!' Danny said. 'It's bullshit, that's what this is! I've told you the truth!'

'No,' Harry said. 'You've told me your version of events, that's all. And I've just told you mine. And right now, I'm putting money on mine being the more accurate.'

Danny went to push past Harry, but the DCI didn't budge.

'You can't do this,' Danny said.

Harry knew, though, from the look in the man's eyes that Danny was fully aware Harry could, and that he was going to.

'Mr Daniel Dinsdale,' Harry said, 'you are under arrest on suspicion of murder. You do not have to say anything, but it may harm your defence if you do not mention when questioned something which you later rely on in court. Anything you do say may be given in evidence.'

Then the door behind Harry crashed inwards and Hannah Dinsdale rushed into the room, and into the arms of her son.

CHAPTER THIRTY-SEVEN

Harry woke to an empty flat, cold and weary. He lay there for a few moments, eyes closed, praying that the sandman would pay him another visit and that the rest of the day would be spent in quiet, unconscious bliss. But it was no good. He was awake and the day was waiting for him outside his front door. Probably sharpening its knives, too, Harry thought, the bastard that it was.

After a short breakfast of toast and coffee, Harry gave Grace a quick call, but she was out and about and clearly had better things to do than wait around to hear from him. So, he typed out a text to send to her, deleted it, typed it again, and deleted that one, too. Giving up on trying to sound in any way romantic in just a few short words, Harry then headed out into Hawes and along to the office, doing his best to try and ignore the ache in his bones reminding him that he'd only had four hours of sleep. Driving Danny to Harrogate hadn't helped, but with no cells any closer, he'd had no choice. And he'd be heading back there today soon enough.

On the way, he'd be stopping in for a chat with Mr Bristow, the vicar over in Leyburn.

At the office, Harry found Matt waiting for him.

'Where's everyone else?' Harry asked.

'Asleep or in hospital,' Matt said. 'Both Liz and Jim weren't back till God knows when, so I've sent them packing. Gordy is over at Harrogate. She's grabbing some sleep in an empty office and will then be on with questioning Danny further this morning.'

Harry was over at the kettle.

'You mind if I say something, Boss?'

'No,' Harry said. 'What?'

'This is only my professional opinion,' Matt said, 'but you look like shite.'

'What gave it away?' Harry asked.

'Everything,' Matt said. 'Why don't you get yourself back home?'

'Do I really need to answer that question?'

Matt shook his head, breathed through his nose, but didn't press the point.

Tea made, Harry went over to one of the chairs and slumped down. He found himself staring at the board Jadyn had filled out a couple of days ago. Other details had been added since, but all Harry could think about was Jadyn, lying in that hospital bed, his face a pulverised mess, the marks on his neck, the cuts in his chest.

'How is he?' Harry asked.

'Awake,' Matt said. 'So, that's something, isn't it? Jen's doing fine at home, by the way. She's at her parents' house. Will be for a while, I think. Says she's aching a lot, but that's about it. Oh, and you'll be pleased to know she's taken Steve with her, so you won't have to be over to check on him again.'

Harry sipped his tea.

'I need to speak with the vicar over in Leyburn.'

'I know,' Matt said, went to say something else, but Harry was still talking.

'So, I'll be doing that on my way over to Harrogate to join Gordy. I'll need to give him a call to let him know.'

'On that, there's no need,' Matt said.

'Why?'

'I've already spoken with him. What with the night you've had, what we've all had, I figured I'd get it done, save you the trouble. Means you can get over to Harrogate quicker, too, doesn't it?'

Harry was impressed and grateful. It was a strange combination of emotions and he didn't quite know how to deal with them so he just ignored them and asked, 'What did he say?'

Matt sat down next to Harry.

'Late afternoon yesterday, Jadyn went to speak to him about the security cameras at the church. He was trying to track down the black BMW, remember?'

'You mean he found it?'

'The vicar's sent through the files for us. I've had a look through and...'

'And what?'

Matt reached over to a table for a thin, brown folder.

'Have a look for yourself.'

Harry opened the folder to find a number of black and white printouts. They showed a crowd of people, a wedding he guessed judging by the number of ill-fitting suits and stupid hats.

'Shuffle through them,' Matt said.

The next sheet was of the same view, except it was magnified somewhat, focusing on an area beyond the crowd.

'That's the car, isn't it?'

'I think it is, yes,' Matt agreed. 'Now look at the next few sheets.'

Harry flipped through and found himself staring at the grainy image of a man climbing out of the car.

'It's not the best image,' Matt said, 'but Jadyn did it. I reckon he was out round at the pubs with these, and whoever they are, they got wind of it and—'

Harry didn't notice that the DS had stopped speaking and was now staring at him.

'Harry? What's wrong?'

Harry lifted the printout up for Matt to see.

'I've seen him before,' he said and was already on his feet.

'What?'

'I've seen him before, Matt!'

'You're kidding, right?'

'At the Rotary on Tuesday! This lanky bastard was there! It was him, I'm sure of it!'

Harry was already at the front door.

'That's a grainy image, Harry,' Matt said. 'You sure about that?'

Harry turned on his heel and stared down at the detective sergeant.

'He wasn't there for long. Henry Turner, the chair of the club, he went to speak with him. I only saw him briefly, I know, but this?' Harry held up the printout. 'It's him. It's definitely him!'

Harry didn't give Matt a chance to answer and was out of the building, racing to his vehicle.

'Where are we going?'

'I need to speak with Adams,' Harry said. 'He knows Turner. He'll be able to at least direct us there. He might even know this bloke here, whoever he is.'

Harry was behind the wheel and clipped in, the engine running, before Matt had even opened the passenger door.

'You know where he lives?' Matt asked.

'I do,' Harry said, and wheelspun out from where he was parked and on through Hawes.

When they arrived at the Adams' house, Harry pulled into the drive, jumped out, and was at the front door with a sharp knock.

The house was silent.

'Where the bloody hell is he?'

Harry knocked again.

The door opened and Mr Richard Adams was standing in front of Harry.

'Officer Grimm? Is something the matter?'

Harry didn't bother with the usual niceties and instead showed Adams the printout from the church security cameras.

'Who's this, then?'

'Pardon?'

'This man? Who is he? Where does he live? Do you know him?'

'I've never seen him before in my life.'

'Well, that's horseshit, and we both know it!' Harry said. 'He was at the meeting on Tuesday. I saw him. Turner went to speak with him. You must've seen him, surely! I need to speak with Turner, urgently!'

Adams glanced at the printout then back to Harry.

'How am I supposed to recognise someone from that?'

'If I can, anyone can!'

Adams had another look.

'It's very hard to make anything out, isn't it?'

'It was before the meeting started,' Harry said. 'Turner spoke with us, remember? Then he walked off. I saw him go over to this man here before they both headed outside. I can't remember his name, but I absolutely remember that face.'

'Did you see him come back in?'

'I don't give a rat's arse if I saw him doing the sodding tango!' Harry roared. 'I need to find him right bloody now!'

Adams, under the barrage of Harry's anger-fuelled urgency, stepped back into his house.

'Well, I don't know who he is, but if you saw him with Henry, then I can call him if you like?'

'You'll give me his contact details is what you'll do,' Harry said. 'And you'll call him now and tell him we're on our way. Understood?'

'Yes, of course.'

'Good!'

A moment later Adams handed Harry a note with an address and a telephone number.

'He might be out.'

'He can be in, out, bloody well shaking it all about for all I care!' Harry said. 'But wherever he is, and whatever he's doing, you call him and you tell him to meet me at this address you've just given me!'

'What if he says he can't make it?'

At this, Harry narrowed his eyes at Matt, and was then back around into Adams, holding the printout close enough to the man's face to touch his nose.

'Do you remember Police Constable Okri?'

'Yes, of course I do. The young constable.'

Harry wasn't interested in what Adams was saying. He was talking and he expected his audience of one to listen.

'You met him Tuesday evening. Lovely lad, a little over-enthusiastic, I'll admit, but otherwise, just a decent human being. Well, I won't go into all of the gory details, but last night, he was assaulted.'

'What? God, that's awful!'

Harry talked over Adams.

'During this attack, which we have every reason to believe was racially motivated, Officer Okri was abducted, tortured, and nearly killed.'

'Killed?' Adams turned pale, which rather surprised Harry.

It wasn't as though he knew the police constable well, but then some people just had a nervous disposition, didn't they?

'But who would do that?'

'He is, I assure you, very, very lucky to be alive! And you see this man here, don't you? Well, I think he's involved. So, can I suggest you point out to your friend, Mr Turner, that unless he helps us with our inquiry I will—and I'm putting this as politely as I can—be his very own personal bloody nightmare!'

'I'll make sure he's there,' Adams said, his voice stumbling on the words.

'I thought you might say that,' Harry said, and he threw his car keys over at Matt. 'You're driving!'

CHAPTER THIRTY-EIGHT

The journey over to Leyburn took too long because Harry wanted to be there now and any slower just wasn't good enough.

'You sure you can't go any faster?'

'Not unless you want us through a wall, no!'

'Just overtake! Come on, bloody well shift it!'

'I can't overtake because that's a blind corner running into a hidden dip!'

'Walking would be quicker!'

'Then why don't you just get out then? And if you're not going to do that, just shut it!'

Harry knew Matt was going as fast as he could. The man knew the roads better than he did, but it wasn't helping with Harry's mood, which was growing darker by the second.

'How long now?'

'Five minutes,' Matt said. 'To Leyburn, anyway. Then it's just another five from there.'

Harry was staring at the printouts.

'I don't understand it,' Harry said. 'Why do that to Jadyn? What's the point of it all?'

'If you're looking for a point, a reason, allow me to direct your attention to the human species as a whole,' Matt said. 'Bit of a reputation for being absolutely horrific to its own kind and pretty bloody awful to every other kind, too.'

'Why risk it, though?' Harry said. 'If they knew he was out looking for them, why go to such an extreme? How does what they did solve anything?'

'They wanted him dead,' Matt said. 'Jadyn wasn't supposed to survive, was he?'

Matt had a point.

'Doesn't make any difference to what we're doing now, though, does it?' Harry said. 'We know Jadyn was at the vicar's place, and we also know that he was then around the pubs with these very same printouts. So, why make it worse?'

Matt eased the vehicle to a stop as they rolled into Leyburn, then was over the painted mini-roundabout and on, heading through the town.

'Maybe they didn't know what he was up to,' Matt suggested.

'What, and they just decided to jump him, take him to a barn, carve him up, then string him up? A bit of a laugh for the violent racists hiding in our midst?'

'I refer you back to my comment about the human species,' Matt said. 'Right, here we are...'

Matt slowed down, easing the vehicle in through a grand-looking gate on the right. They then followed a lane until ahead of them they saw not the usual traditional Dales house of stone and slate, but a building, which to Harry's mind, should never have been allowed to leave the architect's vivid and clearly very strange mind, never mind their sketchbook.

'I'm thinking Mr Turner's the kind of bloke with a few bob and he spends a good amount of it on lining the pockets of the local council,' Matt said. 'No other way I can think of that he'd have been granted planning permission for something that looks like that.'

The building was all angles and flat concrete walls and impossibly huge windows, the roof was lined with vast sections of rusting corrugated metal.

'Not exactly homely, is it?' Harry said as Matt pulled them to a stop.

Harry didn't wait for Matt and was out of his seat and striding to the door. Only problem was, he couldn't actually find it.

'Matt?'

'Boss?'

'Where the hell's the front door?'

Matt looked left, looked right.

'Buggered if I know, Boss.'

Harry scratched his head.

'It has to be here, doesn't it? This is a house and a door is kind of number one on the list of things it needs, isn't it?'

Matt headed off left and Harry went right. He saw another building, this one a sort of earth-covered thing. It looked like a Hobbit house designed by someone who had never read Tolkien. It had the air of an Anderson air-raid shelter about it, only it was considerably larger, a garage perhaps. Harry was about to walk over to it when he heard Matt call to him.

Harry walk on around the house to find Matt waiting for him.

'Ta-dah!'

Harry shook his head.

'Who puts a front door at the back of the house?'

'Someone who paid a lot of money for that view,' Matt said, pointing behind them.

Harry couldn't have cared less about the view at that point and went straight at the door with his knuckles. Then he saw a brass number screwed onto the wood.

'Eighty-eight...'

'Yeah, that's a bit odd, isn't it?' said Matt. 'It's not like there are any other houses about. Anyway, look, there's the bell.'

Matt reached past Harry and pressed it.

Somewhere in the house, a soft tinkle sounded. Then footsteps.

'Let me do the talking,' Harry said, but he was staring at the number in front of him. It meant something, didn't it? He was sure of that. But what? And how did it link to everything else that had happened, not just to Bill, but to Jadyn?

The door opened.

'Yes?'

'Mr Henry Turner?' Harry said.

The tall man in front of him stared at Harry, brow furrowed.

'The policeman!'

'Detective Chief Inspector Grimm,' Harry said. 'May we come in?'

He didn't wait for an answer and pushed through into the house before Turner could protest.

Inside, the house was very much as Harry would have expected, perhaps even a little worse. The architect, clearly not satisfied with the sheer awfulness of the outside of the building, had continued the theme inside, too, only with even more flair and gusto and lack of restraint. To Harry, the house was the kind of place a Bond villain would certainly have appreciated, and no doubt found plenty of places to install hidden trap doors, shark tanks, and large men who don't say much but have teeth that could bite your head off. Everything was concrete and he felt more like he was walking around a bunker than a home.

'Perhaps we should go through here?' Turner said and directed Harry and Matt along an uncarpeted concrete corridor and into a room with a window staring out into a vast world of green.

'Quite the place you have here,' Harry said. 'Certainly impressive.'

'It's not to everyone's tastes, I know,' Turner said.

'Each to their own,' said Matt.

'Now then, Mr Grimm,' Turner said managing, Harry noticed, to sound both overly familiar with his name and also strangely civil and courteous all at once. 'Richard rang me to tell me you were on your way over. He mentioned some trouble with one of your officers, I think.'

'Police Constable Okri was assaulted last night,' Harry said, and handed the printouts over to Turner. 'And I believe this man knows something about it.'

Turner stared at the sheets in his hands, shuffled through them, handed them back.

'And you think I know this man, yes?'

'I don't think you know, I know you know,' Harry said. 'He was there last night, at the Rotary Club.'

'He was?'

Harry was taking a distinct dislike to Mr Turner.

'I saw you speaking with him before the meeting, just after we'd met,' he said, fighting to stay calm. 'You went outside together.'

'Oh, yes, I think you're right.'

'There's no "think" about it,' Harry replied. 'I bloody well know that I'm right because I was there!'

Turner said nothing.

'I'll be needing his contact details,' Harry said. 'By which I mean, either you get them for me right now, or I go for a little search around this lovely house of yours.'

'A search?'

'And I'm not the most careful of people,' Harry said. 'A bit clumsy, you might say. I'm the kind of person who just walks into things and knocks stuff over. Accidentally, of course.'

'Like a bull in a china shop,' Matt added.

Turner smiled, seemingly oblivious to Harry's raised voice.

'Well?' Harry growled. 'Are you going to get those details or not?'

Harry heard a dull thud and a groan behind him and turned to see Matt drop to the floor like liquid. Where Matt had been standing, Harry was now looking at the man whose fuzzy image he held in his hand. He was tall, carrying what looked like an enormous book, and he had the heel of his right foot between Matt's shoulder blades. There were marks on his neck. Scratches, Harry thought, which was when everything started to fall into place.

Bollocks…

Matt groaned. The man dug his foot deeper, turning the groan into a squeal of pain.

'I'm only going to say this once,' Harry said, turning slowly back round to face Turner, 'so my advice is to listen very, very carefully—'

Turner laughed at this, cutting Harry off, and the other man smiled, joining in.

'And I'm going to give you a very simple choice, Officer Grimm,' Turner said, refusing to allow Harry to finish. 'Turn around, walk out of my house, and forget about why you're here.' He paused for dramatic effect. 'Or your friend dies. And before you start overthinking this, please understand that this threat doesn't just end there. It has long claws, long enough to reach beyond you both, to friends, to family.'

Harry nodded as though giving the words some thought. And he was, to some degree anyway, because behind that threat from Turner he could now clearly see how the past few days were linked, from Bill's death through to the accident with Jen, onto what had happened to Jadyn, then finally to where he was now standing at that very moment.

'You're going to need to help me here,' he said eventually.

'In what way?'

'Well, if you want me to walk out of here, you're going to have to help me with the story, aren't you?'

'There is no story, Detective,' Turner said. 'There is only us in this room.'

Harry said nothing, playing for time, trying to piece everything together. The door number was really bugging him, needling its way into his brain and making it hurt, driving its dagger-like point through the events of the past few days, drawing blood. And whether Turner realised it or not, it was that one thing which was now allowing Harry to focus, the piece of the jigsaw which made everything else just slot into place.

'Well, I think there is a story actually,' Harry said. 'But if it's all the same with you, I'll skip the once-upon-a-time...'

CHAPTER THIRTY-NINE

'It's the chapel, isn't it?' Harry said. 'That's what this is all about. But not the chapel as such. No. It's something much bigger than that.'

Turner cocked his head to one side.

'Whatever it is you think that you have, Detective, you don't. And even if you did, it wouldn't matter. This is bigger than you. And if you want to continue with your nice little life in the Dales, with your brother, your dog, your new girlfriend, then I suggest you do as I have already said and leave.'

'You know, right up until this moment, I still wasn't sure,' Harry said, shuffling through the pieces in his mind. 'So far as I could tell, I had three separate incidents. There was the murder on Sunday, of Bill Dinsdale—'

'So sad, so awful,' Turner said, his voice laced with so much false grief it was all Harry could do not to grab the man and throw him through a wall. 'His poor wife.'

'Then there was the hit-and-run the same day. You wouldn't know about that. Well, you *shouldn't* know about that, but something tells me that you actually know all about it, possibly in more detail than I do.'

Turner said nothing but Harry saw a look shoot from him to the man standing on Matt's back. Harry moved back just enough to bring them both into view.

'And finally, there was last night's attempted murder on one of my officers,' Harry said. 'Now here we are and I'm thinking, what's the connection? What could it possibly be? Because on the surface, there isn't one, is there? I mean, there are possible connections, yes, but nothing concrete. And then I saw the number on your door, and it bugged me. I didn't know why, but it was there, in my head, like an itch I had to scratch until it drew blood.'

Turner folded his arms, frowned.

'The number on my door? What on earth are you talking about?'

'It's not actually eighty-eight at all, is it?' Harry said. 'It's eight-eight, which as you and I both know, is code for the eighth letter of the alphabet repeated twice, right? First word *heil*, second word—'

'You have no idea what you're talking about!' Turner snapped back, his eyes thin, mean slits staring at Harry.

'Most people probably wouldn't think anything of it, but I'm not most people,' Harry said, unable to hide the disgust in his voice. 'I've dealt with your type before. Most are skinhead thugs looking for someone or something to blame for their own inadequacies.'

Turner was starting to look awkward, Harry noticed, his confident façade slipping just enough.

'But then there are ones like you, well spoken and with a few quid, not so easy to spot. But you're just the same, aren't you?'

'I've just about have enough of this,' Turner said.

'I could give you even more of a clue,' said Harry, 'but frankly, I just can't bring myself to do anything so grubby as a Nazi salute.'

Turner glanced over at the man with his foot still pressed hard into Matt's back.

'Nigel, would you be so kind as to deal with these two for me, please?'

Harry stared at the other man.

'Nigel?'

'What of it?' the man said back.

Harry didn't believe in coincidences.

'You're Nigel Thwaite, aren't you? Danny's mate?'

Harry saw anger flicker in the man's eyes.

'You're dead, you know that, don't you?'

'And there's another link,' said Harry.

'Nigel!'

Turner's voice was the bark of an angry dog.

'It wasn't the purchase of the chapel you took issue with at all,' said Harry. 'No, it was what it was going to be used for that you didn't approve of. That's what started all this.'

'And what of it?' Turner said.

'What was your problem?' Harry asked. 'Yorkshire just not white enough for you, was that it?'

That got a rise out of Turner, Harry noticed, the man's skin flushing red momentarily.

Nigel stepped over Matt, the weight of his whole body pushing down on the foot between the detective sergeant's shoulders. Harry was sure he heard bone crack.

'At first, I thought I was maybe dealing with a couple of people who had a grudge against Bill,' Harry said. 'A handful of locals who didn't agree with his plans. But it's bigger than that, isn't it? Your grudge is with anyone who isn't Aryan enough!'

Turner's face was red again and this time the colour wasn't going anywhere.

Nigel took a step closer, hands open, ready to grab.

'You tried the soft-touch first, didn't you? Spoke with Adams, maybe persuaded him to go in on the project with Bill? That would make sense, from your perspective. I doubt that he had any idea about your actual motivation. He just doesn't strike me as the type.'

Harry was working fast now, pulling together everything that he knew, trying to knit it into something that made sense. He was saying stuff to get a reaction. If it didn't, he'd change tack. But if it did, then he knew he was onto something and would keep pushing.

'You'd have someone on the inside. Then, when the project fell apart, something could still be done with the building, just so long as it wasn't what Bill had originally intended.'

'You're clutching at straws,' Turner said. 'And the thing about straws, Detective, is that they're easily blown away. Or burned to ash.'

'The letters, now they were a nice touch,' Harry said, ignoring the threat. 'Did you send them?'

Nothing from Turner.

'Maybe Adams did that bit? Thinking about it, they were rather polite, almost as though Adams couldn't quite bring himself to threaten Bill, in the true sense of the word. And you could easily paint that to him as a clever way to help Bill see the error of his ways. You underestimated Bill, though, didn't you?'

Turner shook his head, rolled his eyes, smirked.

'So, he sent them to himself and Bill. Clever, that. But old Bill Dinsdale? Well, he wasn't for budging, was he? So, you had to do something else, up the ante a bit.'

Nigel edged closer. Behind him, though, Harry saw Matt move.

'Adams spoke with Hannah about the threats, had her come over that morning. Which gave you the perfect opportunity to send in a couple of heavies.' Harry remembered something else then, from when he'd first arrived at the field. 'I saw Adams on the phone just before I went to see what had happened to Bill. Now, this is absolutely a guess here, but who'd like to bet that when I get hold of his phone records I'll find that he was talking to you?'

'And why would he do that?'

'Because I don't think he expected to find Bill dead,' Harry said. 'Maybe he did, maybe he didn't, but I just don't see it. Things went a bit too far that day and perhaps he called you to ask just what the hell was going on.'

Harry turned his attention to Nigel.

'Anyway, back to just before Bill was killed, which is where you come in, I think.'

Nigel, Harry could tell, was poised and ready to attack. And he'd be ready for him when he did.

'You'd know where Danny was, and his dad, wouldn't you, Nigel? So off you went, you and your pal, to have a word, give the old man a bit of a scare. But it went a bit wrong, didn't it? Things got out of hand and poor old Bill ended up dead. Then Danny turned up and saw you at the scene. He knew what you'd done.'

Nigel lunged, just as Harry had expected. And he was ready for it, stepping back, allowing the man to fall past him, giving him a helping hand on the way, sending him with a hard shove in his back into a glass shelf attached to the wall on top of which stood a porcelain vase. Both smashed and Nigel crashed to the floor.

'You shouldn't have chased him, you know that, don't you?' Harry said. 'You were wearing balaclavas! No way would he have recognised you! But you recognised him and you probably weren't thinking straight right then. Few people do after they've killed someone, particularly if it's their first. All that adrenaline. It's overwhelming.'

'Shut up!' Nigel roared, spitting blood and pushing himself back up onto his feet. 'Just shut up!'

Glass shards stuck out of his face and he stared at Harry, all sense and caution gone to hell.

'I'm speaking from experience, you see,' Harry said. 'It's not something I'm proud of. Killing another human, that's not something you brag about. If you do, you're either a liar or you should be behind bars. I don't talk about it. It was a job and I knew that when I signed on the dotted line. But what you did? That was cold, calculated. Wrong.'

Nigel charged again, but the blood in his eye had him off balance as soon as he started and Harry stepped back once again, tripping him up on the way. The man went flying, landing only a few feet from Matt. Except that Matt was now back on his feet and before Nigel could do anything, Matt dropped his full weight onto him, knocking the wind from his lungs. Then he cuffed him.

'The hit-and-run, that was unfortunate,' Harry said. 'You ran into one of my officers and, in the process, lost a wing mirror. And if you're wondering where it is—which I know you are, because you or your mate visited her in the hospital to ask about it—we have it. And I'm thinking, if we find that car, which we will with your help, it'll match, won't it?'

Harry turned to Turner.

'So, Jadyn then, Mr Turner. Why?'

'You really need me to spell it out?'

'I do.'

'You know why.'

'Is that a confession?'

'What if it is? I'm proud of our actions! This is war! You wouldn't understand!'

Harry moved quicker than even he had expected to, his left hand twisting Turner's jumper into a knot beneath his chin, the man now up hard against one of his idiotic concrete walls.

'I've seen war,' Harry said, 'and it has nothing to do with what you did to that young man!'

'I didn't do anything,' Turner said, struggling to breathe. 'You have no proof!'

'We have skin,' Harry said.

'Rubbish!'

'Your thugs, like Nigel here, they're certainly enthusiastic, I'll give them that, but they don't really know what they're doing, how to clean up after themselves, leave no trace.'

'I don't understand.'

'Then allow me to explain,' Harry said, and he stepped back, allowing Turner the chance to breathe. The man doubled over, gasping. 'Turns out Police Constable Okri scratched one of his attackers. Now, if you'll look over at our friend on the floor over there, you'll see something...'

Turner turned his head to look at Nigel who Matt had pulled to his feet, hands cuffed behind his back.

'I don't see anything,' Turner said.

'There are marks on his neck,' explained Harry. 'Can you

see them? I know I can. And I'm willing to bet we'll get a match. The scratches will match the profile of Officer Okri's nails and the DNA under them will be Nigel's.'

'That's not enough,' Turner said. 'None of this is anything! You're putting two and two together and making five!'

Harry stepped back, allowed Turner to stand. He pulled out his phone.

'What you've built,' Harry said, as he put the phone to his ear to make a call, 'is a house of cards. And the thing about a house of cards is that it's very, very easy to knock down.'

Turner threw himself at Harry, arms wide, head aimed at his centre mass. Harry was no fool and he'd been ready for it, though he was a little surprised with the energy behind the move. He braced himself for the impact, lifted a knee, heard the dull, hollow crack of Turner's skull connect. Turner dropped to the ground like a puppet with its strings cut.

Harry's call connected.

'Who are you calling?' Turner asked, his voice a shocked, crackling wheeze.

Harry ignored him.

'Jim? I need a favour. Any chance you could pay Mr Adams a visit for me?'

CHAPTER FORTY

HARRY WAS BACK IN HOSPITAL AT JADYN'S BEDSIDE. THE rest of the team, bar Jen, was busy with Swift in making arrests.

As Harry had predicted, Adams had folded under pressure. Though not directly responsible for the murder of Bill Dinsdale, he'd certainly been involved, having written the letters and acted as a funnel of information whenever he could or was asked to. He'd even called Turner from the field after finding Bill in the baler, as Harry had guessed.

Upon initial questioning, he'd sung like a canary, giving out names and addresses and anything else he could think of to take the attention away from himself; it had all gone much further than he had ever expected, and Bill's death had certainly not been something he would ever have had anything to do with. Except, of course, he'd had quite a lot to do with it in the end, and no amount of hot air was going to prevent him from being arrested.

Turner was taken in, though he tried to claim that Harry had assaulted him. Nigel Thwaite had gone quietly and also rather bitterly, cursing Turner under his breath as they'd been led from the house.

Matt and Harry had found both the van used in the abduction of Jadyn, and the BMW that Nigel had crashed into Jen, in the odd Hobbit house structure on Turner's property. The others involved in the death of Bill and the assault on Jadyn were now being quickly rounded up, their names found easily in Nigel and Turner's phones.

As for Danny, he was released without charge. Harry felt a little guilty about what had happened, but at that point in the investigation he'd pushed Danny hard and the answers he'd been given, or not, had left him little choice. In the end, Danny had been surprisingly okay about it all, probably because his attention was easily drawn away by the betrayal of his supposed old school friend, Nigel Thwaite. His father's killers had been caught, that was what mattered, and in the end, all he'd actually suffered was a few hours in a cell.

Harry didn't want to think about the next stage of the investigation though. It was a complicated series of events involving too many people. Getting to the bottom of it all was going to be beyond just his team. Which was why Swift had called in additional help.

'How are you doing?'

Harry looked up to see Grace standing beside him, two steaming plastic cups in her hands.

'I'm doing okay,' Harry said. 'Little sleep and a sore knee from someone *accidentally* head-butting it, hardly compares to what Jadyn's been through, does it?'

'Coffee?'

'No, it isn't,' Harry said with a grim smile. 'But I'll take one anyway.' Harry took a sip, swallowed. God, it was the worst. 'Thanks for coming over.'

Grace sat down beside him.

'How's he been?'

Harry shrugged.

'They've induced a coma. It'll allow his body time to recover apparently.'

Grace reached a hand over to Harry's and gave it a gentle squeeze.

'He knows you're here, you know that, don't you?'

'No, I don't,' Harry said. 'But whether he does or doesn't, that's irrelevant. I need to be here, so here is where I am.'

'You can't stand sentry for the next week,' Grace said.

Harry said nothing, took another sip of the awful coffee.

'You know what this needs?' Grace said. 'Sugar.'

'But neither of us take sugar,' Harry said.

Grace stood up.

'You'll be here when I get back, won't you?'

'Where else would I be?' Harry said.

With Grace gone, Harry looked back at Jadyn. The hospital staff had done their best to make him comfortable and to also make him look less shocking, but there was only so much they could do. His face was swollen, there were bandages and dressings all over, and he was wired up to numerous monitors and machines. At least there was no blood, Harry thought, and that was a relief, because in a couple of hours his parents would be arriving.

Leaning back, Harry closed his eyes. Everywhere hurt, inside and out. All he really wanted to do was head home, crawl into bed, and drift off into blissful nothingness. But none of that mattered. He'd been exhausted before, strung out after ferocious firefights, hunkering down in a scrape in the middle of a blasted landscape, belly empty and a good night's sleep nowhere on the horizon. He may have changed jobs, but what it required of him? That hadn't changed at all. And neither had his dedication to those in his care.

Opening his eyes, Harry looked over at Jadyn. He had no idea how the young officer would be when he came out the other side of this, but he'd be there to help in any and every way he could. And so would the rest of the team, that was a given.

'Here, try this...'

Grace's voice pulled Harry from his thoughts. She was holding out another cup, but this one looked different to what she'd offered before.

'This smells like real coffee,' Harry said.

'It is,' Grace replied. 'I nipped out, found a little place just down the road.'

'But you've only been gone five minutes.'

'Forty minutes actually,' Grace said.

Harry rubbed his eyes.

'I must've dozed off,' he said. 'Didn't realise.'

He sipped the coffee.

'How is it?'

'Strong,' Harry said.

Grace pulled up a chair.

'You're not going anywhere, are you?'

'No,' Harry said.

'Mind if I keep you company, then?'

Harry reached out and held Grace's hand. And that was answer enough.

AFTER EVERYTHING that's happened in Cold Sanctuary, you're not going to want to miss One Bad Turn.

JOIN THE VIP CLUB!

WANT to find out where it all began, and how Harry decided to join the police? <u>Sign up to my newsletter today</u> to get your exclusive copy of the short origin story, 'Homecoming', and to join the DCI Harry Grimm VIP Club. You'll receive regular updates on the series, plus VIP access to a photo gallery of locations from the books, and the chance to win amazing free stuff in some fantastic competitions.

You can also connect with other fans of DCI Grimm and his team by joining The Official DCI Harry Grimm Reader Group on Facebook.

Enjoyed this book? Then please tell others!

The best thing about reviews is they help people like you: other readers. So, if you can spare a few seconds and leave a review, that would be fantastic. I love hearing what readers think about my books, so you can also email me the link to your review at dave@davidjgatward.com.

AUTHOR'S NOTE

I have a very distinct memory of hay timing. It was the summer of 1986, school was coming to a close, and I was spending the weekend with my mate, Phil Guy. He lived on a farm over by West Burton. We were both thirteen, had nothing planned, and that Saturday morning Phil's dad gave us a job to do: a few hay meadows needed raking and we were to go and do it for him.

I couldn't believe it! We were kids! But that was (and is) life on a farm: everyone gets involved. We were handed the keys to an old Grey Fergie tractor, like the one Bill drove in the story you've just read. Then, with the rake attached to the back, off we went.

Imagine it! Two teenage lads, trundling off down the road on an old tractor, to spend the next few hours working the fields. It was amazing! It's a memory that has stuck with me, not only because it was a truly wonderful experience, but also because Phil was a great friend.

I dedicated my first Grimm novel, Grimm Up North, to Phil, and another school friend from the dales, Wayne, both of whom are sadly no longer with us. That memory of the hay fields is a special one. Time, I think, stood still for me and Phil that weekend, or it certainly seemed to. We had no idea of the futures which lay before us, where our lives would lead. All we knew was that we were out that day, under the sun, working the land, and nothing could have made that day brighter.

We none of us know what lies around the corner. We can make plans, pretend to ourselves that it's all laid out before us, but life often has other ideas! I would never have thought that some thirty-five years later I would be drawing on that treasure of a day to write a story, make a living, even. And yet, here I am, doing exactly that.

Thanks, Phil, that was a great, great day...

Dave

ABOUT DAVID J. GATWARD

David had his first book published when he was 18 and has written extensively for children and young adults. *Cold Sanctuary* is his eighth crime novel.

Visit David's website to find out more about him and the DCI Harry Grimm books.

f facebook.com/davidjgatwardauthor

THE DCI HARRY GRIMM SERIES

Welcome to Yorkshire. Where the beer is warm, the scenery beautiful, and the locals have murder on their minds.

Printed in Great Britain
by Amazon